CW01456145

ALONE IN THE DARK

JOANNE RYAN

B

Boldwood

First published in Great Britain in 2024 by Boldwood Books Ltd.

Copyright © Joanne Ryan, 2024

Cover Design by 12 Orchards Ltd.

Cover Photography: Shutterstock

The moral right of Joanna Ryan to be identified as the author of this work has been asserted in accordance with the Copyright, Designs and Patents Act 1988.

All rights reserved. No part of this book may be reproduced in any form or by any electronic or mechanical means, including information storage and retrieval systems, without written permission from the author, except for the use of brief quotations in a book review.

This book is a work of fiction and, except in the case of historical fact, any resemblance to actual persons, living or dead, is purely coincidental.

Every effort has been made to obtain the necessary permissions with reference to copyright material, both illustrative and quoted. We apologise for any omissions in this respect and will be pleased to make the appropriate acknowledgements in any future edition.

A CIP catalogue record for this book is available from the British Library.

Paperback ISBN 978-1-83533-735-6

Large Print ISBN 978-1-83533-731-8

Hardback ISBN 978-1-83533-730-1

Ebook ISBN 978-1-83533-728-8

Kindle ISBN 978-1-83533-729-5

Audio CD ISBN 978-1-83533-736-3

MP3 CD ISBN 978-1-83533-733-2

Digital audio download ISBN 978-1-83533-727-1

Boldwood Books Ltd
23 Bowerdean Street
London SW6 3TN
www.boldwoodbooks.com

For my sister-in-law, Carol, who always looks forward to my next book.

PROLOGUE
NOW

I'm going to die.

The thought runs through my head on a loop, expunging every other conscious thought from my brain.

Escape. There must be a way.

There isn't.

I'm so cold. The biting wind whips my hair around my face, covering my eyes, my mouth. I pull it away and feel wetness on my skin.

It's snowing.

Perhaps it'll be a white Christmas.

I wrap my arms tightly around my body, fumbling to pull my jacket sleeves over my fingers. I'm standing in the furthest corner of the rooftop, as far away as possible from the squat brick building that sits in the middle of it. Small and square, it houses the access to the stairwell. Double doors that open out onto the roof are opposite me and at any moment, he's going to step through them. I fleetingly considered hiding in between the huge heating pipes that snaked around one side of the rooftop – they rise out of the floor and run parallel to the roofline – but decided not to. Besides being too easy to trip over, my feet would still be visible.

He knows I'm here, so it's pointless to hide. He's chased me through every floor of this department store and soon, he'll burst through those doors, intent on ending my life. I was so confident I could outrun him as I raced up the escalators, so sure I'd find an emergency exit to make my getaway from the store. There must be a fire escape, I reasoned, stairs that I could use to get back down to the ground floor. I'd spotted the door marked 'Staff' tucked away in the corner as I'd raced through the china department; dodging around shoppers who'd tutted and glared at me with annoyed glances as I'd passed them. I shouldn't have been able to get into the stairwell because it had a keypad on the door, but someone had wedged it open with a cardboard box so I took my opportunity and ran through, pushing the box out of the way and pulling the door closed behind me. How clever I'd thought I was; he couldn't follow me now. I was convinced I'd lost him.

Only I hadn't.

He's strong, much stronger than me. Seconds after I'd shut the door, I heard him on the other side as he battered against it. I knew it was only a matter of minutes before he'd get to me and, in my panic to get away, I ran up the stairs instead of down. Realising my mistake, I turned to go back, but it was too late. With a crash, he was through the door and on my heels. So I ran. Up and up.

And now I'm trapped.

I look around again, praying that in my panic I've missed another exit that offers an escape from this roof. There isn't one, of course, because no one comes up here except for the maintenance men, and why would they have another exit?

I don't want to look down over the edge, but the brightly coloured lights from the shopping centre far below draw my eyes to them like a magnet. They stretch high across the square, twinkling prettily in the darkness, and the faint sound of Christmas carols carries on the wind. Or maybe I'm imagining it; my brain playing tricks on me. From here the shoppers look like swarms of ants scurrying around. The last-minute panic-buying has begun in earnest.

A Christmas I'll never get to see.

I'm sad about that, but much more than that, so very afraid.

Will it hurt, the moment that I hit the ground below? Will death be instantaneous, or will I feel every agonising second of it? As I plummet towards my death, will each millisecond seem like forever?

I'm not brave; I never have been.

I don't want to die but it's inevitable, so *Make it painless*, I pray to a god I don't believe in, *make it quick*.

Is this building ten storeys high or eight? I'm not sure, there are four retail floors and I've spent a large part of my life shopping on them. This store has been here for as long as I can remember, a constant in this ever-changing retail environment. What are all the other floors for? Offices, stockrooms? I've always assumed so and I still don't know because all I've seen of them is the scruffy, cold stairwell.

Not that it matters, eight floors or ten; it's high enough to ensure my death. I hope. Lying half-dead with appalling injuries would be worse than dying. What if I land on one of the shoppers below? Will I kill them, too? As if it's not bad enough that I have to die, will I murder an innocent person in the process?

A noise breaks through the howling of the wind and I tear my eyes from the scene below to stare at the door. Is he here already? I've pushed a wooden mop through the handles of the doors that lead onto this roof. It was sitting in a bucket nearby, as I burst out there, running for my life. I'd felt a glimmer of hope when I saw it; a lifeline had been thrown to me. Was this an omen that at last, luck was on my side? With a hoot of hysteria, I'd grabbed hold of it, sending the bucket spinning around like a top. Although I'd known the mop would only stall and not stop him, I'd thought it would be enough.

That it would give me the vital minutes I needed to get away.

Except that there is no escape, nowhere else to run, no other way out. The only way off this rooftop is back through the door I came out of, or over the low wall that runs around the edge.

The quick way.

A bang echoes around the rooftop, and I watch as the doors bow inwards, shaking the mop.

He's here.

Maybe someone will hear him and come and help me, but I instantly banish the thought and hope that no one does. They'll die too, he'll make sure of that. No witnesses. No comebacks. The doors swell outwards again, and there is loud thudding as he batters against them. There's a splintering sound and I know that it won't be long now before the mop handle snaps. He's strong; a thin wooden pole won't stop him. I open my mouth wide, draw in a deep breath and scream as loud as I can, but the sound is snatched away by the wind. No one is going to hear me up here, no one can help me and if anyone tries, I'll have signed their death warrant.

But it feels good to scream, so I do it again and as I do so, I wish I could go back in time; return to that day, change what I did. Relive that moment again and make it different; make this not happen, make it all go away. Because life is about choices; there is always a choice.

I made the wrong one.

In just one second, I ruined my life.

1

NOVEMBER

The road is deserted; not a car or a person in sight. Not surprising since it's only a quarter to five in the morning. Too soon yet for the workers who start their day early to begin their commute. This is a busy main road in the daylight hours and early evening, but so deathly quiet now that I could run in the traffic lanes if I wanted to. But I don't; I stick to the path, safety-conscious. There are numerous potholes in the road and I don't relish the thought of a sprained ankle or worse. The road needs resurfacing and the holes get bigger with each hard frost of the winter; it's on the long and ever-growing list of roads in this town that need repairing.

The weak light thrown downwards from the streetlights is just enough to see where I'm going, but I don't need it; I could run this route with my eyes closed, I've done it so often.

It's cold but not raining. Although even if it were, I'd still be here. Running is my therapy, my saviour, without it, I wouldn't be able to function. It keeps me sane. Ish. I run when there is no one else around because I've no desire to meet other people. I want solitude and mostly, I get it, apart from the odd lone fox scavenging for food, or cats on their way home from their nightly prowls.

Occasionally there'll be other people about but, if I see them first, I run the other way to avoid them. One morning, running later than normal as the sun was coming up, I saw a man racing through the scrubland on the edge of the estate where I live. He was completely naked except for running shoes. I don't know who was more shocked, him or me. He stared over at me as he ran, faltering for a moment, a startled expression on his bearded face. Then he turned his head away, picked up the pace, and disappeared from sight. I've never seen him since.

To the right up ahead is the road into the industrial estate. There's a path at the back of it that runs alongside and although it's fenced off, there's a hole in the wire that I can squeeze through. I'm on the home straight and the familiar rush of endorphins course through me at having nearly completed my run. Or perhaps I imagine it; it could all be in my head, that feeling. Whatever it is, it feels good.

I need to feel good about something.

Most people would be horrified at the thought of me running alone in the darkness, especially as I don't take my mobile phone with me. Why bother? If a mad axeman chooses to attack me, he's not going to wait patiently whilst I take out my phone and call the police to report him. A phone is an annoyance, the weight of it in my pocket, an irritation. Weirdly, I feel stronger without it; braver, more in control: a test to myself that I'm not afraid.

Not of running alone, anyway.

Besides, I can outrun most people, man or woman, and if I can't, well, that's my fate. So be it.

I'm almost at the turn of the industrial estate when a movement catches my eye from the left. I turn my head, expecting to see a fox or a cat, but it's a man. He's running at full pelt out of a side road. He's not seen me as he's ahead of me and doesn't so much as glance in my direction. He veers to the left, running up the road, past the turning to the industrial estate and continuing on towards the town centre. The glow of a street light illuminates him as he runs underneath it and I'm surprised that he's not wearing joggers or shorts but a suit, the jacket open and flapping as he runs, a tie flying over his shoulder like a scarf. His arms are punching the air and his legs are pumping up and down. I stop in my tracks, thoughts of getting home forgotten.

Something's not right.

The sound of a car engine breaks the silence and a split second later, a low dark car comes tearing out of the road the man just appeared from. It comes to a brief halt in the middle of the road and, after a moment, turns and zooms off in the same direction as the man. He's still running fast, but the car eats up the distance between them in seconds. As my brain tells me the car will stop, the other part of me knows that it won't.

I know what's going to happen and there's nothing I can do to stop it, not a thing. The sound, when it comes, is sickening and gut-wrenching. No screech of brakes, but a dull thud. When I open my eyes – because somehow, I've shut them – there's the dark shape of the man's body in the road.

A hit and run.

Except that it's not, because the car has stopped and both front doors are opening. Through the darkness I make out two figures getting out of the car – men, judging by the size of them. I breathe a sigh of relief; they're going to help him, call an ambulance and deal with everything.

I won't need to get involved.

They lean over the man, oblivious to me watching them from the shadows, and it dawns on me that of course I'm involved; I'm a witness. I saw it happen. I'll have to make a statement to the police.

One of them kneels down, and although it's too dark to properly see, I guess he's checking the man over to see how badly injured he is. After a moment, he straightens up and walks over to the car, the second man following him. Perhaps he's getting a blanket for him to make him more comfortable until the ambulance arrives.

If he's still alive.

My conscience tells me I should go and help, but my feet are rooted to the spot. What can I do, anyway? I have no medical knowledge, only the vaguest memory of a first aid course that I was forced to attend at work many years ago. Still, I should go, tell them I'm a witness. Offer help, do something. My brain refuses to obey.

The sound of the car doors slamming breaks through my thoughts. The men have got back into the car. It pulls slowly away. No screeching of tyres this time, but quietly, without urgency. I begin to jog towards the car but it's already far from me, gathering speed as it drives off, unaware of me watching as it disappears up the road. I try to make sense of what I've just seen and the only thing I can imagine is that they've panicked; they've knocked a man over and are trying to get away because if they stay, whatever happens next isn't going to be good for them. They don't want to be here when the ambulance and police arrive. They're totally unaware that there is a witness to the accident, although what can I actually tell the police? I couldn't describe the men or the car.

I jog towards the man in the road, selfishly wishing that I'd not seen this occur. One second later and I would haven't been here, I'd already have turned into the industrial estate and if I'd heard the car, I'd have ignored it as unimportant. I'm immediately disgusted with myself and I pick up my speed, determined to get to the man and help him.

It's the least I can do.

As I draw near, I see he's not moving at all. He's lying on his back, one leg twisted awkwardly underneath him at an unnatural angle. It must surely be broken. I kneel down next to him on shaking legs, the grit on the road digging through the thin nylon of my leggings. My breath comes in ragged, panicky gasps as I try to remember how to do CPR. I move slightly to one side so that what little light there is falls on him without me blocking it. For a moment, he seems to be looking right at me and I'm about to ask him if he's okay when I realise that although his eyes are open, he can't see me.

He's dead.

They knew that, the men in the car; that's why they've run. They could have been drinking, and the driver is over the limit. Maybe it's a very late-night session gone wrong, although that would be some session to go on until five in the morning, and why was the man running? Why were they chasing him?

I stop that thought before it can take hold; wild theories won't help. I need to concentrate and decide what to do. *I* can't help him, but I need to call the police, tell them there's been a hit and run, because they might not have rung for an ambulance.

But I don't have a phone.

For the first time, I recognise the stupidity of running without it; what if I'd had an accident or fallen over and injured myself? There must be a telephone box around here somewhere. They're still around, aren't they, even though the whole world owns a mobile phone? I think back over my route and try to remember if there's a telephone box. I usually run in a rough circle, out of the estate onto the main road and on the way back, through the industrial estate, past the two blocks of flats beside the scruffy, run-down pub and the small block of shops with flats above. There's a mini-mart there, a newsagent. A betting shop. Definitely a cashpoint.

And a telephone kiosk.

I see it in my mind's eye, on the brick wall outside the mini-mart. The corner facing the flats. Is it really there or am I imagining it? There's only one way to find out. If it's not there, I'll continue running until I reach home and then I can use my mobile phone instead. I peer down at the man again. He looks dead, but is he? He's young; probably around my age.

There's no blood on him that I can see. His white shirt has no marks on it and his tie is still tied in a knot, the bright stripes on it standing out in the dim lighting. Although when I screw my eyes up,

I think I see a darker shadow on his hair at the side of his head, as if it's wet. I quickly look away, afraid to look again because it could be blood. Or just a shadow. What if he's just unconscious and could be saved? Are people's eyes open when they're unconscious? I don't know. I wish I knew. I wish I weren't so stupid.

I pick up his hand. The skin is warm and dry. That's a good sign, isn't it? I place my fingers around his wrist, but I honestly have no idea what I'm doing, with only the vaguest idea where to find his pulse. I consider putting him in the recovery position because aren't you supposed to protect the airway?

I look down at him and he stares back at me.

I don't think he's breathing. But what if he is? What if he's alive and I move him and he has a spinal injury and I make it worse? What if, because I move him, he's paralysed for life?

I lay his hand down gently on the ground, stand up and strip off my zip-up jacket and lay it over his chest. The material is thin but it's all I have to help keep him warm if there's a chance he's alive. Feeling useless and pathetic, I turn towards the industrial estate; I'll find the phone kiosk, call the police and ambulance, it's all I can do. I take a deep breath and start to run.

* * *

It takes around fifteen minutes to run to the telephone kiosk and miraculously, it's not vandalised. I experience a moment of panic when I realise I have no money to make a call and then remember that, of course, I don't need money to call the emergency services.

'Fire, police or ambulance?' the woman asks when I get through. I'm flummoxed for a moment, panicked, not knowing what to reply. She repeats the question and I wake up and tell her ambulance and police. She asks me if I can stay with the casualty and I tell her I've had to leave him alone to find a phone box. I feel guilty when I say it, because I've deserted him in his hour of need. I ask her if someone has already reported the accident, wondering if the men in the car might have, but she doesn't answer. She takes the details and I tell her I'll go back and wait for the ambulance but that I think he's dead. She asks me why I think that and I tell her his eyes were open and he didn't look as if he was breathing. She doesn't comment. As I answer her questions, I begin to panic less, her business-like manner calming me. By the time I finish the call, my breathing has returned to normal.

I run back the way I came but it seems to be taking forever to get there, as if the distance is much farther than when I ran the other way. Almost as if I'm running on the spot. For a second, I experience the weirdest sensation of dreaming; as if none of this is real. How I wish that today was Wednesday instead of Thursday, because then I'd have been at work and wouldn't have been a witness, so wouldn't have had to deal with any of this. Would have no need of any contact with the police. Again. Stupid, selfish thoughts that make me feel even worse because I'm making this all about me and not the poor man who's been hit by a car.

At last I reach the corner of the industrial estate. It must be around thirty minutes since I left him and that's a hell of a long time when someone is injured. As I turn right towards the street where he's lying, I see flashing blue lights, and the relief is so immense that I need to stop for a moment to catch my breath.

They're here already. He's no longer my responsibility.

Whether he lives or dies now is nothing to do with me.

2

As I jog closer, I see that the flashing light is not an ambulance as I first thought, but a police car. It's parked across the road, blocking it, which is sensible, because people will be starting their commutes to work soon and the man in the road could potentially get run over again. It's dark, and a car would be almost on top of him before he was seen.

A horrific thought hits me; what if that's happened? What if he was alive when I left him and an innocent motorist came along and ran him over because they didn't see him? It would be my fault, because I should have stayed with him and waited for someone to find us.

Shut up, Abi, get a grip.

I approach the police car and see that it's empty. I take a deep breath, readying myself to go around the car and see how the man is. I shiver; it's cold without my jacket but that's not the only reason I'm shivering, I think it's delayed shock.

Where are the police? Where's the ambulance?

A head pops up from the other side of the car. I jump but when I see who it is, I relax; it's a policeman, he must have been kneeling down in the road when I arrived here.

'Hi.' He looks surprised.

'Hi. I called in the accident,' I blurt and feel immediately stupid. Why did I say 'called in' as if I'm in the police force myself? I've watched too many TV programmes.

He nods. 'Sergeant Malone.'

I walk around the car, steeling myself for the sight of the dead man coming into view. I'm hoping the policeman has covered him up. They must carry blankets or something in their cars for that sort of eventuality.

I stop and stare.

He's gone. The space where he was lying is empty; bare tarmac. He's disappeared. Confused and unable to make sense of it, I'm about to ask what's happened to him when I realise that, of course, the ambulance must have already come and taken him to hospital. Although the fact that I didn't hear sirens or see any blue lights means he's probably dead.

'That was quick,' I say to the policeman. It can only be fifteen minutes since I rang 999 but I was talking to the woman for a while after, so I guess she would have despatched the ambulance immediately when she took the call and questioned me afterwards.

'I'm a first responder. I'm usually first on the scene and I was nearby when I got the call. You must be Abigail Redmond?'

'Yes,' I say, impatiently. 'So how was he? Was he alive?' Blunt, but I need to know.

He doesn't answer but looks down at the tarmac and that tells me the man is dead, but he doesn't want to say it. He's going to lie and say he doesn't know because that's what people do; they lie and leave the shit news for someone else to impart. Perhaps he thinks I'll blame myself.

I probably will.

Because there are two types of people in the world: those who blame everyone else for their problems and those who blame themselves for everything, whether it's their fault or not.

I'm one of the latter.

He walks over and stands next to me.

'He was lying here, was he? The man?' He points to the tarmac. I shiver, the early morning air cutting through the thin material of my running top. I remember my jacket; the ambulance crew must have taken it to the hospital with them. I'll buy another one; I'm not going to go and ask for it back because how mercenary would that seem? Do I even want it back? He hasn't said if the man is dead or not, but it doesn't surprise me; the police like to be the ones asking the questions. But shouldn't he know where he is if he was the first responder, whatever that is?

'Yes. Just there. He came running out of that road.' I turn and point to show him. 'And he came up here, running hell for leather even though he was dressed for the office and not exercise. Then a minute or two later, a car came tearing out of the same road and ran him down.'

He nods, studying the ground. The radio attached to his stab vest suddenly bursts into life and he reaches up and presses a button, mutters something into it and then presses the button again to silence it.

'Can you describe the car?'

'Not really. It was dark, darker than it is now, and all I can tell you is that I thought it was a low-down sort of car: sporty, fast. At least that was my impression for the few seconds I saw it, because of the height of it, but more than that, I can't tell you.'

'And the car stopped?'

'Yes. I thought they were going to help him, give him mouth to mouth or whatever, but they didn't. Two people got out – men, judging from the size of them. They walked over to him, stood over him for a minute and then got back in the car and drove off. Did they call an ambulance?'

He shakes his head. 'No, no call from them. You were the only person to call it in.'

'That's awful.' If he's dead, that's murder. Or manslaughter, at least.

'Was the man conscious, did he say anything?' he asks.

'No, he didn't speak. I'm not sure if he was conscious or not. It was darker then and I thought he was looking at me, but maybe I imagined that. I put my tracksuit jacket over him to try and keep him warm and then ran to the phone box.'

'And what time was that?'

I look at my watch and realise that I should have checked exactly when it happened. It would be helpful for the police checking traffic cameras and stuff on the nearby motorway. I'm shocked to discover it's almost six o'clock now and then I realise how much lighter the sky is. Traffic will be starting to come along here at any minute, unless they've blocked it farther down to make it detour around the estate. They do that quite often, even though it annoys the hell out of everyone.

'It took me about thirty minutes to run to the phone box and back, so somewhere between 5.15 and 5.30, I'd say.'

'And you run this route often, do you, early in the morning?'

'Three times a week. When I run in the day, I use a different route. A quieter one.'

He purses his lips slightly and I sense disapproval. There may not be any, it could be my imagination because I often feel disapproved of even when I'm not.

'And you don't carry a mobile phone with you? What about a panic alarm?'

'I forgot my phone,' I lie. 'I usually have it in my pocket.'

'Okay. Well, we'll need you to make a statement.'

I nod.

'You can come to the station or someone can go out to your house, but it won't be for a few days. You'll be contacted.' He smiles and I'm relieved. They'll come to me. There's no need to go inside that police station again.

'You didn't answer my question, though, about how he is? I'm guessing it's not good because I didn't hear any sirens.' He can tell me, now he has all the information he needs. Although I've already given all these details to the call handler, but I suppose he has to hear it from me.

'The ambulance never came. I cancelled it,' he says.

I stare at him in confusion.

'What? Why?'

'There was no casualty here when I arrived. Whoever you saw get hit by the car wasn't as badly injured as you imagined, because by the time I got here, he'd gone.'

* * *

I thought he was dead; I was *sure* he was dead.

But he wasn't.

What a massive relief it was when I heard the officer's words; no more feeling guilty for doing the wrong thing, for leaving him, for having no idea about first aid or what to do. In the time it took me to run to the shops, make the call and run back, he managed to get up and leave.

Cameron, the policeman, was patient and kind. He gave me a lift home in his car, although I told him I was fine to run back the way I'd come. He insisted on driving me; said that what had happened probably hadn't hit me yet. He said that although the man was able to get up and walk away, I'd witnessed a hit and run and shouldn't underestimate the shock I'd suffered.

It took a while for it to sink in because I'd honestly believed he was dead. He obviously wasn't, but even so, that car *hit* him. A ton weight of metal smashed into him and okay, he somehow survived it, but *walk away*? His leg looked broken, the way it was bent underneath him, but even if he could get up, why would he walk away?

He'd just been mown down and left for dead. Why wouldn't he report it or at least get checked over at the hospital?

I said all this to Cameron, and much more, and as I said, he was very patient and explained that things aren't always what they seem. Sadly, he said, he'd been to many road traffic accidents and found casualties without a mark on them who had died, and others where people had miraculous escapes from seemingly impossible situations and injuries. And, as he so rightly said, the man might not have walked away. He could have rung someone, and they came and got him and took him to the hospital. As for not reporting it to the police, a lot of people never involve them if they can avoid it, choosing to sort out their own problems. The accident and emergency department at the hospital routinely inform the police of any suspicious injuries, be they stab wounds or RTA injuries, so if the man should seek any sort of treatment, the police would soon be informed.

I told him that the man's eyes were open. He had looked dead. Cameron nodded and smiled and said, 'But it was dark, wasn't it?' The smile took the sting out of his words. He was right, though. I had had to lean to one side to see the man's face because only the feeble light from the street light was shining on him. The lamp posts are so tall that any illumination is pretty dim by the time it reaches the ground. His eyes could have been closed. They must have been closed. My own eyes were playing tricks on me, my panic and hysteria at what I'd seen distorting my reality.

Before I got out of the car, Cameron said he'd be in touch in a few days to arrange for someone to come and take my statement, and I thought then, *I hope it's him.*

Because he was so nice, and he was about my age and so easy to talk to. Good-looking too. The man who got run over wasn't dead, so it didn't seem disrespectful to be wondering. And Cameron's probably nice to everyone, but it was good to talk to him and him being a policeman, well, I was safe with him.

So, yeah, I hope he comes back.

3

'I'm keeping out of her way. She's got a right mare on.' Sally pulls a face and rolls her eyes. 'For a youngster, she's a right misery. Teenage temper tantrums.' I smile at her conspiratorially, and we giggle guiltily.

She's talking about our supervisor, Kelly. In her early twenties and super keen to 'get on', as Sally puts it, she behaves as if we're children and she's the teacher. I use my cutter to slice open another box, pull out a pack of nappies and shove it onto the shelf. It's eleven o'clock on Sunday night and I'm just over an hour into my shift. Sundays, Mondays, Tuesdays and Wednesdays, from ten at night until 6.30 in the morning, I can be found at the Sainsbury's on the high street stacking shelves, or picking and packing shoppers' online orders.

Or *not* be found, which is the actual point. This store is a smaller branch and closes to the public at nine o'clock, so there is no danger of anyone popping in and seeing me. Not that I'm ashamed of working here, far from it. I'm very grateful. Without this job, who knows where I'd be. But I just don't want to see anyone I know if I can help it.

'So...' Checking over her shoulder to make sure the dreaded

Kelly is not around, Sally leans in towards me, lowering her voice: 'How was your time off? Do anything exciting, go anywhere, see anyone?'

'Mostly running, not much else. Thursday night, Spanish as usual. And I popped in to see my parents this morning.'

I walked there and stayed for exactly forty-five minutes. An hour's walk to stay for less than an hour. Adam, my brother, was ensconced in the lounge drinking tea when I arrived and, had I realised that, I would never have gone there. When I saw his shiny red Alfa Romeo parked in the driveway, I wanted to turn around and go straight home without even going inside the house. The only thing that stopped me was that the security camera would have already picked me up. Dad goes through the footage with a fine-tooth comb and there would have been some explaining to do when he found me on there. So I went in, gritted my teeth, drank a cup of tea and put up with my big brother treating me like an idiot. I was planning on telling Mum and Dad about the accident, but I didn't mention it because Adam would have taken over the conversation and lectured me about going running alone. I could have been vague on times with my parents and got away with it because they don't demand every minute detail, but I knew Adam, with his lawyerly eye, would cross-examine me about it. He'd use it as another excuse to bring up my own accident and we'd have to go over everything in excruciating detail, yet again.

I couldn't tolerate it.

There's a nine-year age gap between me and Adam but he behaves as if I'm still a child and not a thirty-five-year-old woman who, until a year ago, had a thriving and lucrative career. He'd got used to being the only child until I made a surprise appearance when Mum was thirty-nine, and it put Adam's nose massively out of joint. He's never recovered from the shock and has made it his life's mission to disapprove of me, joined in his disapproval by his wife, Eve. Yes, really, Eve.

'Keeping well, are they?' Sally asks and for a moment, I have no idea who she's talking about before remembering I've told her I'd visited my parents.

'Oh, yes, they're fine. Dad's still getting over a bout of flu, but apart from that, they're good.'

'That's nice. You're so lucky you've still got your mum and dad.' Sally looks a bit wistful. She's sixty-three herself but only lost her mum last year. She was nearly ninety but, as Sally always says, she still had all her marbles.

'I am.' I give her a sympathetic smile and we resume our shelf stacking in companionable silence. I don't mind this job because it passes the time and Sally is a good workmate. I'm usually teamed up with her and we get along well, despite our age difference. She's a nice person and although she's aware of the reason I ended up working here, she doesn't judge me for it.

Not like some of the others.

Kelly, for one. She likes to make vague hints and snide comments about my past, but I choose to ignore her. I think she does it because she feels threatened. This time last year I had a career in retail management and spent my working life going around stores much bigger than this, for a major supermarket competitor, trouble-shooting problems and initiating new work practices.

It came to an abrupt end because an area manager who can't drive isn't much use.

'Are you still enjoying learning Spanish?' Sally asks quietly. 'Because my doctor keeps on at me to try to get out a bit more or take up some sort of hobby; reckons it could make all the difference. I mean, it seems to be working for you, getting out, but you're a lot younger than me.'

Sally's on anti-depressants and has been since her mother died. She wants to get off them but is terrified of falling into a pit of depression again. She knows that I've had a similar major life-change, coming out of a long-term relationship, but I haven't told her any of the details.

'It couldn't hurt to try, could it?' I say. 'Find something you're interested in and give it a go. I mean, you've got nothing to lose because if you don't like it or find it's a waste of time, you don't have to keep going.'

'Hmm, you might be right. Every time I see him for my prescription, he suggests it. Maybe I'll try it. "Give it a whirl", as Mum used to say.'

Kelly appears around the end of the aisle and we turn our attention to shoving the nappies onto the shelves.

'Nearly done, are we, ladies?'

Facing the shelf, Sally rolls her eyes. *Ladies...* Who does Kelly think she is? She could use our names because it's not as if she doesn't know them.

'Nearly there,' I say cheerfully, turning around to face her as she walks up behind us, determined not to let her rattle me.

'Good, so you can hop on to dog food, yes?' She arches one of her perfectly drawn eyebrows at me, a slightly challenging look on her face. 'There's a delivery in that needs shelving. Immediately.'

'Hopping now.' I push the bag in my hands onto the shelf in one swift movement and head around to the next aisle, leaving Kelly standing there. As I turn the corner I mutter 'woof, woof' under my breath, and I hear Sally giggle.

God, I'm so childish sometimes.

* * *

My alarm goes off and I pull up my eye mask and squint into the half-light. Heavy curtains cover the windows, letting only the faintest of light filter through. I'm lucky that despite working shifts, I rarely have trouble sleeping in the daytime. My alarm is always set for three o'clock in the afternoon on the days I work and although it's daylight now, it'll be getting dark again in about an hour and a half. Once December comes, on my working days I'll barely see any daylight at all. But I'm not bothered, I quite like the winter; it's cosy. With the curtains drawn and the heating on, I'm quite happy in my own home with my own company. The only thing I truly hate about winter is the rain. Running in the rain isn't the most pleasant thing to do.

But I won't let it stop me, I'll still do it.

I get out of bed, pull open the curtains, and the room brightens slightly. I peer through the window to see unappealing low, grey sky and drizzle. Usually, I get straight out of bed, pull on my joggers, go for a run and have a shower when I come back, but today, I'm not.

Sergeant Malone – Cameron – is coming round to take my statement.

I could have set my alarm for earlier but decided not to; I run enough and, when I'm not running, I pretty much walk everywhere, so a day off isn't going to hurt. Now that I don't drive, it's my normal method of transport.

I go through into the en suite, strip off my pyjamas and step straight into the shower. The hot water takes a while to come through and I grit my teeth and stand under the freezing water until it runs warm. It has the desired effect of waking me up and by the time I turn it off and towel myself dry, I'm alert and ready for the day. I go into the bedroom, dry my hair, open the wardrobe and stare at the contents. Jogging pants and a jumper are not going to cut it; that's fine for normal days when I get up, run, come back, and put my work uniform on, but today is different. After a moment I pull out a pair of jeans, a pale cream and green jumper and put them on before assessing myself in the mirror.

Perfectly presentable.

I used to criticise myself constantly and was never satisfied with how I looked. My hair was a mess, my face too pale, my stomach too flabby. I'd weigh myself every single day and convince myself that if I could just lose ten pounds, my life would be much better. The list of my faults went on and on. Years of constantly being told I wasn't good enough had battered my self-confidence until it was rock-bottom. Now I have no need to worry about my weight; the pounds dropped off after the court hearing. Taking up running has ensured they've stayed off, although I didn't do it for that reason. Also, there's no one constantly telling me that I'm crap.

If anything, now I'm a bit on the thin side, but I'm not going to beat myself up about it. I am what I am and I won't linger in front of the mirror to start bringing myself down and finding fault.

I shake the duvet, pull it over the bed and then go downstairs. As I get to the bottom, my eyes, as they always do, go straight to the bolts that I had fitted on the top and bottom of the front door. I never push them across and almost instantly regretted having them installed. I thought they'd make me feel safe but then realised that although they could stop anyone getting in, they could also stop me from getting out. I'd be trapped.

I have a fear of being trapped.

So I never bolt the door because then, if I need to, I can run.

I go into the kitchen, flick the kettle on and drop two slices of bread into the toaster. I've no idea how long this statement thing is going to take, so I'll need to pack something extra in my lunchbox to eat later tonight. The appointment is for four o'clock – surely this won't last any longer than two hours? If it does, I'll have to tell him I've got to leave for work at six.

After I've eaten and cleared the debris away, I loiter around the lounge window and at four o'clock exactly, a police car pulls up outside. I imagine the curtains twitching from the other residents in the street. This house is the only rental property around, all the others are owner-occupied and I consider myself fortunate to be living here. The house belongs to my best friend Mel's dad, who's doing a buy-to-let as an investment for his pension pot. If he weren't renting it to me, I'd be living back home with Mum and Dad. The house is bigger than I need – three bedrooms – but the rent is reasonable as there's no agent involved and it's not far from town, which is a bonus.

If I were renting through an agency, I'd have had to declare my conviction for drink driving. With rentals as scarce as hen's teeth in this town, they can pick and choose their tenants and I wouldn't have stood a chance once I'd put that on the form.

The police car door opens and I'm relieved to see that it's Cameron who's come to take my statement. He rang me to arrange the appointment, but I still had a fear that someone else might turn up instead of him. I tell myself I wanted it to be him because he was so easy to talk to – and he is – but the main reason is that I didn't want it to be anyone whom I've met on my one and only previous visit to the police station. The embarrassment would be too much.

When the doorbell rings, I go and let him in, lead him through to the lounge, asking if he wants a tea or coffee. To my surprise, he accepts. I go out to the kitchen to make it and when I return, he's looking out of the window. He turns when he hears me come in.

'Probably set your neighbours gossiping, parking right outside your house,' he says with a smile.

I laugh, placing the mugs on the coffee table. 'Well, as I don't ever talk to any of them, it's not a problem.' He looks surprised and I realise how it must sound.

'We're like ships that pass in the night,' I add. 'Most of them are at work during the day and I work nights, so I don't really see anyone.'

'Really?' He sits down in the armchair underneath the window and I sit opposite him on the sofa. Mel's dad's sofa, because this house came furnished. 'Where do you work?'

'In town.'

He nods as if I've told him something, when clearly, I haven't. I wonder if he's heard about me; a female drunk driver is still rare enough that it made the local newspaper, even though no one else was involved or hurt. Although that was more luck than anything else; a second later, and it would have been a very different story.

One second later and I'd be serving a prison sentence.

'So.' He opens the bag he's brought with him and pulls out a pad of paper. 'Tell me about it all, in your own words. I'll write it down and then you can sign it. How does that sound?'

'Sounds fine. Did the man ever turn up at the hospital?'

'No, he didn't.' He looks down and writes on the pad. 'Although he still could because it was only a few days ago, but to be honest, the more time that passes, the less likely that becomes.'

'So what's the point in making a statement?'

'Well, you were a witness to an accident and there could be consequences that we've not thought of. The driver of that car may appear on our radar at a later date, if he does it again. Besides, it needs to be documented because you reported an accident, despite the casualty not coming forward.' He picks up his pen. 'Are you ready?'

I nod, and after giving him my full name, date of birth and address, I repeat the events of that morning and the room is quiet, except for my voice and the noise of his pen.

I haven't told anybody else what happened. I thought of telling Sally but then didn't because talking about cars and accidents would remind her of what I'd done. There's no need to remind people about my own mistakes, I want them to forget about them. Mum and Dad would have been different because only they know the truth about what happened the night I crashed my car.

Well, most of the truth. Some things I've never told a soul.

I wanted to talk with them about seeing the man run over and, if it hadn't been for my annoying, high and mighty brother being there, I would have done so.

As Cameron writes it all down, I notice that he's not wearing a wedding ring. I wonder if he's single. It doesn't mean a thing, him not wearing a ring; he could be happily in a relationship but not married. Someone so handsome is bound to be spoken for and anyway, I'm not even looking for anyone.

I'm not sure I ever will.

He looks up and catches me gazing at him and I feel my cheeks flush.

'All done.' He holds the pad out to me. 'Read it through and if you're happy with it, sign and date on the dotted line.'

I read it through, to see that incredibly, there are two pages. His writing is neat and clear, obviously a prerequisite for this job. I sign and date each page and return the statement to him, and he tucks it back into the box file.

'Thank you for your time.' He stands up and hands me a sheet of paper with a mobile number scribbled on it. 'My direct number. If you remember anything else you think might be important, just give me a ring.'

I glance at my watch to see that it's gone half past five. I need to leave for work in half an hour.

'I hope I've not made you late.'

'No, it's fine. I don't start for another hour. I suppose you're finished for the day now?'

'I wish.' He grimaces. 'Two more calls to make, then back to the station to type everything up. That's why I'm ancient but still single; no one can put up with the job.'

'Hardly ancient.' Not married then.

'A couple more years and I'll be staring forty in the face.'

'Never!' I grin. He grins back, and it hits me that I'm flirting.

And so is he.

4

THURSDAY NIGHT

Spanish class night.

It would be so easy not to bother going; to turn on the TV, draw the curtains, lock the doors and stay home. To not trudge to the community centre, which is a good forty-five minutes' walk away.

Would it matter if I didn't go?

It wouldn't. Not at all. I'm not planning on going to Spain any time soon and, if I ever do, I'll have forgotten what little I've learned. I have this same internal argument with myself every week, and every week I force myself to go because in my optimistic moments, it's a diversion from work and I need to develop interests and hobbies. My plan is to do a different course every year. It's not about learning, it's about making myself a more sociable person and getting back into real life. It's working, too, because didn't I almost flirt with Cameron, the police officer?

Yes, I did, and that would have been unthinkable six months ago, so going to the evening class is helping me. It's two hours a week, so it's no hardship to go and if nothing else, it's making me talk and engage with other people, which is something that's been lacking in my life for the last three years. It's only now, since I've been inter-acting more with others, that I realise how insular I'd become. I have friends – of course I do – but aside from Mel, I've not seen any of them since the accident. My fault, not theirs, because they've all checked in on me countless times. I just don't feel up to socialising but I'm aiming to remedy that at some point in the near future.

Before I can change my mind about going tonight, I pull on my big, padded puffa coat, slip my phone into my pocket and open the front door. It's two hours, that's all. One hundred and twenty minutes in a classroom that smells of plimsolls and chalk, practising basic Spanish phrases. Afterwards I can come home and watch TV, feeling better for having made the effort.

I shut the door behind me and lock it. It's dark and there's no moon, or if there is, it's obscured behind thick cloud. I have considered getting myself a panic alarm. Cameron seemed surprised I didn't have one. What's the point if there's no one around to hear it? Although I suppose the noise could potentially stop an attacker if they thought someone might hear. I'll give it a bit more thought.

I set off down the street, looking at my neighbours' houses as I pass by. They're all closed up for the night, curtains drawn, doors closed. Only the flickering light of a television behind the flimsy curtains of one house shows that there's any life in the street at all.

I haven't seen Cameron since he came to take my statement on Monday and why should I? He said he'd contact me if he needed anything else, but honestly, what could he need? I remind myself, yet again, that he has my phone number. If he were interested, he'd call me.

I don't know if *I'm* interested. Actually, I'm not sure if I'm ready to even consider dating or if I'll ever be ready. I absolutely am not going to make the same mistake again.

My phone vibrates from my pocket with an incoming message, and I stop and pull it out.

CELIA

Please just think about what I said, give it some
serious thought xx

I slide it back into my pocket, trying to work out whether I'm disappointed that it's not Cameron. No. Yes. Maybe.

I've just spent over an hour talking to Celia on the phone; she was trying to do me a favour. Again. She used to be my boss and, if it weren't for her, I'd have been fired without notice and come away with absolutely nothing to show for over ten years' loyal service. I couldn't drive, therefore I couldn't do my job, and that's without even taking into account the fact that a criminal record meant instant dismissal, according to the HR rules. Luckily for me, the company were 'rationalising'; cutting down on staff, in other words. Somehow, and at some cost to her own reputation, Celia managed to wrangle redundancy for me and for that, I'll be eternally grateful. The very healthy severance package I received is now lodged safely in the bank and when I get a permanent, decently paid job again, I'll be using it as a deposit on a house. For now, my shelf stacking pays enough that I can eat and pay my rent without dipping into my savings.

Celia rang because she's still looking out for me; one of her old colleagues approached her and asked if she could recommend anyone for an area manager's job for a large DIY and garden centre chain.

She wants to give them my name.

As she says, I'll be getting my licence back in a couple of months and the recruitment process takes at least three months, so I need to start looking for another job now. The way she put it, she's pretty sure she could swing it for me, despite the drink-drive conviction. Everyone is allowed a second chance and apart from that, I have an exemplary record. I was the best performing area manager out of the seven in the country – earmarked for promotion. If I hadn't completely stuffed up my life, I'd have been UK manager by now, with all the area managers reporting to me.

Celia's talking sense, but when she told me about the job, the thing I felt most was fear. As if somehow, I'd be taking a step back into my old life. I couldn't explain this to Celia without telling her about the other stuff, the stuff that came before the accident.

The stuff that *caused* the accident.

None of my friends know about that; no one, not even Mel. Mum and Dad are the only ones who know anything close to the truth, but even they aren't aware of everything. I lived a lie for almost three years and, as far as anyone else is concerned, I had a happy, normal life.

I want everyone to continue to believe that.

I wasn't intending on burdening my parents with any of it, but when they collected me from the police station, a lot of it came out. I couldn't *not* tell them. Mum had half-guessed, anyway. With the sixth sense that all mothers possess, she'd suspected for some time that something wasn't right, but as long as I hid the truth and refused to acknowledge what was happening, there was no way for her to help me.

Mum and Dad were incredible; horrified, but so calm and reassuring and there for me, and they have been ever since. My fears that they were old and frail and wouldn't be able to cope with the truth were completely unfounded. They got me back on my feet and made me believe in myself again. And the relief of being able to talk almost freely about it to them after three long years was immense.

But I'm not ready to share what happened with anyone else.

I don't know if I ever will be.

And I am moving on. This year it's learning Spanish and next year it'll be something else. I'm meeting people and learning something new into the bargain. I'm only six weeks into the course and I've met sixteen new people whom I wouldn't have if I hadn't joined the class. A couple of weeks ago, quite a few of them went to a nearby pub after the lesson finished as it was Jax's birthday, and she asked everyone if they wanted to join her for a drink. I didn't go but I've promised myself that next time it's suggested, I will. I absolutely will.

And somehow, I've arrived at the community college and I don't even recall walking here, I've been so deep in thought. All the way on autopilot without even noticing my surroundings, or the fact that it's now raining. I pull open the heavy swing door and go inside.

The class is in one of the classrooms on the second floor. The college is huge and slightly worse for wear; built in the seventies, it's showing its age with the worn grey tiling on the floor and yellowing paint on the stairs. I walk past the lifts and head straight up the stairs, climbing them quickly. When I arrive in the classroom, Josie, the tutor, is already there, chatting with my classmates. I call out '*Hola*' to everyone, shrug off my coat, and settle myself in my normal seat.

Josie pulls all the desks together for her class so that we're essentially sitting around one big table. I sit at the end, directly facing the front. Jax, whom I sit next to, is deep in whispered conversation with Caro, who sits on the other side of her. She looks up and grins before resuming her conversation. This is the good thing about evening classes; in real life, Jax and Caro would never have the opportunity to speak to each other because they come from vastly different backgrounds. Caro is textbook posh; clipped vowels, velvet headband, and private boarding school, whereas Jax is a mishmash of punk with pink hair, combat trousers and a ragged T-shirt. She must be in her fifties but hasn't changed her style in thirty-odd years. She's always telling everyone that she's going to sell up and move to a cave house in Almería to live the dream.

'How are you, Abigail?' Arthur asks from the chair beside me.

'Good.' I smile. 'And how are you? Been practising your Spanish?' He won't call me Abi, no matter how many times I ask him to. It doesn't bother me, but every time he calls Josie Josephine, I see her frown. He can't help himself, he does it with everyone, refusing to shorten names. It's his generation because my parents are the same. He must be getting on for eighty.

'Not so bad. I've been practising my words, but it doesn't go in so well when you get to my age.' He smiles and I laugh.

'That's not so. You put the rest of us to shame.' I smile.

Arthur hasn't shared very much about himself, but reading between the lines, he's been widowed and is floundering on his own. Learning Spanish is a way to fill some of the lonely hours. He always does his homework, unlike some of the others, and listens attentively to everything that Josie says.

He leans sideways towards me.

'Looks like there's someone new joining us.' He nods in the direction of an empty chair that's been added at the side of the desks closest to the front, a printed handout placed on the desk in front of it. So, we have a new class member. 'They'll have a bit to catch up on.'

The new member could already know some Spanish, like the couple who always arrive and sit together. None of us know if they're a couple or mother and son, and they seem to pick up Spanish way too easily to be on a beginners' course. Their hands are always up in the air first to answer any questions, and some of the class can't hide their annoyance at them. The faces in this room have become familiar to me over the last six weeks and, whilst I assumed some would drop out over time, I hadn't considered new people joining.

I'm prevented from answering because Josie has finished scribbling on the blackboard and is looking around expectantly at us.

'*Buenas noches a todos!*'

We all respond, mimicking her. The classroom door opens and a tall, fair-haired man comes in and looks around uncertainly.

'*Mis amigos...*'

Josie speaks in rapid Spanish and I catch only the first two words before she repeats it in English. 'My friends, I want you all to give a big Spanish welcome to John.' She holds her arm out towards the new man and pulls the chair out for him. Amidst a chorus of '*Hola*' and '*Bienvenido*', he makes his way to his seat and sits down.

'If you can all introduce yourselves to John in Spanish?' Josie looks around expectantly and Jack, who's seated next to him, obliges.

'*Hola, John, me llamo Jack.*'

We go around the room until everyone has introduced themselves and I experience a flashback of all the courses I've attended over the years and wonder why we're doing this. No one ever remembers anyone's name and personally, I find it excruciating. I suppose at least we're spared from telling John something about ourselves because what the hell would I say?

'Okay,' Josie says, once we're done. 'Let's get started.' She's always full of enthusiasm and never minds if we don't remember any of the words we've learned from the previous week. Everyone picks up their handouts and studies them. Jax nudges me.

'He's a bit of all right, isn't he?' she whispers, leaning towards me. 'The new bloke? I mean, look at those gorgeous blue eyes.'

It's a loud whisper and John must have heard her. Jax *is* loud. I surreptitiously study his profile whilst Josie talks, and notice that several others are sneaking a glance at him. His cheeks redden because Jax and Caro are being so obvious about it. He looks very together, is my first thought, his well-cut suit suggesting that he's come straight from work and I wonder what his job is. He looks to be in his late thirties, early forties, and seems slightly out of place here.

'So, who's going to be the first to recap on last week's lesson?' Josie asks.

The woman from the couple who are always first to answer everything puts her hand up immediately and Josie asks her to begin. We listen as she recaps on last week's lesson in Spanish much better than it should be for only six weeks' lessons.

I never volunteer to answer anything. I'm content to merge with the crowd, usually remembering to do my homework on the day of the lesson. It's enjoyable though, and my fellow students are a mixed bunch of people and whilst I'm here, I try to concentrate and give it my all.

The two hours fly by quickly and as Josie is winding up the lesson and giving us this week's homework, she announces that as next week is her birthday, she's planning on a drink after class in The Rolling Mills if anyone wants to join her. From the response, it appears that everyone is going to go, including Arthur. I say yes, I'll be going too, reminding myself that I can easily change my mind because it's a week away.

Class over, once I'm out on the street on my walk home, I think about next week, about what excuse I'm going to use for not going and then I stop myself. Why wouldn't I go? I've no reason not to; I should go.

It's time to move on. Properly.

Time to get out there.

5

'That was delicious.' I lean back in the dining chair and breathe out. 'You're such a good cook, Mel. Anyone would think I'm the one eating for two, not you.'

'It was just a roast and a quick pudding I threw together,' she says in a casual manner, but she can't hide the pride in her voice. This is the girl who could burn toast when we were teenagers and whose idea of gourmet cooking was a curry pot noodle.

Owen beams at her, patting his flat, non-existent stomach. 'It's her fault I'm so fat. I just can't say no. I'm going to be an elephant by the time the baby arrives, with all these recipes she keeps trying out.'

We all laugh and I'm so happy for them; after five long years of IVF, they're finally having the baby they've longed for.

Mel and I have been best friends since the day we started in year seven at Headingham Comprehensive school. We were in the same class; two eleven-year-olds floundering in a huge school where everyone seemed bigger and more grown-up than us. We palled up that day and have stuck together ever since. I remember the overpowering feeling that everyone else knew what they were doing and where they were going except for me. It was a massive relief to find out that Mel felt exactly the same way. I'd come from a small primary school around the corner from where I lived, where I'd pretty much stayed in the same classroom since the day I'd started school. Headingham was huge; all the small local primaries fed into it and it seemed as if my name had been thrown into a huge pot with everyone else's and given a good shake-up. I was put in a class with hardly anyone I knew except for two girls from my old school who were already best friends and were clinging to each other for dear life. There was no room for anyone else. Everything was strange, from changing classrooms every time the bell rang, a different teacher for every lesson, to the huge boys in year ten who seemed like men.

'As if!' Mel demands. 'You're at the gym every day so there's no chance of *you* ever getting fat. *I'm* the elephant in the room. My body will never be the same again.' She points at her six-month bump and we all laugh. I can see it in her expression though, the need for reassurance. She's beautiful, blooming, and loving every minute of her pregnancy, but she's insecure, and always has been. Owen's blessed with good looks and charm and Mel's never quite believed that she's good enough for him.

'You look gorgeous,' I say. 'Positively blooming. And the apple crumble was to die for, too. Do we have the baby to thank for you turning into a domestic goddess?'

She giggles, picks up the empty bowls from the table and carries them over to the dishwasher.

'I wish. Anyway, going back to this accident you saw, are you sure you're all right, Abi?' Owen asks. 'Bit of a shock, seeing someone get run over.'

'I'm fine.' I shrug. 'Just glad that the man who was hit managed to get up and walk away, because like I said, I thought he was dead.'

'It's incredible that someone can survive getting hit by a car,' Mel says, coming back to the table. 'Like a cat with nine lives. Must have been horrible to see.'

'It was.'

We've discussed the accident over dinner and whilst they've been very sympathetic, I can sense what's coming next; the telling-off.

'Although you probably shouldn't go out running at night on your own, because you could have been the one getting run over. You could have been killed,' Mel says, a worried look on her face.

'It's fine. I'm fine.'

'Or worse.' Owen frowns. 'You've no idea who's around, who's watching. A serial killer or a rapist could be keeping tabs on you and just waiting for his chance to jump you.'

'Owen!' Mel glares at him disapprovingly.

'I'm just saying it how it is. Abi, you shouldn't be running alone in the middle of the night because God knows what weirdos are about. Go in the daytime when there are other people around, at least give yourself a fighting chance.'

'God, you're worse than my parents.' I laugh.

'We're just worried about you,' Mel says. 'I don't want anything to happen to my best and oldest friend.'

'Yeah, she's right.' Owen says. 'Not to mention we've got you lined up as our babysitter, and they're like absolute gold dust.'

I laugh as I stand up and begin collecting some of the remaining dishes. 'I'll be more careful and go when it's daylight,' I lie. 'No way do I want to witness any more dodgy accidents.' I carry the dishes into the kitchen and Mel follows behind me. I hope they drop it now. I don't like lying but equally, I have no intention of changing my running hours. I like running in the dark. Besides, I reckon I could outrun almost any attacker.

Although not a car.

Mel stacks everything neatly in the dishwasher and I ferry the rest of the stuff from the table while Owen quietly sneaks off into the lounge. The kitchen is huge and state of the art and, whilst I've never coveted a huge house, I can't help being impressed by it. There are so many cupboards that I want to open some of the doors to see if there's actually anything inside them. I can't imagine owning enough kitchen stuff to fill even half of them. The smooth lines of the duck egg blue units and white quartz worktops are top of the range and look as if they belong on the pages of a glossy magazine. Which I suppose they do, because this is a newly built house on an exclusive development of executive houses.

In no time at all, the kitchen is as immaculate as it was when I arrived. Yet again I marvel at Mel; she was never super tidy before they moved here. I wonder if it will last.

'Shall we leave it a while before coffee, or rather, green tea for me? Let the food go down a bit? We could have a breather and then I'll show you the baby's room. It's all finished now,' Mel says as I follow her through to the lounge. Owen is stretched out on the sofa, remote control in hand.

'I'll make the coffee,' he says with a yawn. 'Give it five.'

'He's only offering because he wants to show off his new, flash, all-singing, all-dancing coffee maker.'

'Guilty as charged. Slap on the cuffs.' He holds his wrists up whilst simultaneously managing to point the remote at the TV and navigate to a football match.

'Why don't you show me the baby's room now?' I ask. 'I need to walk around a bit after all that lovely food. Help digest it.'

'Mel can show you my handiwork,' Owen says. 'Because I'm officially a master decorator after all the painting I've done in this house.'

'I can't wait to see this,' I say.

I follow Mel out into the hallway and up the stairs, my stockinged feet sinking into the deep carpet. Their house is large, beautiful and very expensive and still has that new smell about it. They moved in just over a year ago and the contrast between this five-bedroomed executive house and their old terraced two-up, two-down in the oldest part of town is incredible. Their old place was nice. Always warm and cosy, but it was small and quite knocked about. This is in a different league. Mel still hasn't got over having such a beautiful house and everything is super neat and tidy without so much as a cushion out of place. I feel a small pang of envy and then tell myself not to be so selfish; they thoroughly deserve it. They've not had it easy and everything they have is down to their hard work.

We walk along the vast landing, which is big enough to fit a sofa, past two doorways and then into the baby's room. It's stunning; pink wallpaper dotted with elephants on one wall with the remaining walls painted a pale pink. A white cot stands against one wall, already made up with bedding that matches the wallpaper. A dresser and changing station stand opposite the cot with a wide, pink velvet-upholstered nursing chair on rockers in the corner. I wander around the room and glance into the en suite to see baby bath toys are already arranged around the bath.

'Oh, wow, Mel, it's beautiful. Stunning.'

'It is, isn't it?' She lowers herself into the nursing chair and begins to rock it gently. 'I've gone a bit mad with everything, but Owen said, "Have what you want", so I have. He did all the painting, but we got someone in to do the wallpapering because neither of us has done it before. We didn't want to mess it up because it was a hundred pounds a roll. We're so lucky he got such a good promotion and we were able to move house. I never thought we'd live in a house like this. It's a dream come true.'

'You deserve it. And your baby's so lucky: you two as parents and a fabulous bedroom, too.'

'Well, they say good things come to those who wait so maybe it's true. All those years of Owen getting nowhere at work and suddenly they're practically throwing money at him. Remember how pissed off he used to get whenever he was passed over for promotion? It seems like a distant memory now. God, how he used to moan and rant on.' Mel rolls her eyes and we giggle guiltily.

I wander over to the window and look outside. The front garden is mostly block-paved apart from a small patch of grass at the front nearest the pavement. Mel's Fiesta sits next to Owen's huge black BMW. Things are working out so well for them and their life is soon going to be completed with the birth of a desperately wanted baby girl.

'And how are you, Abi?'

'Good.' I turn around and give her my brightest smile. 'I'm going to start applying for proper jobs soon. Remember my old boss, Celia? Well, she rang me the other day, and it's set me thinking. According to her, my conviction shouldn't be a major problem, not with my experience and track record. In the grand scheme of things, she says, as long as I'm contrite and acknowledge it and don't attempt to hide it, it shouldn't be an issue. It's all about diversity these days and apparently that includes giving people a second chance. And I *am* contrite, very, so I wouldn't be lying. I'm genuinely disgusted with myself for what I did and feel so guilty about it. Thank God I never hurt anyone else because I'd never have been able to forgive myself. I know I have to move on and I'll get my licence back in a couple of months, so I need to start looking ahead.' It's a bit of a lie about looking for a job, but I want to sound positive. If I keep saying it to other people, I might be able to convince myself.

'Really? Well, that's great. It's good to hear you being so positive, and you need to remember you weren't that much over the limit. It wasn't as if you were legless when you got in the car. It could have happened to any of us.'

But it didn't; it happened to me. And people don't want to know how much over the limit you were, because that's no excuse and doesn't make it any less bad. If you're going to drink alcohol, even one, don't drive. And I'd had more than one.

'Well, anyway, I'm moving on.' I run my fingers over the velvety curtains, turn around and lean back against the windowsill. Mel stares back at me.

'I just want you to be happy, Abi, because you deserve it, more than most. Especially after Will.'

I shrug, pretending nonchalance, but inside I feel sick just hearing his name. Like everyone else apart from Mum and Dad, Mel has no idea of the truth about him. She's my best friend but I can't tell her, because Will and I made a deal.

Will. My ex. The man I lived with for three years.

'I still think he's a pig for treating you like that,' Mel says.

'I can't blame him.' I shrug. 'It was his house. He didn't love me any more, so why would he want me living there?'

'You're too nice. Will behaved horribly. He practically threw you out onto the street; after all that time you were together, he treated you like you were nothing.'

I fold my arms and mentally grit my teeth. Mel is convinced that Will cheated on me, absolutely convinced, even though it's not the truth. It looks like we're going to have to talk about him, which means I'm going to lie. Lying doesn't come easily to me, especially not to Mel.

'Honestly, it's fine. I'm over him now and I'm so lucky to be living in your dad's pension pot. But for your dad, I'd still be living with Mum and Dad and although I love them to bits, it gets to be too much after a while.' I grin and Mel laughs. I want to get off the subject of Will; I don't want to talk about him.

'Don't you ever wonder, though, if he had someone else? I mean, you said he didn't, but it was all so sudden, the way you split up. He had to be cheating to finish with you so suddenly.'

I've had this same conversation with Mel several times over the past year. She can't understand that Will and I were fine one day and the next we were over. We weren't fine, of course.

'I don't believe he was cheating, but I really don't care now if he was or not. It's done. In the past. I've moved on.'

'I saw him,' she says suddenly. 'Will. I saw him last week in town.'

My stomach flips when she says it. Ridiculous, because of course he still lives in the same house, here in this town. He still works at his father's company. Will hasn't gone anywhere, so it's quite possible for Mel to bump into him. It's a large town and I avoid the area where he lives and works so luckily, I've never seen him since that day.

I hope I never do.

I went to school with people that I've never seen since the day I left, so why should I bump into Will? I hope I never see him again, but I know there's always the chance our paths will cross. We made a deal, and I won't renege on it if he doesn't, and that's what I'm holding on to.

'You saw him? How did he look?' I don't care how he is, but it'll seem strange if I don't ask her.

'Just the same. He had someone with him. A girlfriend.'

There it is again; the flip of my stomach.

'Really?' It could be a date, a casual date. It doesn't mean anything.

'He stopped and chatted with me.'

Mel has a strange expression on her face that I can't quite figure out, and a sense of impending doom hits me out of nowhere.

'He obviously cheated on you, Abi.'

'I don't care, Mel, it doesn't matter.'

'It matters to me,' she says angrily. 'You should have seen him, he made me fucking sick. He was so full of himself, showing off his new girlfriend to me as if I'd be interested! He even had the nerve to congratulate me on the baby and ask how Owen was.'

'Honestly, Mel, it's ancient history. I couldn't care less about him.'

'Well, I care. He's a liar. He treated you like shit and was blatantly cheating on you. It's so obvious.'

'Why is it obvious?'

'Because he's living with her already, the girlfriend, and has been for the last seven months and you only split up, what, ten months ago? Seven months! Didn't take him long to find someone else, did it? I know you moved in with him quickly, but he hadn't just come out of a three-year relationship then, had he? So tell me now that he wasn't cheating.'

6

I leave Mel and Owen's house at five o'clock and power-walk home. Once inside, I quickly get changed into my uniform, pack my rucksack and leave for work. Mel offered to drive me home from hers, but I told her I liked to walk. I *do* like to walk, but the real reason was that once we'd had the conversation about Will, I just wanted to get out of there, so I could think things through on my own.

Mel had no idea, but what she'd told me about Will blighted the rest of the afternoon. I told her that I was sure Will hadn't cheated, but she wouldn't have it. She's got it into her head that his cheating was the reason we split up so suddenly. She's fixated about it and I couldn't persuade her otherwise. He was on my mind the whole time and it was all coming back, everything that had happened, and I was constantly trying to push it all away. It was a relief when I left because I could stop pretending that everything was okay; stop making small talk about anything other than Will.

He'd ruined the day for me.

I relived it all on the walk home; the three years with Will. How he swept me off my feet. How those first few months when I fell head over heels in love with him were perfect.

He was the man I'd been looking for all of my life and I couldn't believe that he wanted me. Drop-dead handsome, funny, kind and as much in love with me as I was with him. When he asked me to move in with him after we'd been seeing each other for only three months, it didn't seem too soon at all. Why wait, we both agreed, when we felt the same way about each other?

And it was great, that first year, better than great. I worked long hours and so did Will, but at weekends we spent every moment together, making up for the time we'd been apart in the week. Will had recently taken over control of his father's chemical supplies company and was revelling in his new responsibilities, even though it was hard work taking it all on. But that was the way he wanted it, he said, because he was the boss now and had total control. His father had stepped completely away from the business, enjoying his retirement on the golf course, taking expensive holidays with his second wife, happy just as long as the income from his share didn't diminish.

We were quite insular, Will and I, because all we wanted was each other. We couldn't get enough of each other. We'd been out for dinner a few times with Mel and Owen and some of my other friends, to parties and birthday celebrations and the like, but Will never seemed quite the same man that I knew and loved when other people were around. He was polite and engaged in conversation, but he never really gelled with any of them. I put that down to them being my friends. Occasionally we socialised with his, but not often; I excused this by telling myself that a lot of his mates were still single. After a while, the get-togethers tailed off, but even now, I still can't pinpoint the exact moment that things began to change between us, when life became a little less perfect. It was insidious and so gradual as to be barely noticeable.

Or I just got used to it.

I never thought of Will as the jealous type, but he was never keen on me seeing my friends. He would pout and say that he'd be lonely without me; jokily ask me why I wasn't enough for him. He said that he loved me so much that he wanted me all to himself.

I felt flattered.

When we celebrated our first anniversary together, I was still happy, and the only thing niggling at the back of my brain was that although I'd lost touch with most of my friends, the same didn't apply to Will. He still went out at least once a week on his own, played rugby most weekends and went for drinks afterwards whilst I stayed home alone. Mel was the only one I continued to see on a regular basis; we've never gone more than a few weeks without seeing each other. We'd meet for lunch whenever I worked in town, but I couldn't remember the last time I'd had a night out with the girls.

It was my own fault, I decided, and easy to put right.

I arranged an evening out with my girlfriends and Will seemed fine about it. I remember being relieved about that because it was the only small doubt that I had about him. I kissed him goodbye, went out and enjoyed a meal and a few drinks with the girls. It was great to catch up with them and we all promised that we'd do it again soon, because I wasn't the only one who'd let things slip; we all had busy lives, and it was sometimes difficult to pin down a date when we could all get together. When I arrived home, as I paid the taxi driver, I noticed the house was in darkness. I assumed that Will had gone to bed and I was a little surprised because I'd been sure he'd wait up for me.

I let myself into the house and quietly closed the front door so as not to wake him. On my way to the kitchen to get a glass of water, Will stepped into the hallway directly in front of me from the darkness of the lounge, and it was such a shock that for a moment, I thought he was an intruder. I screamed. When he quietly spoke my name, I laughed in relief. He didn't laugh and I knew instantly that something was wrong. It flashed through my mind that something had happened to his father, an accident or a heart attack; something bad. I asked him what was wrong. He did laugh then; a bitter, nasty laugh. He said that he'd been waiting all night for me to come home and whilst I'd been out enjoying myself, he'd been in pieces because he knew I'd been with another man.

Shocked at the person in front of me, who bore no resemblance to the Will I loved, I told him he was wrong, that of course I hadn't been with another man. Even as I said the words, I could see he wasn't listening. Grabbing me roughly around the top of my arms, his fingers biting into the flesh so hard that I thought he'd draw blood, I thought he was going to hit me.

He didn't.

That time.

He roughly pushed me along the hallway, stumbling and tripping, opened the door to the understairs cupboard and shoved me inside. I banged my head on the low door frame as I tumbled in, nearly falling, only the vacuum cleaner and assorted junk inside the cupboard preventing me from hitting the floor.

'Stay in there and think about what you've done, bitch,' he said. 'Because I can't even look at you right now.'

He slammed the door shut and, in shock, I stared into the darkness, unable to believe what was happening. The top of my head throbbed where I'd hit it, and I could hear him doing something to the door outside. Then there was silence. I pulled myself upright and pushed the door, but it wouldn't open. I hammered my fists on it, shouting for him to let me out. Part of me still wanted to believe that it was some sort of sick joke, even though it wasn't in the least bit funny. I stopped after a while, because there was only silence. Will didn't answer me and try as hard as I could, I couldn't push that door open.

I had no concept of time. It was pitch-black inside that cupboard and my phone was still in my handbag, sitting on the console table in the hallway where I'd left it. I fell asleep at some point, sitting on the junk, propped up uncomfortably against the wall. When I awoke, the faintest slither of light was showing underneath the door and, just as I raised my hand to hammer on it again, I heard movement outside. When Will finally opened the door – he'd pushed the console table across the front to keep it closed – it was six o'clock in the morning.

One look at his face told me that the old Will was back; he was contrite and near to tears and begging me for forgiveness. Still in shock at what he'd done, I stumbled past him without speaking, desperate to use the bathroom. When I came out, he was still standing in the hallway. I ignored him and strode past him into the kitchen to find my handbag and its contents strewn across the floor. Will came in and I glared at him and demanded to know what the hell he thought he was playing at.

He was crying. He tearfully told me that he'd been beside himself with fear whilst I'd been out; convinced that I'd be swept off my feet by another man. He said he knew he wasn't good enough for me and was just waiting for me to realise it. To say I was shocked would be an understatement, I couldn't reconcile Will with the bully who had locked me in a cupboard for the night and rifled through my handbag.

I knelt down on the floor and began putting everything back into my bag, pushing Will away when he attempted to help. Then I went upstairs to get ready for work. I had an important meeting in Manchester that day and had no intention of missing it. I showered with the bathroom door locked so that he couldn't come in. When I came out and sat in the bedroom drying my hair, Will was telling me how much he loved me. Begging me over and over again not to leave him. The only time I spoke to him was to say that I'd talk to him later.

Incredibly, I went to the meeting at work as if the night before had never happened.

I spent the day in a daze; in disbelief at what had occurred. At times, it seemed like a dream, because it was so surreal. Will messaged me constantly to tell me he loved me, how sorry he was. I never replied to any of his messages. When I got home late, he was waiting with a huge bouquet of flowers and a meal that he'd cooked for me.

So clichéd.

I forgave him. He promised on his life to never, ever behave in that way again. I told him that it was his one chance. If anything like it ever happened again, then I would leave him immediately. He was pathetically grateful and although I pretended to be tough, I loved him so much that I just wanted things back as they were.

I could *pretend* it had never happened; forget about it, put it to the back of my mind.

Life settled down and went back to normal, but over the coming weeks, there was a subtle shift between us. At first, we never spoke of that night but after a while, Will began mentioning 'our little blip', as he started to call it. He would bring it up in conversation and make light of it, make less of it. He normalised it, I see that now. It had been a silly joke, he insisted, and I could have got out of that cupboard anytime I wanted to simply by pushing the door open. He'd gone to bed, fallen asleep and had no idea that I'd stayed in there all night. His begging for forgiveness, his crying, my threat to leave him, were gradually forgotten.

History was being rewritten.

Slowly, the narrative changed: I'd overreacted to what had happened, I'd made a big fuss about nothing; a hysterical fuss, because all I had to do was push the door open. Was being put in a cupboard such a terrible thing? No, it wasn't; he hadn't hit me, for God's sake. I was making a mountain out of a molehill. Okay, he had been a bit rough when he'd grabbed hold of my arms, but I'd imagined how tightly he held onto them. I was exaggerating. I needed to get a grip and stop being such a drama llama, as Will became so fond of saying. If I kept on like this, I would ruin our relationship. Will's begging and pleading for forgiveness was conveniently forgotten because it didn't fit the new reality, that it was a joke. Horseplay, a bit of fun that I'd massively overreacted to.

On some level, I realised what Will was doing, but I chose to ignore it. I wanted our relationship to work, to get back what we had at the beginning. Will was very clever, but I was so sucked in by him that I didn't see it.

I didn't want to see it.

If the doubts did resurface, I'd convince myself it didn't matter. It would never happen again, so it was best to forget about it and there was no need to dwell on it. Although, deep down, a part of me knew that I should have left him immediately and never given him another chance, I ignored it.

I stayed.

But none of it mattered because it was already too late; I was trapped.

* * *

The first night back at work after a few days off is always hard. There's something about getting back into the swing of being stuck indoors stacking shelves after a few days of freedom that takes a few hours to get into. Thankfully, we were busy last night; lots of Christmas stock to put out despite it only being early November. Christmas comes early in retail. I knew this from my previous job where the Christmas plans would be made in June.

Sally was working alongside me in the new seasonal aisle, taking all the usual stock of herbs, spices and suchlike off the shelves to be replaced with boxes of Christmas chocolates, Santas and selection boxes. Anything chocolate and remotely Christmas-themed had to go onto those shelves. There wasn't much time for chatting because there was so much to do, and that was without Kelly constantly appearing behind us to see how we were 'getting on'. *Much better if you'd leave us alone*, we wanted to shout at her. We didn't, of course.

I made myself concentrate on the job in hand, lining up every-thing extra neatly so Will couldn't get into my head any more. And I pretty much succeeded at work but now I'm here, back home, making myself some breakfast before I go to bed and he's there, again, in my head, waiting to ambush me.

I don't want to go to bed and toss and turn with him on my mind. I generally sleep well and I don't want *him* to be the reason I don't. I usually manage to put him out of my thoughts because that's the deal; I leave him alone and he'll leave me alone. It's what we've agreed and we've both kept to it. So far. As long as I don't ever have to see him again, and there's no risk of him coming for me, that's enough for me. Because Will isn't the only one who has things to hide.

But Will has a new girlfriend now, and she's living with him.

I wish Mel hadn't told me.

At first, when she said it, my instant feeling was relief. Will had found someone else so I would be truly safe now. There would be no possibility of him changing his mind. No chance of him coming after me, because now he had someone else. Milliseconds later, the abso-lute shame of what I was thinking hit me; I was happy for another woman to go through what I did, just so long as he stayed away from me.

And didn't I always know he'd meet someone else? Of course I did, but if I didn't know about her, it wasn't my problem. I'm not responsible for the whole world, I'd tell myself when my guilty conscience pricked me. People make their own decisions.

Has she found out what he's really like yet, the new girlfriend? Mel said she seemed happy but that doesn't mean a thing.

Everyone thought I was happy, too.

Because that's what you do, you lie. For you. For other people. You lie for the life you want, for the life everyone else thinks you have, not for the life that is truly yours. Is it some kind of weird pride? Yes, at first. You don't want to admit what a disaster your life has become. And after a while you lie because you're afraid to tell the truth. Afraid of what he'll do to you if you confide in someone. Afraid of what he'll do to the people you love because now you know what he's capable of. If the new girlfriend hasn't seen the true Will yet and I told her the truth, would she believe me? Of course not. I would never have believed anything bad an ex-girlfriend had told me when I'd just met Will.

I thought he was perfect.

My toast pops up and I chuck it onto the plate and slather it with butter.

Besides, if I even attempt to tell her, I've broken our deal.

He could be different with her. Maybe he won't do it to her and will treat her right. It could be me; there could be something about me that made him the way he was. He always told me I was the problem, that everything was my fault.

Even as this is going through my head, I'm disgusted with myself.

So *I* made him do it now, did I?

I pick up my plate, walk into the lounge and flop onto the sofa, pick up the remote control and point it at the TV. I can't think about it any more. I need to get something else into my head to push Will out. I can mull it over again when I go for my run this afternoon. If I have to. Some sleep will put it all into perspective.

There I go, lying to myself again; this is perspective.

I scroll through the channels and settle on the news, turning up the sound to drown out all thoughts of Will. The female newsreader looks annoyingly wide awake and perky for seven o'clock in the morning and, bleary-eyed and miserable myself, I munch on my toast. What she's saying barely registers, and it's only when a man's face flashes onto the screen that my interest is piqued. I pause, toast in mid-air.

Something about him seems familiar. Do I know him?

The photograph disappears and the newsreader returns and this time, I pay attention to what she's saying. The man's name is

Dominic Newton. He's been missing since the first of November. The name doesn't mean anything, although the date does. I resume eating my toast as she repeats his name and a telephone number is displayed on the screen. As she requests that anyone who has seen him should call the number, it suddenly hits me.

I know exactly where I've seen him before.

7

Dominic Newton is the man I saw run down by the car. His face as he stared up at me is imprinted on my brain from that night. He has the same-shaped eyes, the same slightly crooked nose. In the TV picture he was smiling and the man in the accident obviously wasn't, but it was him.

I'm almost certain.

So what do I do? I should tell someone. The police. What if he crawled off somewhere and is lying there, injured?

He'd be dead by now.

Of course he would. The accident was nearly two weeks ago. And where would he go that he'd have lain undiscovered for that amount of time? It's an unlikely scenario, even for my overactive imagination. Maybe it's not him at all, because I'm putting two and two together and making five.

But he's been missing since the first of November; the day I witnessed the accident.

I could just call the telephone number given out on the news and tell them. But if I do that, they're going to tell me to go to the police station because I've previously reported the accident. I've reported seeing a man run over who I was convinced was dead, whose body then miraculously vanished. Now I'm telling them it's the missing man from TV.

It sounds far-fetched and dramatic.

But it's not that, not really. If I am convinced it's him, I'll have to go to the police and tell them, and I'm trying not to panic at the thought of it, but anxiety is billowing up from deep inside, threatening to swallow me whole. All thoughts of Will's new girlfriend are pushed aside, and the only thing I can think about is how I'm going to be able to make myself walk into that police station again.

It's overwhelming.

The events of that night still haunt me and I do my utmost not to even think about them. Going to the station will bring it all back. Do I really want to do that?

No, I don't.

But this isn't about me; it's time to face up to things and deal with them instead of burying everything, as if that'll somehow make it all disappear.

I crashed my car into the railings of a primary school because I was over the drink-driving limit. Sometimes I wonder if on some level, I meant to do it. I'm not sure. I wasn't going fast. The road was quiet because it was 10.30 at night so thankfully, the school was empty. There was no one around. I damaged the railings and wrote off my car, but I didn't kill or hurt anyone, although a few seconds earlier or later and it could have been a different story. Apart from a few cuts and bruises, I even escaped injury myself.

When the police arrived at the scene, I was still slumped in the driver's seat. Dazed and shocked, but mostly uninjured. I was checked over by a doctor before being helped out of the car and into the back of the ambulance. The doctor insisted I was in shock. I was; and not just from crashing the car. Even now I can remember the humiliation and shame when the police officer climbed into the ambulance and insisted that I take a breathalyser test. The doctor and paramedic weren't impressed with him, looking on with frowns as he pushed the breathalyser bag towards me. I sat with a blanket around my shoulders and blew into that bag, fully aware what the result was going to be. I'd drunk three quarters of a bottle of wine; there was no way that test wasn't going to be positive. Once the result was apparent, the sympathy shown by the doctor and paramedic quickly vanished, and rightly so. Somehow, despite the lateness of the hour and the lack of any people about, word quickly spread that there'd been an accident. The power of social media, or the person who rang the police to report the accident, could have spread the word. However news got around, a few onlookers began to gather on the path in front of the school. Breathalyser test failed, I clambered down the steps of the ambulance to be taken to the police station, frantically scanning the people watching to see if Will was there.

Of course he wasn't.

But I was still afraid he'd get to me, even though I knew that wasn't possible.

And still I never said one word about Will to the police, not one, speaking only to give my name and address. I walked to the police car and as the officer held the door open and I climbed into the back seat, one of the onlookers shouted out 'Shame on you' and 'Fucking drunk driver.' I looked over to see one of them holding a mobile phone in the air and in shock, I saw I was being filmed. My car and face would be splattered all over social media within minutes and there was nothing I could do about that. I realised that I didn't care; I deserved it.

That night was the one and only occasion that I've been inside a police station. When I arrived there and was led in, I can remember the utter shame and remorse that I felt for what I'd done, but there was something else I felt, too.

Relief.

Because whilst I didn't relish spending the night in a cell, it meant Will wouldn't be able to get to me. Even though the rational part of me knew that he wouldn't come after me, I was still terrified that somehow, he'd try.

In a police cell, I would be completely safe.

And now, if I have to go into the station to report the missing man, I might see one of the officers from that night; they could recognise me. It would be utterly humiliating. Shameful. And it would take me right back there, to that night. I'm trying to move on, not go back. I've been trying so hard to forget what happened before even I got to the station, before I got into the car. I've spent the last ten months trying to forget.

Pictures flash though my brain; Will's face contorted with anger as he screamed at me, the open cupboard door as he tried to force me inside.

The blood.

That night was nearly two years after the first time he locked me in the cupboard. Two years of trying – and failing – to leave him.

The familiar feelings of fear, disgust and shame rear their ugly heads and I jump up from the sofa and take my plate out to the kitchen, throwing the rest of my toast into the bin.

There'll be no sleep for me now.

Time to go for a run.

* * *

We're on our break – we call it lunch even though it's 2.30 in the morning – and the lack of sleep is really kicking in. Despite running for so long that my leg muscles were screaming for me to stop, sleep was elusive and I tossed and turned for hours. I finally dropped off about half an hour before the alarm rang.

'Something or someone I should know about keeping you awake?' Sally asks with an arched eyebrow.

'No.' I laugh. 'It's single all the way for me now.'

'Never say never,' she says. 'What about that nice man at Spanish? Didn't you go to the pub with him last week?'

'No, that's this week and who's saying he'll go? He only joined last week so he won't know anyone. I might not even go yet.'

'Hmm.' Sally takes a bite out of her sandwich. 'You should definitely go. Get out a bit and enjoy yourself. And you mentioned him, so he must have made an impact.'

'I only said that we had a new starter. He hasn't made an impact at all. That's how dull my life is; someone new in my evening class is a big deal. I haven't even spoken to him. Not one word.'

Which is true.

'You never know when you might meet *the one*,' she says. 'Broken hearts mend.'

Sally's been married forever to Dave, her high school sweetheart, and she wants everyone to be as happy and settled as she is.

'You don't have to marry him,' Sally says with a grin. 'I'm happily married but I know it's not for everyone. It's different nowadays, you don't have to settle down with one man. There's no reason you can't have a bit of fun with him. You don't need to be in a relationship to have sex.'

'I don't think I'm ready yet.' I roll my eyes and laugh. Sally smiles and gets up to get more coffees and my thoughts return to the missing man. I could ask her opinion about it, but that would mean I'd have to tell her about the accident and the only people who I've told are Mel and Owen. I'm not sure why I've not said anything, because Sally's a good sort and it's not as if it's a secret. I've nothing to hide. She knows about my driving ban because I've told her. I don't wear it as a badge, but there's no point in trying to keep something like that covered up because word gets around; one of the joys of social media and a local newspaper that is desperate for anything printable.

She's doesn't know the truth about Will, though. I told her the same lie as I told Mel; we simply fell out of love.

I have to make a decision about whether I'm going to report that I think the man I saw run over is the man from the news or not, because I need to get it out of my head. If it *is* him, it could be important. I can't stop thinking about it and I wonder if my accident is part of the reason I feel that way. Do I think that helping the police find the driver of that car will soothe my own guilt for what I did? Make amends somehow? I don't know. I pull my phone out of my pocket and open up the local newspaper app. I'll look at the picture of him one more time, make a decision, and stick to it. I scroll through the articles and right at the bottom, there it is. I tap on it and the photograph appears. Is it him? I'm not so sure now; he looks familiar, but is that because I've looked at this picture so many times?

'That's really sad, isn't it?' Sally peers over my shoulder as she puts the coffees on the table. She slides into the seat opposite.

'Thanks, Sally.' I pull the mug closer. 'What's really sad?'

'That missing man.' She nods at my phone. 'My next-door neighbour works with his wife. Although she hasn't been into work lately, what with him being missing and everything. They have two little kids, too. My friend can't understand it because they're a respectable family and you know, just normal.'

'That *is* sad.'

'She says the wife's going out of her mind with worry, and there's loads of gossip and nasty stuff all over Facebook about him running off and starting a new life with another woman. Aren't people vile? My neighbour says they're a nice, ordinary family, both got good jobs and then he goes to work one morning and never comes home. The police say he apparently left the office as usual after work but after that there's no clue where he went. He just vanished. Poor woman, I feel so sorry for her.'

I look down at the photo but I don't see the man, I see a woman with no idea what's happened to her husband. I click the screen closed and put my phone back in my pocket. Whether it is him I saw or not, it's for the police to decide. It's not about me, it's about a missing man. Any information could be important, even if it turns out to be nothing.

As soon as I get home, I'm ringing the police.

8

'They're looking into it, but Cameron says it's unlikely it's the same man.'

'And does that make you feel better?' Mel asks.

'Yes. It does.'

It's Thursday afternoon and Mel and I are in Boasters cafe having a very late lunch while I bring her up to speed on the missing man situation. I kept the promise I made to myself on Monday night to contact the police and, although I'd intended to go to the police station, I decided to ring Cameron, the officer who took my original statement, first. I'd been panicking so much that contacting him never occurred to me, but he had given me his number and said to ring him if I needed anything – so that's what I did. I was massively relieved when he told me that he could do the report himself and that there was no need for me to actually go into the station.

I kept to the facts when I told him, simply saying that from what I could remember, the man in the accident looked like the photograph of Dominic Newton.

'How does he know it's unlikely to be him?' Mel asks.

I shrug. 'I don't know; maybe they have information that I'm not privy to.'

'You weren't tempted to get him to come round to your house and take a statement?' Mel grins.

'No.' I laugh. 'He seemed different this time when I spoke to him, a bit distant and formal. Not at all how I remembered him. Or I could have remembered wrong; whatever it was, by the time I got off the phone I felt a bit stupid. Like I was wasting his time.'

'Really? That's not very nice; you were only trying to do the right thing.'

'I was. I mean, he wasn't rude or anything, but he did stress – several times – that it was extremely unlikely to be the same person.' When I sat and thought about it afterwards, it crossed my mind that maybe Cameron didn't believe I'd seen an accident in the first place because by the time he arrived, the body in the road had gone.

'You could have caught him at a bad time or something,' Mel says.

Possibly, or I could have it all wrong. Perhaps he has me pegged as some sort of fantasist, because I'm sure they must come across people like that all the time. Whatever gave me the idea that we'd flirted when he came to take my statement? Because the way he spoke to me on Tuesday, it was as if we'd never met. I was a bit disappointed by his attitude, although at least now I can forget about it all. I've done my duty so I can stop agonising over it. All that angst about going into the police station and they're not even interested. I could have saved myself a sleepless night if I hadn't made such a drama out of it.

Drama llama, Will's voice says. I push the thought away.

'That's possible, I suppose. I expect they've been inundated with calls since it was on the news and are ploughing through thousands of time-wasters. Anyway, it's done now, so it's out of my hands.'

That's what I do; make more of things than they are. Not to other people, but in my head. That's why I'm refusing to even think about Will and his new girlfriend. It's not my problem. Besides which, I can't do anything about it anyway.

'It does make you wonder, though.' Mel drags the tea bag around her mug thoughtfully. 'About what's happened to him. Could be he was living a double life and has gone off to live with the other wife. Or he's dead; been murdered.'

'Or lost his memory.' I join in with her musings.

'Or gone into hiding because the mafia are after him?'

'Honestly, Mel.' I laugh. 'This pregnancy has made your imagination even wilder than it used to be.'

'It's rampant. Uncontrollable. Owen only has to glance at a woman on the telly and I'm convinced he fancies her. Or anyone in the street; I get it into my head that he's having an affair with her and is going to leave me. I don't know what's wrong with me.' She bites her bottom lip and looks close to tears.

'Hey.' I reach across for her hand. 'Owen would never cheat on you. Never. It's all those hormones whizzing around making you unsettled, that's all.'

She sighs. 'I'm so fat and unglamourous at the moment though, Abi. And I've gone right off sex. What if Owen gets so desperate that he starts looking elsewhere?'

'Of course he won't look elsewhere. He adores you. It won't kill him to go without sex for a while. He's longing for this baby as much as you are, so a few months without is a small sacrifice to make.'

'The signs are there.' She looks down at her tea.

'What signs?'

'He's always working late. And he gets text messages at all hours of the day and night. When I ask him what they are, he says it's work. At night? And he never leaves his phone lying around any more. Takes it with him every time he leaves the room. You tell me that's not suspicious.'

'Mel. Stop it. Owen's mad about you and always has been. Don't start seeing things that aren't there. He's had a massive promotion at work so things are bound to be different. I expect he has to jump to it whenever the boss needs him. He's not nine to five any more, is he?

Not with his new job. He probably takes his phone because he has to be available 24/7.'

'That's what I keep telling myself, but I can't seem to stop getting so jealous. I've seen the way women look at him. He's always been way out of my league and now the gap's even bigger.' She sighs.

'He's not out of your league at all. Talk to him. Tell him how you feel.'

'How can I? I'll sound needy and pathetic. I don't want to doubt him, but the signs are all there.'

'No, they're not. They're in your head. Owen's not a cheater.'

'I wouldn't blame him. I can't stop myself from thinking about it and then I start imagining what she looks like and my insides twist into knots and I can't breathe. I'm fat and ugly and I don't want sex. What have I got to offer? Varicose veins, stretch marks and leaking boobs.'

'Stop it. You're gorgeous, and Owen is the luckiest man alive, and he knows it. You need to stop beating yourself up about gaining a few extra pounds because you're pregnant. Don't let your imagination spoil what you and Owen have. Talk to him, Mel.'

'I know I'm being stupid.' She sighs and reaches across the table and takes hold of my hand. 'I wish I could be as level-headed and clear-thinking as you.'

I wish; if I really were level-headed and calm, my life would be a lot easier.

'That's what best friends are for,' I say with a smile. 'To tell you when to stop imagining the worst and appreciate what you've got. You need to get all of those doubts out of your head and into words and tell Owen. You'll feel so much better when you do.'

* * *

The entire class is going to the pub and there's an almost festive atmosphere as we all put on our coats and gather up our belongings to leave the college. Caro has made Josie a birthday cake and brought it in, along with paper plates, napkins, and a knife. She insisted on everyone having a slice and, as we all sat and ate it, we learned the Spanish word for birthday cake. *Pastel de cumpleaños.*

'Do you want a lift?' Caro asks as I wind my scarf around my neck. 'I'm taking Jax and Josie but I've room for one more.'

'Thanks, that would be great.' I'd intended walking, but if Caro's offering, I'm not going to refuse.

As we hurry down the stairs, John walks behind us with Arthur. I can hear them chatting and I'm pleased for Arthur, he gets a bit left out of things due to the difference in ages and he's also a bit deaf, so misses chunks of the conversation. I'm sure he sometimes pretends to hear when he can't.

It's cold and starting to rain when we get outside, so I'm pleased to clamber into the back of Caro's Range Rover. It's battered and old, but very comfortable. With Josie beside me on the back seat, we zoom out of the car park and up Prospect Hill towards The Rolling Mills.

Josie chatters the whole time, translating everything she sees out of the window into Spanish. She's bubbly, animated and as she talks, I study her. I come to the conclusion that she must be about the same age as me, although she seems much younger in her manner. I feel suddenly old and jaded before reminding myself that I'm here to enjoy myself, not navel-gaze and overthink everything like I normally do.

When we arrive at the pub, most of the class are already ensconced at a table, drinks in front of them. I offer to get a round for the four of us, and head to the bar. Tables and chairs are moved around so we can all sit together. Aside from us, the place is pretty much deserted, so the landlord won't be too bothered by us rearranging the furniture.

I haven't been in a pub for a long time; this is the first time I've been out in the evening and can do exactly what I want without worrying whether it's okay with Will. Going out together – with his friends, never mine – happened less and less until it stopped altogether. It was a relief. I'd come to dread going out because I was so afraid of doing or saying something wrong. It was all too easy to displease Will; talking too much, not talking enough, saying the wrong thing, or not appearing happy enough. Drinking too quickly, not drinking quickly enough, being a party pooper. Wearing the wrong clothes, sitting the wrong way, spending too long in the toilets. Talking to the barman or waiter for too long. Looking at other people. The list went on and on. Being out with Will meant several hours of being on a knife edge, never knowing what mood he'd be in once we were home and the door had closed behind us.

'Yes, love?'

The barman is standing in front of me with a quizzical expression on his face.

'Sorry, miles away.' I smile and give him the order, including a large gin and tonic for me. I'm not driving, so I can drink what I like. I've got into the habit of having a few glasses of wine at home on the evenings I'm not working. Is it bad to drink alone? It is, but tonight, I don't need to worry because I'm not alone. A gin and tonic is perfectly acceptable.

'Hi. Abigail, isn't it?' John, the new guy, is leaning on the bar smiling at me.

'Hi. Yes, it is, although I prefer Abi. Hi John.'

'Right. Abi.' He smiles; a nice smile revealing white, even teeth. He's not wearing a suit tonight, but casual trousers and a hooded sweatshirt. It makes him look younger. For the first time, I notice his eyes; piercing and crystal blue, the beginnings of crow's feet making him seem more approachable, less perfect. His eyes are, as Jax said, gorgeous.

'So,' he says. 'Let me guess, you're either emigrating to live the dream in Spain or you want to be able to ask for a glass of wine on holiday?'

I laugh; one of those is pretty much the answer you'll get from anyone else in the class.

'Nope, neither. I decided that I needed to take an evening class, and Spanish was one of the few left with vacancies. It was either this or flower arranging. How about you?'

'My company has a branch in Spain, so I pop over there quite a lot. They all speak excellent English but I thought it only polite to learn the basics. Unfortunately for me, I dithered around and left it a bit late, hence why I missed the first six weeks.'

'Oh, I see. What do you do?'

'Project manager. Deadly dull. I won't bore you with the details. The Spanish trips are the only thing that makes it bearable.' He grins. 'How about you?'

'Retail,' I say. 'Also deadly dull, but without the Spanish trips.'

He laughs and I find myself smiling. The barman coughs and I turn to see the four drinks I've ordered lined up on the bar. I tap my card on the proffered machine and tuck it back into my pocket. Without being asked, John picks up the drinks, transfers them to the tray holding his own, and carries it over to the table. I follow behind and as the only two vacant seats left are next to each other, I sit down. John pulls the other chair out and sits down next to me. There's a hum of conversation and everyone seems to be enjoying themselves.

'Cheers,' he says, picking up his Coke and holding it up. 'Or should that be "*Salud*"?'

'*Salud*.' We chink glasses and I take a sip of my gin and tonic. It tastes divine and the comforting warmth of the alcohol spreads through me. I steal a glance at John to find him looking right at me, his eyes holding my gaze. My face flushes and I wonder if he knows about my drink-driving conviction.

There I go again; making everything a drama, all about me.

Shut up, Abi, and enjoy the moment.

9

'So, how's it going at the supermarket?'

An innocuous question, if it were from anyone other than my brother Adam. He can't speak to me without sounding condescending.

'Okay. Can't complain. How's soliciting?'

There's an annoyed press of the lips at my cheap joke; how dare I belittle his grand profession?

'Very busy. Thankfully, I'm not involved in the criminal side of the business because it's off the scale at the moment. The senior partner seems to spend most of his day in court. It's mad, isn't it, Eve?'

'It is. Ridiculous.' Eve barely looks up from her plate. Eve never has much to say to me, or Mum and Dad, either. Even having known her for fourteen years, I've never figured out whether she's naturally reticent or just can't be bothered with us. Serious-minded and a bit worthy, she rarely engages in conversation and as soon as lunch is finished and the TV goes on, her head will be buried in a huge law textbook that she has a constant supply of. Mum's cooked roast beef with all the trimmings and it's delicious; the only downside is having to eat it in the company of my brother and his wife.

'I suppose you'll be looking for something else once your ban is spent and you can start driving again?' Adam says.

I put my knife and fork down on the plate as if I'm giving it serious thought.

'Possibly. Although I quite like it at Sainsbury's.'

Adam laughs. 'Well, it's all right as a fill-in, but it's hardly a proper job, is it?'

'It pays wages and I have to turn up on time and actually work, so yeah, I think it *is* a proper job.' I'm being facetious, but can't seem to stop myself.

'I don't mean it like that, Abi. You work shifts, which can't be easy. Why do you always take offence at every single thing I say? I'm just asking, that's all.'

I open my mouth to respond and catch a warning glance from Mum. I close it again. I don't want to spoil lunch; Mum's been slaving away all morning and all she wants is for her family to have a nice meal together. 'I've started looking at similar roles to my old job and put a few feelers out, so I'm sure something will crop up, eventually.' I can't quite bring myself to say sorry, even though I should.

Adam smiles. 'Excellent. It won't take long, because you had a good reputation and work ethic before.'

Wow, almost a compliment, albeit a backhanded one. I smile and try to look pleased at his remark. Neither Adam nor Eve know the truth about Will, although obviously they know about the drink-drive charge. Adam was desperate to get involved in it and tried his utmost to persuade me to let him represent me in court, but I wouldn't allow it. I was guilty, so why try to wriggle out of it? Mum and Dad begged me to tell him about Will. They said he'd be able to help. They were right about that; Adam would have had Will up in court before he'd had a chance to mouth the words 'not guilty'. He's good at his job and he'd have done his very best for me, even though we've never really got on.

Which is precisely why I didn't tell him.

My parents don't understand why I couldn't tell Adam, because they don't know the entire story about what happened that night. As far as they're concerned, Will should be punished for what he did to me. My dad, at seventy-two years old, was fully ready to go round to Will's house and punch his lights out. They know nothing of the deal I made with Will, and it has to remain that way. There is no reason for me and Will to ever see each other again.

I'm safe from him just as long as I stick to our deal.

I eventually persuaded my parents to drop it, telling them that I just wanted to move on and put the past behind me. I also made them promise not to tell Adam any of the real details, either. As far as Adam is aware, Will and I broke up because we fell out of love.

We continue eating in silence and once the main course is finished, I help Mum clear the plates and take them out into the kitchen.

'He's only trying to help.' She peers at me as I push the scraps off the plates into the bin. 'Your brother,' she adds, as if there were a dozen men she could be talking about.

'I know he is. I'm sorry, he just rubs me up the wrong way. Talks to me as if I'm a naughty schoolgirl. Dad doesn't speak to me like that and he *is* my dad.'

Mum makes a humph sound. 'He's always been like that, so he's not going to change now. He's been trying to boss *me* around since he was ten years old.'

We exchange a glance and giggle conspiratorially, jumping apart guiltily when Eve appears behind us with her plate.

'That was fabulous, Anne. The beef was to die for.' She stands there awkwardly and I take the plate from her. She studies me for a moment through her glasses, her brown eyes huge behind the thick lenses. 'You're looking super trim, Abi. Have you been on a diet?'

'What? No, no diet. It's probably all the walking now I can't drive. I run most days now, too, so that might be it.'

'Well, whatever it is, it looks good on you.' She smiles and then turns and walks back into the dining room. Mum and I stare at each other in shock, our mouths open.

'Was that a compliment?' I whisper in disbelief.

'I rather think it was, dear.'

* * *

It's the post-lunch lull; the TV is showing boring football and the temptation to close my eyes is almost overwhelming. I've got to leave for work at half past five and the thought of the thirty minute walk it'll take to get there doesn't fill me with joy. I could always ask Adam for a lift. He'd say yes.

Dad's head is lolling on the back of the armchair, his eyes closed, but he still has a firm grip of the remote control. Adam and Eve are sitting on the sofa together and for once, Eve doesn't have her nose in a book but is having a whispered conversation with Adam. Mum is bustling around in the kitchen making cups of tea and I really should get up and help her but can't make myself. I'm so comfortable and have eaten far too much food to move.

'Hey!' Dad's woken up and is looking at Adam, who's leaned across and deftly removed the remote control from his hand. 'I was watching that!'

'Just want to catch up on the news, Dad.'

He points the remote at the TV and flicks through the channels until he gets to 24 hour news. I glance at my watch to see that it's a quarter to five. Far too late for a nap, now.

'Hey, it's the missing man,' Eve says to Adam. The picture of Dominic Newton flashes onto the screen, replaced almost immediately by the police telephone number. 'His poor family.'

'What's that, dear?' Mum appears with a tray of tea and biscuits. Strangely, although I'm stuffed to the gills with food, I find myself wanting a biscuit.

'The man who's disappeared,' Adam says as Mum doles out the tea. 'I doubt they'll find him now.'

'Oh, don't say that,' Eve says. 'He might turn up.'

'Unlikely. From what I've heard, the police have no leads. He's either dead or he's run away to start a new life and doesn't want to be found.'

'Adam!' Eve looks shocked.

'Sorry, darling.'

I'm about to tell them about the accident and my notion that it was the man who's gone missing, but quickly decide against it. It'll take forever to get to the point and I'll be opening myself up to getting a lecture about running on my own in the dark.

'Not for me, thanks, Anne.' Eve waves away the tea that Mum's offering to her. 'Sorry, I should have said, I'm cutting down on tea.'

'Oh, okay. What about a coffee?'

'Too much caffeine.'

Adam gives Eve a look and they grin at each other. I watch them, astonished at their behaviour. It's as if two strangers have replaced my normally uptight brother and sister-in-law.

Compliments, sitting together and whispering, no caffeine...

The possible reason for their weird behaviour hits me and Mum at the same moment. Mum puts the tray down on the coffee table and stands there, hands on hips, in front of them.

'Have you got something to tell us, you two?' she demands.

Dad looks at me, then Mum, then Adam and Eve in bewilderment.

Adam puts his arm around Eve's shoulders, pulling her gently towards him.

'Okay, we were going to wait until the twelve-week scan, but as you've guessed, yes, we're having a baby.'

* * *

I stride along, the cold air on my face blasting away the last of the post-lunch sleepiness.

What a surprise.

I'd always assumed they didn't want children; that they were too career-driven to allow a child into their lives.

It seems I don't know my brother as well as I thought.

They're quite rightly delighted and I'm genuinely pleased for them, despite my surprise. Eve is only a couple of years older than me and Adam is forty-four – not old at all.

I'm going to be an auntie.

Mum and Dad are absolutely thrilled, and I knew Mum would be getting her knitting needles out the very minute we'd all gone. Adam was uncharacteristically emotional when we all hugged them both. He mumbled something about 'it's been a long time coming', so I guess they've been wanting a baby for quite a while. I think Mum and Dad had given up on having grandchildren, especially after my break-up with Will. I'd always assumed that if there were to be any grandchildren, I'd be the one providing them. Just shows how wrong you can be.

I'll confess to being a little jealous.

Will and I never discussed having a family; I always imagined that to be a topic we'd discuss when we'd been together for a while, but assumed that in the future there'd be children. A natural progression. My thoughts changed when Will turned into a man I no longer recognised. No way would I have children with him because there was no future for us.

I'm only thirty-five; it's not too late for me to meet someone else and have a family. Mel's having a baby and I'm sure she'll want to have more if they can. We're the same age and lots of people delay having children until their late thirties and early forties.

And I have been asked out on a date, so anything is possible.

John messaged me. Everyone exchanged numbers on Thursday night because Jax decided that we needed a Spanish class WhatsApp group. I was surprised when I saw his message this morning, asking if I'd like to go out for a drink one evening. The first thing he said was that if I didn't want to, I just had to say so. He wouldn't take offence. I haven't replied yet, because I can't decide whether I want to go or not. He's nice and very attractive. I like him and it's just for a drink, that's all. We chatted for ages when we were at the pub for Josie's birthday and I discovered that John's very easy to talk to and we're on the same wavelength, humour-wise. It was only after Caro dropped me off and I got home that I realised I'd hardly spoken to anyone else all night except for John.

Is it too soon to start seeing someone? It's been less than a year since I left Will, but in reality, we hadn't been in a loving relationship for a long time. For two years he made me feel like shit; two years of nastiness and living on a knife edge.

I hated him.

No, it's not too soon.

I'm lonely. I want what everyone else has; a loving partner, someone I can trust. A family of my own one day. Why shouldn't I have all that?

And it's just a date, that's all. There's no need to get ahead of myself.

So I should go, get out there, and move on, because John is good-looking, charming, and funny.

But so was Will.

10

I'm taking a week's annual leave from work. I didn't want any time off because I've got nothing planned, but I have to take it, apparently, because those are the rules. I'll still have two more weeks left after this, and that shows just how sad my life is that I'd rather go to work than take time off. I'm trying to plan something to fill each day so that it doesn't seem a complete waste.

My activity today is going to the police station.

Why?

Because I need to see if there's any new information about the man who's missing. I want to reiterate to the police that I'm sure the man I saw run down by the car is Dominic Newton. I'm not relishing the thought of going in there again, but Eve's remarks about the missing man have been running through my mind all night. I can't just let it go.

It matters.

He has a family and, from what I've read, he's a normal guy who's disappeared for no reason. There's a niggle inside of me that won't go away until I've done this. What I saw didn't *seem* like an accident. The men in the car didn't make any attempt to help him or call for an ambulance. They drove off and left him for dead.

Was it deliberate? Did they drive at him because they wanted to kill him?

Yes, it sounds like the plot from a movie, but I can't ignore it any more or pretend it didn't happen. Cameron's dismissiveness when I phoned him convinced me that I was overreacting, because I *wanted* to believe what he was saying. It was much easier to believe him than stand my ground and insist that the police investigate it properly. Cameron let me off the hook; giving me a way out of having any further contact with the police. I'd done my duty and I could forget about it. But the more I've thought about it, the more I believe that the two things *must* be connected. I'm starting to believe that Cameron saw me as an unreliable witness – or not a witness at all, because there was no body in the road when he arrived, and he must have got there pretty quickly. He could have me down as a fantasist; an attention-seeker who makes things up. Was he so nice to me when he took my statement because he was humouring me?

It's not a comfortable thought. But whatever he might think of me, it's not important; I know what I saw. I've allowed Cameron's attitude to make me doubt myself, just as I allowed Will to make me believe that his treatment of me was somehow my fault. I turned from a confident woman who spoke her mind into a meek mouse who was too scared to voice an opinion for fear of upsetting him.

I am not that woman any more.

I'm going to the police station to report that the man I saw run over looked like Dominic Newton. Because if I don't do this, I'm allowing someone to tell me what I'm thinking and I'm not having that.

Not again.

I power along the street, almost at a run, focussing on getting through the next few hours. It's a miniscule amount of time in the grand scheme of things and it'll soon be over. I'll be back home tonight and it will be behind me and my conscience will be clear and I'll have done all I can.

Ten more minutes and I'll be there.

My phone bleeps. I stop and pull it out of my pocket, ignoring the voice in my head that asks me if I really need to read it now? It's a delaying tactic. I ignore the voice and open the message.

It's from John.

JOHN

> That's great! How about Wednesday night for a drink? Pick you up at 7ish?

Yes, I'm going on a date with him.

I finally replied to him on Sunday night during my break at work. It's time to stop dithering and get a life.

Because not everyone is like Will.

Most men are *not* like Will; he was the exception, not the rule.

I need to start enjoying life again, and dating is one aspect I need to get back into. Before I met Will, I had an active social life and besides going out with friends, I also dated. No one serious, until I met Will, but I enjoyed myself and met new people. It's time to start doing that again. I type a quick reply to say seven o'clock is fine, slip my phone into my pocket and resume walking. Suddenly optimistic as I march along, I realise that I've got nothing to wear. Am I really going to buy something new to go out for a drink?

Maybe I am. Nothing amazing. Just something casual that I can wear again. Mulling this over in my mind as I turn the corner, I come to a halt as I'm confronted by the huge building in front of me.

The police station looms out of the ground, a multi-storey seventies cement and glass monstrosity that's seen better days. Weirdly, it stands directly opposite a hotel of the same height, with only the main road and the police station car park separating them. Do the people staying in the hotel feel safer for having the police in such close proximity? I've never thought about it before now because this building has been a constant in my life for as far back as I can remember. I've passed by it thousands of times but taken absolutely no notice of it.

Until that night.

Although I've been here before, the part of the station I remember most is the double doors that lead into the reception. It was dark, of course, when I was here the last time. I kept my head down when I got out of the police car, both from shame and from the fear of someone I knew seeing me; unlikely though it was, as it was so late at night.

But that was then and this is now.

I push the memory away and stride purposefully across the half-empty car park. Without stopping, I continue past two rows of police cars towards the double doors, falling into step behind a middle-aged man heading inside. He pulls open the door, turning and holding it open for me. Taking a deep breath, I follow him in.

I wait for the panic to engulf me and am surprised when it doesn't. I follow the man to the counter and stand behind him, feeling astonishingly normal as I wait my turn. I look around and take in my surroundings, remembering little of them from that night. The counter has Perspex screens running along the length of it, a grille with holes to speak through along the entire front. Two of the chairs behind the screens are empty, the others occupied by two women. They're not in uniform and they don't look like police-women. The place has the ambiance of a building society rather than a police station with the bank of metal chairs bolted to the floor opposite the counter, and the beige walls so typical of public buildings. I could be in a council office, a hospital, or a doctor's surgery, all of them have the same feel. It's quieter than I thought it would be too; for some reason, I'd expected the place to be buzzing with members of the public keen to report crimes. Perhaps like everything else, it's all online these days.

'Yes?'

A woman behind the counter to the right of the one I'm standing at is staring at me. The person she was dealing with has gone and she's now free. I walk over and lean in towards the Perspex grille.

'I'd like to speak to a police officer, please.'

'Is it to pay a fine?'

'No.'

'Make a complaint?'

'No.'

'Okay.' She taps on her keyboard. 'Name?'

I give her my name, followed by my address, and her fingers fly over the keyboard.

'Reason?'

That throws me a little. I don't want to go into detail, so I keep it brief.

'I have information about Dominic Newton.'

She types it in without missing a beat and then tells me to take a seat and I'll be called when they're ready, informing me that there might be a bit of a wait, as they're busy. I sit down on one of the line of chairs set against the wall, squeezing in between a woman who constantly sniffs and a teenager with his nose practically glued to his phone. Five other people are already there and, from a quick glance at their faces, they're fed up and bored. I assume they've been there for a while.

I could be in for a long wait.

I check the time. Three o'clock. How long am I prepared to sit here? I hadn't thought about this before I arrived, but now I make the instant decision that I'll stay for as long as is necessary.

I'm not coming back. This is a one-time-only visit.

I take out my phone, open the Kindle app and continue reading a book I started a few days ago. I marvel at how calm I am; all that worry over returning here and I'm absolutely fine.

All that hysteria for nothing.

Drama llama, Will's voice taunts. I push it away.

The minutes tick by and at 3.35, not one person waiting has moved. I continue to stare at my phone screen but find it difficult to concentrate. I can't remember a single thing that I've read. It's something to focus on, though, instead of gazing into space. All I'm hoping is that it isn't Cameron who's going to interview me. That would be beyond embarrassing. I'd have to ask to speak to another officer because he didn't seem to believe I'd even seen an accident.

The door next to the counter opens with a clicking noise and a harassed man wearing a crumpled white shirt and black trousers steps into the room, holding a piece of paper in his hand. I look up hopefully, as does everyone else on the row of seats. Even though I know I'm going to be last, because I was the last to arrive.

'Abigail Redmond?' he calls, looking up from the piece of paper.

I jump up in surprise and walk towards him, the sound of discontented muttering behind me. From the talk I've heard whilst sitting here, some of these people have been waiting for hours. With a tight smile, the man turns back to the doorway and goes through. I assume I'm to follow so I fall into step behind him, the door locking with a click behind me. I follow him along a narrow corridor into a small room containing just a table and two chairs. He closes the door and motions for me to sit down.

'I'm Sergeant Timpson and I'll be dealing with you today.' He settles himself in the chair opposite me. 'Are you happy to proceed, or would you prefer a policewoman to interview you?'

'No, this is fine.'

He glances at the piece of paper. 'I understand you have information about Dominic Newton?'

'Yes. I'm almost certain I saw him get run over by a car.'

'Okay,' he says without emotion, as if I've just told him it was raining. 'And when was this?'

'The night of the first of November, or rather the morning of the second. At about a quarter to five in the morning.'

He frowns. 'And why have you waited until now, over two weeks later, to report this?'

'I reported it at the time, when it happened. I phoned the emergency services, and the police came out, but by the time they got there, the man hit by the car was gone.'

'Gone? So a car hit him but he wasn't injured?'

'No, he was injured. Stunned, at least. I thought he was dead at the time. He was lying on the road with his eyes open. He looked dead to me but obviously he couldn't have been, because by the time I got back from the phone box, he was gone. But I got a good look at his face and he looked like Dominic Newton. Although I didn't know it was him until much later when I saw him on TV.'

'Right,' he says slowly. He seems confused by what I'm saying and I can't blame him; it sounds all jumbled up.

'I didn't have my mobile on me, you see, so I had to run to a phone box which was quite far away and when I got back, he wasn't lying in the road any more.'

'Okay,' he says, slowly. 'Let's start from the beginning. Tell me exactly what happened.'

I push down my irritation and relay the events of that night, being as thorough as I can. I only want to say this once.

'And you've already told the police all of this?' he asks when I've finished.

'Yes. As I've told you, when I got back to where the accident happened, a policeman was there. I told him. A few days later, he came to my house and took a written statement from me so I wouldn't need to come into the station to do it.'

'Right.' He stares at the paper for a moment. 'I'll need to go and pull the statement and read it. What was the officer's name?'

'Cameron Malone.'

'I've got his phone number, too,' I add. 'He's a sergeant, and he was on first response. I phoned him about it last Thursday and spoke to him about it being Dominic Newton, but I've been giving it a lot of thought since then and I'm more sure now that it was him. Which is why I'm here.' I'm starting to gabble; repeating myself.

He nods again, scribbling down what I tell him. Too late, I realise that I should have told the woman on the desk all this, and they could have got the statement out ready. It sounds convoluted and ridiculous.

'Okay.' He stands up. 'I shouldn't be long.'

And with that, he's gone.

I sit back and wait, confident that once he's read the statement, what I've told him will make more sense. I resist the urge to check my watch, knowing that once I start, I won't be able to stop. Everything will be on the computer so he should find it quickly.

But he doesn't seem to.

He's been gone for ages, or am I imagining it? I've just given in and looked at my watch when the door opens and he comes back in. He's holding a buff-coloured file in his hands and has a serious expression on his face as he slides into the seat opposite. I sense a change in him; something slightly off. His manner is different to when I first came in here, but I can't put my finger on what it is.

'Sorry it took a while.'

'That's okay.'

'So...'

I wait for him to continue.

'Okay.' He sighs heavily. 'The thing is, Miss Redmond, what you're telling me doesn't match what you said in your statement.'

'What?'

He opens the folder, pulling out several sheets of paper. He pushes them across the table to me. I pick them up and immediately recognise the neat handwriting of Cameron. I begin to read, my eyes racing over the words, unable to take in what I'm seeing.

'This isn't what I said! This isn't my statement. There must be some mistake.'

'You're saying the signature at the bottom of the sheet isn't yours?'

'No! I mean, yes, it looks like mine, but it can't be because this isn't what I told him. It's all wrong.' I study the signature, bringing it closer to my eyes. It must be forged. Traced.

What the hell is going on?

I push the statement across the table towards Sergeant Timpson as if it's burning my fingers. 'I don't know what's happened, but that's not my statement. That,' I point at it, 'is most definitely *not* what I told Cameron Malone.'

'This statement is an exact account of what you told Sergeant Malone, Miss Redmond. You signed it. As I'm sure Sergeant Malone explained to you at the time, the police don't punish people for making a genuine mistake.'

'I didn't make a mistake, and I wasn't confused! That,' I tap my fingers on the paper, 'is wrong. It's a forgery, a fake.'

'Okay,' he says. 'Let's just recap. According to your statement, you saw a car racing out of a side street at speed, which you say hit someone whom you saw running up the road. You immediately headed towards the shops where you knew there was a public telephone. You called for police and an ambulance. When you arrived back at the scene, Sergeant Malone was there. You then admitted to Sergeant Malone that due to squeamishness on your part, you hadn't actually checked on the man in the road but had run straight for help.'

'No. I did check on him. I knelt down on the ground right next to him. I took my jacket off and laid it over him to try to keep him warm. He was staring right at me and he looked dead. I remember saying as much to the call operator.'

He nods. 'Yes, you did say that, but in your statement you admit that you were panicked, hysterical even, and that you ran to the public telephone without checking on the man and may have been exaggerating when you spoke to the call handler.'

'No.' I shake my head and try to remain calm. 'That's not right. I didn't say that. I've no idea why Sergeant Malone would write that, because it's not what happened.'

'These are your words, Miss Redmond. You read the statement after Sergeant Malone wrote it and you signed it. You admitted that you were hysterical on the night you made the call to the emergency services, but after a couple of days of reflection, admitted that you hadn't seen an accident at all. The weak lighting and your imagination got the better of you. According to this signed statement, you apologised, Miss Redmond, for wasting police time.'

'No, no, I didn't. I didn't. It wasn't like that.'

'Sergeant Malone arrived within minutes of your emergency call. There was no evidence of any accident. There was no victim. No sign of a hit and run. Had there been any evidence of an accident, he would have found it.'

'He's lying.'

'That's a very serious allegation, Miss Redmond. Why would a serving police officer lie?'

'I don't know.'

'Did you bring your copy of the statement with you?'

'I haven't got one.'

'We always give a copy of a statement for your records.'

I recall the day Cameron came round; I clearly remember signing it, but don't recall him offering me a copy.

I take a deep breath and attempt to push down the rising panic.

'There's something not right,' I say, as calmly as I can. 'That's *not* the statement I made. I never said any of that.'

He sighs and closes the folder with an air of finality.

'I'm sorry, but you signed the statement and we have no evidence that there was an accident.'

'There was. I'm telling the truth. You have to investigate because there must be a reason why Cameron's lying. I need to make a complaint about him.'

He shakes his head. 'I suggest you go home, Miss Redmond, and consider whether that's something you really want to do. I've spoken to Sergeant Malone and whilst he was willing to give you the benefit of the doubt that evening, you did make an unnecessary emergency call, which you later admitted to. Given your history, the CPS wouldn't look too kindly on your complaint. It's my duty to warn you that should you persist in making a complaint, you may well find yourself charged with wasting police time.'

11

THEN

After the first time Will locked me in the cupboard, nearly six months went by until it happened again. By then, I'd almost managed to convince myself that I'd imagined it all and that it was, as Will kept telling me, a joke that had gone wrong. We were getting along fine and it was good between us. We were good.

Except that we weren't; I was fooling myself. In those six months, I'd not once been on a night out with the girls, aside from catching up with Mel and a few others at lunchtimes – meetings that Will didn't know about because they happened whilst he was at work and I never told him about them. I lied to myself and pretended that I didn't need to tell him every trivial detail about my life. When invitations came from my friends for nights out and evening meet-ups, again, I pretended to myself that I was busy and didn't have the time but the truth was, I was afraid.

Not of Will, not then, but of us being over.

I loved him so much and I didn't want us to finish. I knew that if he ever behaved like that again, there would be no more chances for him. I wouldn't forgive him a second time. I would leave him immediately and that would be the end of us, and I didn't want that.

Incredibly, I believed that I still had a choice.

And it didn't even matter whether I went out with my friends or not, because as I discovered, Will didn't need a reason.

The night it happened again, I'd arrived home from work before him and was prepping dinner in the kitchen. I heard the front door open and close and I called out hello. I waited for him to come into the kitchen to give me a kiss because that was how we always greeted each other. A part of the day that I loved and looked forward to. But my greeting was met with silence. Then the blare of the television came from the lounge as he turned it on and I realised that he'd gone straight in there without even coming to see me.

I knew immediately that something was wrong. I felt the first stirrings of unease, but I shook them off; he was ill, he'd had bad news, he'd had the day from hell. There would be a valid reason for his behaviour and all I needed to do was ask him. I stopped what I was doing and hurried into the lounge to find him slumped in the armchair, staring blankly at the television screen. Concerned, I asked him what was the matter, and he turned and stared at me for a moment before turning his attention back to the screen. I asked him again, and he ignored me this time, not even glancing at me. It was as if I'd never spoken. I felt like I was in the room with a stranger. Trying to convince myself that something terrible had happened, I rushed over to him and put my arms around him. He pushed me roughly away without speaking.

I returned to the kitchen, hurt and bewildered, with no clue to what was going on. Scenarios were running through my head about what could have happened for him to be like this. I stood at the window, staring out over the back garden, all thoughts of cooking dinner forgotten, wanting to believe that there'd been some sort of disaster and Will couldn't find the words to tell me. I never heard him come up behind me. The first I knew of it was when I felt a blow to my back, right between the shoulder blades.

Winded and doubled over the sink in pain, I was unable to catch my breath; the pain was so bad that I saw stars. After a moment, I crumpled to the floor and curled up into a ball and closed my eyes. When I opened them and saw Will's feet, I stared up at him. He looked down at me coldly and it gradually dawned on me that he'd punched me in the back. Although I didn't want to believe it, I knew then how things were going to play out. On some level, I'd always been expecting it, despite my attempts to pretend nothing had ever happened.

He never spoke, not one word, and he only hit me once, that time. He leaned down, grabbed hold of my hair, hauled me up from the floor and dragged me into the hallway. I stumbled after him in shock, crying and begging for him to let go. I was met with stony silence. He twisted and pulled my hair so much that the next day I found a great clump of it missing. I made no attempt to try to get away; Will was much bigger and stronger than me, and easily overpowered me. It was almost a relief when he forced me inside the cupboard. I hit the opposite wall and collapsed painfully onto the assorted jumble of junk in there. The door slammed, followed by the sound of the console table being pushed in front of the door, making it impossible for me to get out. Time crawled by and I spent an uncomfortable night curled up inside the cupboard, falling asleep, only to wake minutes later, disorientated and not knowing where I was. The night seemed to last forever.

But I was safer in there, away from Will. Until he'd calmed down.

But I was distraught; not only because of what he'd done, but because that was it, we were finished now. I would be moving out immediately that day, as soon as he'd let me out of the cupboard. No matter how much he said sorry, I was leaving him, there would be no more chances. I honestly believed he was the love of my life and all of my hopes and dreams were in tatters. I spent that night planning for the morning; I'd ring work and feign illness for a few days, which would give me time to pack up all my belongings and move back to Mum and Dad's. By the time daylight started filtering underneath the tiny gap at the bottom of the door, I was calm and knew what I had to do. I wouldn't tell Will I was leaving him; I'd listen to his apologies and pretend to forgive him, pretend that I was going to work.

But I'd be gone by the time he came home and would never be coming back.

When I heard him coming down the stairs, I braced myself and waited for the door to open.

It didn't.

In mounting disbelief and horror, the sound of the front door slamming penetrated my brain. He'd gone out; he'd left me alone and gone to work. It was a Wednesday. I was supposed to be at work. I had no phone to call anyone. I began to push and hammer on the cupboard door. I lay down and put my feet on it and pushed with all of my strength and when that didn't work, I started kicking it. If I did it for long enough, it would eventually give way, or I'd manage to move it sufficiently to knock the console table over. I thought of screaming, but Will's house was detached and set back from the road so it was doubtful anyone would be able to hear me. I lost track of time in the semi-darkness, kicking, resting, and then kicking again.

I didn't hear Will come back into the house.

I stopped kicking when I heard the table being dragged away from the door. When Will opened it, I pulled myself up and started to come out, but he shoved me roughly back inside.

'You thought I'd gone, didn't you?' he snarled at me.

I was shocked; I'd expected him to be contrite and begging for forgiveness, but I could see from the look in his eyes that I couldn't be further from the truth.

He laughed and dangled something in front of my eyes that he had in his hand. It was a padlock and a metal hasp. I stared at the stranger in front of me and wondered if this was some sort of nightmare that I couldn't wake up from. 'Because you tried to get out,' he said, 'you'll have to spend another night in there to teach you a lesson.'

He stepped forward and crouched down to face me.

'And if you think that someone at work will worry where you are, they won't. I rang them and said you were ill.' He smiled, and at that moment I knew he was truly insane. 'If you behave, I might let you out tomorrow. Or maybe I'll go away on a little trip and forget all about you. Who knows?' He stood up and pushed the door closed, but this time, I pushed back. It flew open and knocked him sideways. I raced towards the front door, intent on getting out of that house and away from him.

But the door wouldn't open; it was locked.

We always left the key in the front door. It couldn't be opened without it, but there was no key in sight. I turned towards the stairs, thinking I could escape to the bathroom and lock myself in, but Will was already there, blocking my way. He grabbed hold of me by the throat and, as his fingers tightened, I thought he was going to strangle me. He stared down into my eyes and there was no trace of the Will that I knew. He was gone, replaced by a madman. He pushed me hard and I stumbled, hearing a crack as the back of my head hit the front door. Bursts of light exploded in front of my eyes and then the world turned black. When I awoke, a long time later, my head throbbing, I opened my eyes to darkness.

I was locked in the cupboard again.

And this time, there was no escape.

12

'Miss Redmond?'

My head is spinning and I gawp at him, unable to corral the facts together in my head to make sense of what he's saying.

'I wasn't mistaken,' I whisper in shock. 'I know what I saw and I didn't imagine it.'

He doesn't respond but looks down at his hands, shuffling the papers around, avoiding eye contact with me.

He's embarrassed.

He thinks I'm lying. Why would he take my word over that of a fellow police officer?

He wouldn't.

He sees me as an attention-seeking, hysterical woman. Maybe he's seen my drink-driving prosecution so has me marked down as a habitual boozer who can't remember what she's done, or who or what she's seen. Maybe he thinks I'd been out drinking all that night but didn't want to admit it.

But I have no doubt about what I saw, and now, I'm more certain of it than ever.

The burning question for me is, why is Cameron Malone lying? Why has he faked my statement to make me look unreliable – no, worse than that, he's made me out to be a liar. He was different though, wasn't he, when I spoke to him? He was cold and distant, nothing like the friendly police officer who'd visited my home.

But why?

The room feels suddenly claustrophobic, the walls closing in on me. I have to get out of here.

'Miss Redmond?'

'I'm sorry. I should go.' I stand up on shaking legs.

'There is help available.' His voice is softer and for the first time, he meets my eyes. 'If you're struggling with your mental health. We all have our problems and there is support if you're prepared to accept it.'

There's pity in his voice; sympathy. He has no idea how wrong he's got it.

'I don't have a mental health problem,' I say calmly. 'I know what I saw, I didn't make it up or imagine it.'

He stares at me without speaking and I force myself not to squirm under his scrutiny. I want to reinforce what I've just said; convince him somehow that he's wrong about me but I stop myself, because there would be no point. No one at this police station is going to believe a single word that I say.

He looks away first, making me feel as if I've won some small victory. 'Thank you,' I say. 'I'm sorry I've wasted your time.'

'I'll show you out.' He's relieved to be rid of me, and who can blame him?

He gets up and I follow him. We walk down the corridor to reception and I check wildly around me, suddenly paranoid that I'll see Cameron Malone; that he'll jump out of a doorway and demand to know why I'm accusing him of lying. He must be aware of my visit today because Sergeant Timpson said he'd spoken to him. If Cameron Malone is prepared to falsify my statement, what else is he capable of?

Fear swamps me, my brain telling me to run, now, get away from here because somehow, I've stumbled on something dangerous. But as I think that, the truth hits me.

He knows where I live.

* * *

I'm walking so fast that I'm practically running.

All I want to do is get home and lock all the doors, bolt all the windows, make it impossible for anyone to get in.

I'd be safer at work.

I debate calling a cab because it's already dark when I come out of the police station, but immediately dismiss the idea. The thought of standing outside in the car park waiting for the cab to arrive is too much. What if Cameron Malone is watching me from a window, plotting what he's going to do next? Who can I trust if not the police? Do I really want to be trapped in a cab with no escape? I tell myself that I'm catastrophising, that the world is not out to get me, but as I race through the streets of the town centre, my thoughts are in turmoil. I should go somewhere busy; there's safety in numbers but the shops are closed now, the only people around are those leaving work to hurry home to warmth, normality. I could get a bus; they'll be crowded at this time of night. I reject the idea. I'd be unable to sit still. I'm twitchy and jumpy. I'd be viewing my fellow passengers with suspicion, wondering if they're in on it too.

Because I stumbled across something on the night of the accident. I saw something I wasn't supposed to.

I witnessed a murder.

That missing man, Dominic Newton, is dead. He was the man hit by the car that night and it was deliberate. How stupid was I to be persuaded that it was an accident; it was murder, plain and simple, and I allowed myself to be convinced otherwise. His staring eyes looking up at me as I knelt over him; he was dead. Whoever killed him had removed him by the time I got back from phoning for an ambulance. Or was his body still there, hidden in the boot of Cameron's police car? Is that why he arrived so quickly, so he could clean up? After Cameron took me home, did he take the body away so it could be disposed of somewhere that it would never be found? I can't make myself believe that; Cameron was so friendly and normal both on that night and when he came to take my statement. He wouldn't have been able to behave like that if he'd been hiding the corpse of a man in his car boot. Something happened after that because he was different when I spoke to him on the phone, something that made him change my statement.

I'm the only witness to a murder and now I'm being cancelled; made to look unreliable, a liar. Will an accident be arranged for me too, to ensure no one ever gets the chance to believe me?

I come to a stumbling halt, my breathing ragged, the enormity of what I've witnessed hitting me like a physical force. I bend over, hands on my knees, gasping for air. I want to scream into the night. Someone must be able to help me, wake me up from this nightmare.

But there is no one. I can't trust the police, so what am I going to do?

I stand up slowly, gripping my waist with my fingers to ease the stitch in my side. My lungs are burning, my heels and the soles of my feet sore from running in leather boots instead of the comfortable trainers I normally wear.

Calm yourself, Abi. Stop panicking, because it won't help. Think.

I look around; I've run blindly, my body on autopilot. I'm now on the perimeter of the estate where I live. The streets here are dark, and most of the street lights don't work. They've been broken for a long time. No one bothers to report them, I assume, or if they have, the council never get around to fixing them. Most people drive when it's dark; few, like me, walk. I wish I could drive. I've stopped myself from dwelling on the impact of losing my licence because I couldn't do anything about it, but now, I long for the safety of a car. Locked doors, the ability to speed away from danger.

I do this all the time; set rules in my head for myself.

Don't think about driving, or about Will being an abuser, or about being trapped, or the man who was run over, pretend that none of it is happening so you can have an easier life. Put it all out of your mind; pretend everything is normal and bury it. Deep.

It's the reason I'm in this mess.

Occasional cars pass me by but there are no other pedestrians around because normal people are tucked up cosy and warm, safe in their houses for the evening. No one else is as stupid as me, running at night, inviting disaster.

I'm vulnerable.

And scared.

I've witnessed a murder, but that knowledge doesn't do me, or the victim, any good. I can't go to the police because they don't believe me. I'm an unreliable witness; a drunk, a woman with issues. But worse than that is the fact that Cameron Malone, a serving officer, has lied and covered up a murder. He already knows I've been to the station. It may already be too late for me; one man has died. What's stopping whoever killed him from killing me? How I wish now that I'd never gone to the police station today. If I'd stayed away, perhaps whoever killed him would have continued to leave me alone, believing that I was no threat to them.

I fear that now, they won't.

Oh God, why did I have the misfortune to be there that night? Why me? Why couldn't that car have come tearing out of that road a second later, when I'd have been running through the industrial estate and oblivious to it all? Hasn't my life been bad enough for the last three years without this?

I'm a coward.

A car passes and toots its horn and I jump, my heart pounding. I resume walking, fast. Another ten minutes and I'll be home. I march along, forcing myself not to look over my shoulder to confirm there's no one following me. When I reach the corner of my street, I keep up the pace but reach into my handbag and root around until my fingers find my key. I walk quickly up the path and the outside security light comes on. I push the key into the lock with trembling fingers and turn it, open the door and step inside, quickly shutting it behind me. I turn on the hallway light, blinking in the brightness as I click the latch across and bolt the door. Suddenly exhausted, I lean against it, my legs weak. I close my eyes, slowly lower myself to the floor, and slump into a heap on the doormat.

Safe.

Sort of.

I open my eyes and ease my feet out of my boots, stand up and go into the lounge and pull the curtains tightly closed, checking that all the windows are locked. I've not opened them for weeks, months even. It's been too cold to open them, but that doesn't stop me from checking.

Next, I go through to the kitchen, lean over the sink and pull the blind down over the window, shutting out the darkness. I make sure the back door is locked and bolt it. It probably wouldn't stop someone if they really wanted to get in, but the noise it would make would give me some warning, at least. I turn, intending to head back to the hallway to go upstairs when the knife block catches my eye.

Five sharp knives; should I take the smallest one out and keep it with me from now on? Hide it in my pocket in case I need it? Would I have the guts to use it to defend myself?

I already know the answer to that question.

But a weapon could be used against me. I shudder at the thought of what could be done with a knife. I stride purposefully past, refusing to stop, go out into the hallway, turn on the landing light, and head up the stairs.

I go into my bedroom, pausing at the switch, but continue into the room without pressing it; otherwise, I'll be illuminated as I close the curtains with the light on. I pull the thick, beige material across the windows, and only then go back and turn on the ceiling light.

The neatness of the bedroom comforts me; my cosy, colourful duvet cover, the warmth from the radiator, the familiar contours of the room. The battered but serviceable furniture.

I'm safe.

But am I? This house may be homely and warm, but my brave new life disappeared the second I read that fake statement.

This house is now a prison.

I'm back inside that cupboard, and this time, there's no escape.

13

I'm going to see Mel later this afternoon; she's invited me to stay for dinner, too, so it means I won't have to stay here all day and evening on my own. I'll have to come back tonight, of course, but I'm not dwelling on that now. If I were at work, it wouldn't be so bad, but without that normal routine, I'm adrift and unable to fill the hours.

What a sad life.

Mel only invited me because I'd messaged her and dropped massive hints about being free all week. I told her I was on annual leave and a bit bored. Too early to start my Christmas shopping and too late to take a mini-break, I explained, in what I hoped was a casual way.

As if I have anyone to go on a mini-break with.

She responded immediately with the offer of dinner, but if she hadn't invited me, I'd have gone to Mum and Dad's for the evening. I don't want to spend too much time on my own.

I'm going on a date with John tomorrow night, but I barely have the headspace for it now. I could make an excuse, put him off, feign illness. Romance and men are the furthest things from my mind at the moment.

I slept last night, so well that it was past ten o'clock when I awoke. A deep and dreamless sleep since I'd drunk several glasses of whisky from a bottle I found lurking at the back of the sideboard in the lounge. I never bought the whisky; I don't even like whisky. It was left by a previous occupant of the house and I almost had to hold my nose to get it down.

But it had the desired effect because it pretty much knocked me out.

I have no idea what time I fell asleep on the sofa, but when I woke with a start, the television had turned itself off; the heating had gone off and I was cold. I dragged myself off the sofa and up the stairs, stumbled along the landing and collapsed into bed. The glass and bottle are still on the floor in the lounge where I left them. I was so intent on getting to bed that I never even bothered to brush my teeth for fear that it would wake me up. I lift up the duvet to see that I'm still wearing my clothes from yesterday. My mouth is desert dry with a disgusting taste, and the headache promised last night is in full flight; pounding against the inside of my skull with the force and regularity of a sledgehammer. I feel like shit, which is no surprise because if I drink a lot, I always get a hangover.

I can't drink alcohol every night to make myself sleep. That's not the answer. I could go and stay with Mum and Dad, but to do that, I'd have to give them some sort of explanation and they'd start worrying. I can't put that on them. I've caused them enough anxiety this past year.

I need to stop catastrophising and not get hysterical about it all. Stop imagining the very worst that can happen.

Be braver.

But I'm not brave; I never have been. In my darkest moments, when Will locked me in the cupboard and I could see no way out of my situation, I prayed for death.

Will's, not mine.

I escaped, I remind myself. I wasn't a complete coward. It took me a long time to summon up the courage, but I got away from him.

For every problem, there is a solution. Apparently. I heard that somewhere. So there is an answer. I just have to find it, but for now, I carry on.

As normal.

I consider going back to sleep, but it's a fleeting thought. My mind is fully awake now, even if my body feels like it can't move. I sit up. My head throbs but I ignore it, get out of bed and walk on wobbly legs to the bathroom. I try to convince myself that I'll feel better if I turn on the shower and get underneath it but can't bring myself to do it.

I strip off my clothes from the previous day and then head back to the bedroom and pull on clean underwear, a pair of joggers, a T-shirt and a zip-up fleece. The fleece is old and bobbly and I'm reminded of the night of the accident and my missing jacket that I laid over Dominic Newton. I push the thought away, swallow down the bile rising in my throat and head downstairs and into the kitchen. After a rummage around in the cupboard, I find a rogue packet of paracetamol and swallow two down with a half a glass of water, gagging on the second tablet. Picking up my house key, I tuck my phone into my fleece pocket and go out into the hallway. I stare at the front door.

Fear prickles my spine. They could be outside; what if they're out there, waiting to get me? Will I end up on a slab in the morgue, run over by a person or persons unknown, or will I vanish, my body never to be found, as Dominic Newton has? The panic starts to rise. I'm wondering if I'll ever feel safe again and if my life will ever be the same, when it hits me.

I'm no threat to them, am I? I'm not a reliable witness because my reputation is trashed. There's a statement in my name where I've pretty much admitted that I'm an attention-seeker with mental health issues. The police don't believe a word I say and never will. Whoever murdered Dominic Newton will be secure in that knowledge. To make me disappear could draw attention to them, which is clearly something that they won't want.

So the solution that I've been searching for is already there; carry on as normal and keep my mouth shut. Keep my head down, forget it ever happened, forget what I saw. As long as I appear to be no threat, I'm safe.

It never happened. Bury it, like you always do. Deep.

I open the front door and step outside, pulling it closed behind me and locking it carefully. *One foot in front of the other, Abi, that's all. Keep going. You can't do anything; you can't help the missing man, or his family, it's out of your hands.*

It's done.

Keep calm and carry on.

* * *

So here I am; bathed, dressed and waiting outside Mel and Owen's house. I'm even wearing make-up. I ran for nearly two hours and when I got home, I drank three cups of tea and wolfed down four slices of toast before wallowing in the bath until the water turned cold. I feel almost human again now, and the headache has eased to a faint thud. Although the temperature has dropped significantly and the cold spell we've been promised has arrived, it's a nice day. No rain. A little sun. It took an hour to walk to here, which is nothing to the distance I normally run, but the thought of walking back home tonight doesn't appeal. Perhaps I'll treat myself to a cab.

I've decided to start running in daylight in the future; go out straight after finishing work in the morning before I go to bed for the day. And, like this morning, I'll definitely be taking my phone with me from now on.

I press the brass button for the doorbell and wait, admiring the glossy paint on the door and the huge driveway that could easily hold four cars. I marvel again at how well they've done.

'Come in!' Mel pulls the door open and I step into the warmth of the hallway.

'You've brought the cold in with you!' She hugs me. 'God, you're freezing!'

'And you're like a boiler.' I kiss her on the cheek and she laughs, but she looks tired, the skin around her eyes, dark. The consequence of being six months pregnant, no doubt.

'It's these bloody hormones. Who needs heating when you're pregnant? Thank God it's not the summer, because I couldn't cope.'

I shrug off my coat and look around for somewhere to hang it.

'In here.' Mel presses her fingers against the wall and a door springs open to reveal a wardrobe. She pulls out a coat hanger and hands it to me. I put my coat on it, drape the scarf around the top and stuff my gloves into the pockets. Mel picks up my boots from the mat and puts them inside the cupboard.

'Wow, are these new?' I gaze at the doors that I can now see run the entire length of the hallway. 'I don't remember these from last time.'

'Had them done last week. The guy's amazing. We're going to get him to build something similar in the dining room so we can use it as a playroom in the day and hide all the toys away when we have guests for dinner. We eat mostly in the kitchen. The dining room isn't getting much use except when we have people round.'

'They're lovely.' I smooth my hand over the doors. Pale cream, there are no visible handles on show at all. I hadn't noticed them until Mel opened the door. I open my mouth to comment that they must have cost an absolute fortune, but then close it again. It would sound rude, and whilst it's the sort of thing that we always used to say to each other, it no longer seems appropriate now that Mel and Owen have clearly moved up in the world.

We go through to the kitchen and I settle myself on a chair at the table while Mel busies herself filling the kettle.

'I thought we'd eat about seven. Owen's promised to be home by then.'

'Sounds good. How is he?'

'Okay. Do you want tea or coffee?' She doesn't turn around and I detect something in her voice that I can't quite put my finger on. I noticed it in the hallway, despite her complimentary spiel about the wardrobes; a brittleness, an edge. 'I can make you a proper one with the machine if you like?'

'No, tea is fine, but not that green muck.'

She takes two mugs down from the cupboard and places them on the counter. She still has her back to me.

'Is something wrong, Mel?'

I see her shoulders tense for a moment before she turns around to face me.

'No, of course not. Just not sleeping well, that's all.' She smiles, but it doesn't reach her eyes. She's not herself.

'Everything's okay, isn't it? With the baby?'

'Oh God, yes, absolutely fine. No worries there, blood pressure and everything is all good.' It slips then, the smile. She turns back to the counter to make the tea and I watch her in silence.

'There you go.' She walks over, puts both mugs on the table, and slides onto the chair opposite me.

I pick up my mug and watch as Mel does the same.

'What?' she asks.

'Sure you're okay?'

She sighs, putting the mug down.

'It's nothing. Hormones, probably. They're playing havoc with my emotions. Owen says I should speak to the doctor about it because he can tell something's not right. He must be sick to death of me, and I can't blame him. We've got everything we could possibly want and I'm still not satisfied.'

She's close to tears and I stretch my hand across the table and take hold of her fingers.

'Hey, come on, what's wrong? A problem shared and all that.'

'Nothing.' She swallows, clearly fighting back the tears. 'It's me. *I'm* wrong. I'm going to ruin everything if I don't get a grip.'

A tear rolls down her cheek. She brushes it away angrily.

'I'm a stupid, fat, jealous cow. I wouldn't blame Owen if he did leave me for someone else.'

'Stop it, Mel. Don't talk about yourself like that.'

'It's true.' She's crying now, big fat tears. 'I'm going to drive him away with my stupid jealousy, but even knowing that, I can't seem to stop myself from harping on at him. Every time he works late, every time he gets a text message, I'm wondering if he's found someone else and is cheating on me. I'm constantly questioning him and even though I pretend to do it casually, he's not stupid. He won't put up with it. Not after the last time.'

'Oh, Mel, of course he's not cheating on you. Owen loves you to bits.'

She pulls her hand away from me.

'He's done it before, though, hasn't he?'

'But he hasn't, has he?' I say gently. 'You convinced yourself he did, which isn't the same thing, is it?'

'Okay. He told me it was all in my head, but what if it wasn't?' She gets up and walks over to the sink, pulls a sheet of paper from the roll and wipes her face with it. 'He would never admit to it but I was so sure at the time, Abi, so sure. The signs were all there and if he can do it once, he can do it again.'

'You don't know,' I say. 'You *think*. Two very different things.'

'I was so sure. It was just after he got his first promotion and he was secretive. Evasive. Not Owen at all. He couldn't even make eye contact with me; I didn't imagine that. He changed. We've been together since we were eighteen years old and he was different, no doubt about it. Just because he never admitted it doesn't mean he didn't do it.'

'You were under a lot of stress then.' We've had this conversation so often; every time Mel feels insecure, it raises its ugly head again. 'Owen thought you'd changed, too, didn't he? It was a difficult time for both of you.'

'It was. Four years ago. Eight months after we started IVF. Those months felt more like eight years. I wasn't sure if I was imagining it because I was all over the place. And even though I had a horrible feeling he was lying, I ignored it because I love him and I wanted a baby so much. And then, somehow it all got turned around and became about me and my jealousy, as if I were the one at fault. But what if he did cheat, what if I was right and he's doing it again?'

She sits back down at the table, twisting the paper towel between her fingers and shredding it into tiny pieces. Would Owen cheat? I can't imagine he would, he adores Mel. But his twisting it around to make it seem like Mel's fault is exactly what Will did to me. No, surely not. I can't believe it of Owen, I don't *want* to believe it.

'What makes you so sure he's cheating?'

She shrugs. 'It's the same as before. The phone calls I catch him making that he quickly ends when I walk in on him. His phone's always on silent, so I can't tell when he gets a call or a text. Why would he do that? I don't do that. He's always working late. And he stays downstairs for ages after I've gone to bed. Just like before.'

'He's been promoted, Mel. He has to work late. Look at this lovely house, how hard he's working for you and your baby. He's a high-flyer now. He's hardly going to be working a regular nine to five when he's earning enough for all this, is he?'

'He's got a new credit card.' She looks up at me. 'And I can't see the statement for it. He says he needs it for work, for expenses, but what if it's so he can spend money on another woman without me finding out? It's all online and I can't access it, so I can't see what's on it. Isn't that very convenient for him?'

'That's normal, Mel. Completely normal. In my last job, I used to have one to put all my work expenses on too. It makes claiming them back easier. There's nothing suspicious about it and it certainly doesn't mean he's having an affair.'

'See, when you say it, it sounds perfectly reasonable, but when I'm on my own, I convince myself he's cheating, that he's hiding something. I blow everything up and I can't get rid of it; it's there constantly, going around and around like a bloody washing machine.'

'He's besotted with you, Mel. You're overthinking things. He wouldn't risk everything you have. He just wouldn't. He wants this baby as much as you do.'

'You think?' she asks hopefully.

'I *know*,' I say, hoping that I'm right. 'Owen loves you. Stop doubting him and enjoy what you have.'

She sniffs. 'Hormones, eh? Absolute bastards.'

'They are, but you'll soon have your lovely baby girl and then you'll be back on an even keel.'

'I'll be on a starvation diet as well.' She gives a shaky smile. 'It's just when it's all rattling around in my head, it gets bigger and bigger. Do you know what I mean?'

'I definitely do,' I say with a laugh.

'The trouble is once it gets in here.' She taps her finger on her forehead. 'It drives me mad and before long, I'm just going to blurt it out and start accusing and then it'll be like last time; me all needy and demanding he tell me the truth and Owen losing patience with me. He'll leave me and I wouldn't even blame him because I nearly drove him away last time.'

'Well, next time you feel like that, as if it's overwhelming you, promise me you'll ring me. Get it off your chest and out of your head.'

'You won't want me whinging to you all the time.'

'You're my best friend. We'll talk it through and Owen need

never know about it.'

'Never know about what?'

Mel and I turn in shock to see Owen standing in the kitchen doorway. He looks at Mel and then glares at me.

'Owen!' Mel smiles nervously. 'I never heard you come in. I thought you weren't home until seven.'

He doesn't return her smile. 'So I'll ask again. What, exactly, need I never know about?'

14

Owen's words hang in the air, and I try desperately to think of something to say. Mel should tell him the truth, but one look at her face tells me that's not going to happen; there's genuine fear in her eyes. She's afraid if Owen finds out about her jealousy, she'll drive him away for good. I remember the last time Mel was like this; the downward spiral of accusation and denial that nearly destroyed them. Her refusal to believe Owen when he said he wasn't having an affair and his mounting anger at her jealousy. It went on for months and nearly broke them, it was only the fact that she got pregnant that saved them.

It wasn't the first time, either. Since the day they met, Mel's been fighting her paranoia that Owen is going to cheat on her. She loves him desperately and simply cannot believe that she's good enough for him.

'It's not Mel, it's me,' I say quietly, making the instant decision that I'm going to tell them about my visit to the police station to get my best friend out of this predicament. 'And it's something I shouldn't really be talking about, which is why I asked Mel to keep it to herself.'

Mel's eyes are fixed on my face, surprise and relief evident in her eyes. Owen studies me for a moment, his expression grim. 'Fine,' he says eventually, turning away. 'I'll make myself scarce, then. Get out of your way. I wouldn't want to intrude.' His voice is ice cold.

'No. Wait. Stop. You listen too, please. But you have to promise not to tell a soul.'

He turns back and looks at me, unsmiling, and I try not to flinch under his gaze.

'Well, if it's that big a secret, maybe you should keep it to yourself.'

'Owen! Don't be so rude,' Mel admonishes him. He glances at her briefly but doesn't speak, before turning his attention back to me.

'No, it's fine,' I say. 'You're absolutely right to say that, Owen, but if I don't tell someone, I'll go completely mad. But you can't tell *anyone* what I've told you because I don't want either of you to get into trouble.'

'Trouble?' Owen frowns at me. 'You mean you were about to tell Mel something that could get her into trouble? Thanks for that, Abi, putting my pregnant wife at risk.'

'Oh, God, I'm so sorry. I'm making such a mess of everything.' I hold my head in my hands and stare down at the table.

'Please, Abi, tell me what's wrong.' I feel the warmth of Mel's fingers on my arm and I marvel at how the tables have turned, because now she's trying to comfort me. Just my luck that Owen walked in right then. I don't want to put them at risk by telling them about the dead man but also, I'm ashamed for them to know that the police think I'm a liar.

I sit up straight, rake my hair back with my fingers, and calm myself. 'Come and sit down, Owen. I'll tell you both about it all but be prepared; you're going to find it hard to believe.'

There's silence for a moment, and then Owen speaks.

'Okay.' There's the slightest hint of warmth to his voice now and the tension eases from my body. 'I'll just hang my coat up. Back in a minute.' He shrugs off his coat and goes out into the hallway. Mel and I sit and stare at each other across the table.

The sound of the door opening to the downstairs cloakroom tells me Mel and I have a few minutes alone.

'Thank you,' Mel mouths. 'I'm so sorry.'

I smile and whisper, 'No worries,' but inside I feel sick. Why did Owen come home early and overhear us? Why couldn't he have come in a second later? Now I'll have to tell them the police falsified my statement and I didn't want to tell anyone about that. The fewer people who know about it, the better. I want to pretend it never happened.

Will I be putting them in danger?

Only if they tell other people, and they won't if I ask them not to. They're good friends, not garrulous gossips who'd enjoy spilling every detail of my life to other people.

Owen comes back into the kitchen and slips into the seat next to Mel. He turns to her with a smile and I sense her relief. I remind myself again that they're my closest friends; they won't judge me or blab to the world.

'Okay.' I take a deep breath. 'You remember I told you about that accident I saw? The man being run over?'

'When you were out running?' Mel asks.

I nod. 'Yes. Well, there's been a development.'

'What sort of development?' Owen asks.

'I've recognised him. The man I saw being run over.' As I utter the words, I realise there's no way to play this down, no way to make it less than it is. As I realise that, the relief at being able to actually talk about it and get it out of my head is immense.

'You mean you knew him?' Owen asks.

'No. I didn't. I mean, I know who he was now, but I didn't at the time. It was over a week later, when I was watching the news and a picture of a missing man flashed up on the screen, that I recognised him. The more I looked at the picture, the more I realised it was him;

the man who got run down. His name is Dominic Newton, and he's apparently been missing for several weeks.'

'Wow.' Owen looks stunned. 'And what did the police say?'

'Well, they asked me why it had taken me so long to report it, but it hadn't really because I'd already phoned Cameron Malone, the officer who came out to the house to take my statement. The thing was, he didn't seem very interested when I told him and I let myself be persuaded that it was unlikely to be the same man. I dreaded the thought of going into the station again because of my drink-driving charge and it was just easier to believe him. I cringed at the thought of anyone recognising me.'

This is where it starts to sound incredible. I glance at Owen. His expression is impassive, unreadable. Mel is looking at me wide-eyed.

I plough on. 'So. Anyway, the more I thought about it, the more convinced I became that the man I saw run over was this Dominic Newton, so I went to the police station yesterday and told them. I'm not sure what I expected them to do about it, I just knew that I had to report it. Do the right thing and get it off my conscience and then whatever they did was up to them. It was out of my hands.'

'Hang on, though,' Owen interrupts. 'You saw that accident weeks ago. How can you be so sure it was him? It was dark, you were panicked. Are you sure you're not jumping to conclusions? No offence, Abi, but it sounds a bit implausible.'

'It does, but this is where it gets really weird. I thought, well, whether they take me seriously or not, I've done my duty. It's up to them to look into it. So I explained everything to a sergeant, and he wrote it all down and then went off to get the statement that I'd made after the accident.' I stop, aware that once I've told them, there'll be no going back. 'You remember the policeman who was at the scene?'

Mel nods and Owen stares at me, his eyes searching my face.

'Well, the statement the sergeant brought back, it wasn't the one that I made.'

'What do you mean?' Mel looks confused.

'It wasn't the same one. It was nothing like what I'd said, the one I'd signed. The statement he showed me said I'd been mistaken about the accident. Said I hadn't actually seen an accident at all and it was my overactive imagination and I'd got confused. It had my signature on it, but I never signed it, so it was forged.'

'And you told the sergeant this?' Owen asks.

'Yes. And he didn't believe me. Obviously. Because that would make the officer who took it a liar.'

'Oh my God.' Mel is open-mouthed in shock, but when I look at Owen, he's calmly studying my face.

'So what you're saying is that the officer lied and falsified your statement?' Owen asks.

'Yes. Cameron Malone replaced the statement I made with a fake one. I didn't imagine anything. I saw a car run that man down and two men get out of the car, look at him lying in the road and then get back into the car and drive off. When I knelt down next to him, I saw his face clearly, and I thought he was dead. I told Sergeant Cameron Malone this and a couple of days later he came to my house, and he put it in my statement and I signed it. Which means he's covering up an accident. Or more likely, a murder; it was deliberate because that car never even braked. But I can't do anything about it, can I? No one is going to take what I say over the word of a policeman, are they?'

'Christ.' Mel mumbles.

'I think he's dead,' I state. 'The missing man. And whoever killed him has made sure that no one is ever going to find out.'

'So what are you going to do?' Mel asks.

I shrug. 'Nothing. If I go to the police again I'll be charged with wasting police time.'

'But that's not right! If that poor man is dead, whoever's done it is getting away with murder.'

'There's nothing I can do.'

'What about the newspapers or the media?' Mel leans across the table. 'They'd listen.'

'No. I'd rather not do that.' No way am I stirring it up and making myself a target.

'It's probably best to let it go,' Owen says quietly.

'What? Are you mad?' Mel demands. 'Let someone get away with murder?'

Owen shrugs. 'You heard what Abi said. She signed a statement.'

'No, she didn't. It was forged.'

'You'd not had a drink, Abi? That night?' Owen asks.

'No.' I'm shocked that he's even asking me. 'It was early in the morning. I was running.'

'So you never drink, is that right?'

I cringe when I remember the whisky I drank last night. What if Owen can smell it on me? I could always smell it on Will if he'd been drinking the night before, no matter how many times he brushed his teeth.

I've taken too long to answer and Mel jumps in, sounding indignant. 'I can't believe you're saying this, Owen. Are you calling Abi a liar?'

'No. I'm just playing devil's advocate. It's what the media and a court would do; they'd try and tear Abi's story apart. Drag up every bit of dirt they could find, every tiny detail of her life, and twist it. They'd discredit her, Mel. The drink driving conviction would come out and when the media can't find any more dirt to report on, no doubt they'd make a load of stuff up, too, because it's what they do. It's their job. I'm just telling it how it is, that's all.'

'But if someone's been killed, she can't keep quiet, can she?'

Owen shrugs.

'Well?'

He sighs and turns to her, and it's as if I'm no longer in the room. 'Abi could have got it wrong, Mel. She could be mistaken. Because it all sounds incredible, doesn't it? Like something out of a movie. *The body vanishes.*' He turns to me. 'I'm sorry, Abi, I'm not calling you a liar. I'm just saying that you could be mistaken. When you told us about the accident, you never mentioned anything about the man being dead, did you? Or the car driving at him on purpose. You said he got up and walked away, didn't you? All I'm saying is that you've been under a lot of strain this last year and maybe it affected you more than you realise. I'm not wrong in saying that, am I?'

I shake my head. Mel looks at Owen and then at me, shock clear on her face, but as well as shock, I see something else.

Doubt.

She's not sure whether to believe me or not.

15

THEN

My actions on the night I left Will were premeditated. Not the car crash, but what came before.

I intended claiming self-defence but make no mistake, I'd planned every second of it; Will was going to die.

In the days before, I'd hidden the knife in the cupboard. In my head, I'd planned exactly what I was going to do and when Will was out of the house, at work or out with his friends, I practised. Standing in the hallway in different positions, I'd pretend Will was forcing me inside the cupboard and I'd rehearse my stumble inside, practise reaching my hand for the knife, hidden underneath empty boxes in just the right position for me to grab hold of it. Hundreds of times I'd practise the pivot and the turn towards him, the lunge to thrust the knife into him as I aimed for his chest. All of it rehearsed over and over again.

Will was much bigger and stronger than me, but I had the element of surprise because I'd never fought back before.

He wouldn't be expecting me to attack him.

I had one chance only. If I didn't succeed in killing him, there would be no second chance and I would be the one who ended up dead.

In the days preceding that night, I had a fear that somehow he would read my mind; would know what I was planning and discover the knife and use it on me. I was terrified that without meaning to, I would give away what I was going to do. I was on tenterhooks. The signs that he would attack me were all there, it was coming; if not that night, then the next. Soon. Will hadn't attacked me for over a month and the space between his attacks was growing shorter each time. The long silences when he refused to speak to me, the strained atmosphere between us, the coldness in the air; they were all signs that the tension was building. The atmosphere was unbearable and almost palpable. Laughably, even though I intended killing him, I still talked to him in an attempt to try and avert what was going to happen, even though I knew it was pointless.

And I hated myself for even trying.

I excused my pathetic pandering to him by telling myself I was giving him an opportunity to live, to change his behaviour.

Giving him one last chance to stop me from killing him.

Why didn't I just leave him, escape before he had the opportunity to lock me up again? I had all day when he was at work, ample opportunity to run away. If I left him as soon as he'd gone to work, it would be hours before he'd discover I'd gone. I went to work every day; I drove my car; I went shopping and left the house like a normal person. To everyone else, my friends, my family, I could do as I liked, come and go as I pleased because no one, except for me, had witnessed the real Will. There were numerous opportunities to escape from him, but I stayed. He was so sure of his power over me that he never checked where I was in the day when I was supposed to be at work.

I could have run.

That's what a jury would say, wouldn't they? If things were so bad, if he was so abusive, then why was I still here waiting for him to attack me again?

Because I was afraid. More than afraid. Terrified.

Will would kill me, I knew that. He'd told me so. Many times. Wherever I thought I could hide, he would track me down. He'd promised me that he'd never let me go until he decided he didn't want me any more. I belonged to him. He told me that if I ever left him and he couldn't find me, he knew where my parents lived. They would pay for my misbehaviour. That's what he called it, 'misbehaviour'. I never doubted he meant every word of it, and that was the sole reason I stayed with him.

So I had to make sure that he could never come after me or my parents and the only way to do that was to kill him.

I'd been documenting his abuse on my phone for months; photographs of my injuries, exact dates and times, descriptions of what he'd done, things he'd said. This, I hoped, would be enough to prevent me from going to prison for murder. I had my defence ready: I'd been making plans to leave him, but he'd discovered what I'd been doing. When he'd attacked me in a rage, telling me that this time, I'd be going in the cupboard and never coming out, I'd grabbed the knife from the worktop and stabbed him in self-defence.

So if I had the evidence against him of everything he'd been doing to me, why didn't I go to the police? Why did I try to kill him?

Because he had to be dead.

I needed him to be dead.

All the evidence in the world wouldn't stop Will from killing me. My evidence would never see the inside of a courtroom because I would no longer be alive. Will would make sure of it. The police, no one, would be able to protect me or my family from him. While he was alive, I would never escape him. Even if by some miracle he was convicted and sent to prison, once freed, he'd want revenge, he'd come after me.

I would never be free of him.

He told me so often that he was the one who would decide when he was done with me, not the other way around. Bizarrely, when he said that, he gave me hope. It meant that one day, he might let me go.

He must hate me, I reasoned, to treat me the way he did, so why was he so adamant that I stay? I couldn't understand why he still wanted me living with him. Was it the total power that he had over me? Did the complete control over another person give him pleasure?

I never knew; I still don't know.

In his normal times, which were becoming fewer and fewer, he still told me he loved me. But even then, he quantified it by always saying he loved me despite my failings. Where previously he – and I – had laughed off his attacks as my being a drama llama, they were now acknowledged. It was my fault he attacked me; I goaded him, misbehaved, nagged at him relentlessly. I did none of those things, but I had to agree and promise to try harder to be a better person. Occasionally, he would be loving and considerate and I had to pretend to love him too, for fear of him turning. I cringed at his touch, feeling utter disgust at myself for allowing him anywhere near me, but I was trapped. Besides, if I refused, it was much worse; if he detected the slightest hesitation on my part, he would violently force himself on me and afterwards push me into the cupboard to think about what I'd made him do to me.

One day soon, he would kill me. Bury me somewhere I'd never be found.

Get away with murder because no one knew what he was really like, how he treated me, because I had never told anyone.

So I had to kill him before he killed me.

We drank wine that night. Before. Will opened a bottle of red and in no time at all, it had gone. He opened another. I didn't want any, but to refuse would have accelerated what was to come. There was a part of me that still had a tiny sliver of hope that a drink would relax him. It didn't, of course. It seldom did.

When it finally happened, it went like clockwork and it was almost as if I were watching another person push that knife into Will. His eyes widened in surprise and he made a low grunting noise. Pushing the knife in was much harder than I'd imagined it would be. There was no blood in those first few seconds, but then it gushed, spreading over his shirt in a red bloom. I recoiled in horror as he reached out towards me for help.

After a few moments he slumped to the floor and I ran from the house, convinced I'd killed him and it would only be a matter of time before he was discovered. The sensible part of me recognised that I should call the police immediately, tell them what I'd done, say I hadn't meant to do it. Plead self-defence; it would go better for me.

But I didn't.

Because I wanted to make sure he died.

If I rang the police, an ambulance would be dispatched immediately. What if they managed to save him? Will had to die; I couldn't risk him living because it would be worse for me afterwards. But I'm not a monster. I couldn't stand there and watch him take his last breath, so I ran. Running from that house as if I were being pursued by demons, throwing myself into the car with no thought of being over the limit, no thought of anything other than my desperation to get as far away from him as possible. I was still in shock from the horror of it. The amount of blood was horrific; when I'd imagined killing him, I'd had no concept of the reality of it.

So I drove with no clear idea of where I was going, only that I had to get away. When I crashed outside the school and the police arrived, I could have confessed then, but I didn't.

I wanted there to be no possibility of Will surviving.

What sort of heartless bitch does that make me?

I never spoke about what I'd done; not one word. My parents collected me from the police station the next morning and I still hadn't told anyone. I hadn't spoken at all when the police charged me, except to give my name and address. What was there to say? I kept telling myself that I'd tell the police soon, before the day was out.

But I didn't.

Three days after I fled that house, still, I'd told no one what I'd done. I knew Will must be dead and I was just waiting for someone to discover his body. Every morning when I clawed my way out of bed, I spent the hours waiting for the knock on the door from the police. Will's staff would try to contact him when he didn't turn up for work, I reasoned. Eventually, someone would go to the house. At some point, unable to get an answer to their incessant knocking or repeated telephone calls, a decision would be made to break in and they'd find Will's body.

By then, I was beginning to go slightly mad, realising I should have confessed the next day and used the excuse that I was in shock, but it was too late now. No one would believe the self-defence story. No one pleads self-defence and leaves someone to die for three days.

I was in a zombie-like state and unable to think coherently, and one day merged into another. If not sleeping, I spent my time sitting in my parents' lounge on the sofa, staring unseeingly at the television. My mother would bustle around, bringing me cups of tea and putting blankets around me as if I were a patient and not a drunk driver. There wasn't a word of recrimination from either of them about the crash, just concern. They knew that I'd left Will and that things had gone badly wrong between us for me to have been drinking and driving. I intended telling them the truth but couldn't summon up the energy and they didn't push me, wanting to let me tell them in my own time. Later, I promised myself, later. Although I would tell them the self-defence lie, too, so not the complete truth. But not yet; I wanted just a few more days of semi-normality before my entire world exploded and became a mess of police and courts.

And on the fourth day, my phone rang.

Even now, I can remember the absolute terror I felt when Will's name flashed up on the screen. I stared at it disbelievingly, and then it stopped ringing and voicemail clicked in. Seconds later, it rang again.

He was dead. I'd plunged that knife into his chest with every bit of strength I possessed, and by the time I fled, his shirt was soaked red. He lay in the hallway, a bewildered expression on his face as I turned my back on him and bolted.

He must be dead by now.

I pressed the button to answer the call, meeting silence from the other end and then Will spoke. One word, my name.

He sounded normal; just the same as he always did.

He was alive.

16

I march along, thoughts of yesterday's visit to Mel and Owen whirling around in my head. It was a shock when I realised that they weren't sure whether to believe me or not and I was embarrassed for them and for myself. They did their best to hide it, but once I'd seen the doubt in their eyes, I knew I needed to stop talking about it. After an awkward silence, they agreed on how bizarre it all was, but they were simply being polite. I stayed for dinner but the conversation felt stilted and I didn't hang around for long afterwards, refusing the offer of a lift home from Mel.

Do I appear slightly unhinged to other people? Because that's how I felt.

Maybe my mind *was* playing tricks on me that night.

No. It wasn't. I know with absolute certainty that the statement Sergeant Timpson showed me was not the one I signed. I shudder at the thought of the dead man and push the thought away. That's how I think of him now; dead, not missing. I've done all I can. There's nothing more I can do because no one believes me, not the police, not my best friend.

Forget it all and move on.

It was light when I went out running this morning, but going in daylight wasn't intentional; I slept in far later than normal. I had trouble getting to sleep last night, but I was determined not to resort to using alcohol as a sleeping aid. Besides, there was only the disgusting whisky that I drank the previous night and I couldn't face it.

It's dark now, though. I'm on my way to meet John and, as the pub is only a forty-five-minute walk away, I'm walking. I've decided against changing my entire life and routine because of that stupid accident. Why should I? Unfortunately, my subconscious keeps imagining a stalker behind me in the darkness, an attacker lurking in every shadow. I have the sensation of being watched and even though I've tried to convince myself that it's just the echoes of my own footsteps, the hairs on the back of my neck are standing on end. Shivering from the cold, I can't shake off the thought that someone is behind me. It's all in my mind, there's nothing to fear, I tell myself, but with each passing moment, the sensation that I'm being followed grows. For the third time since I set off, I swing around to look behind me.

There's no one there.

Of course there isn't; just as there wasn't anyone there the first and second time.

Well, not anyone I can see, the voice of doubt whispers. They could be hiding. There are plenty of shop doorways to hop into out of sight.

I power on and shake the thought off, annoyed with myself. That's what happens when you let a random thought into your head; it takes root and grows like a weed. No one is after me and no one is following me. I'm an unreliable witness. No threat to anyone.

Get a grip.

I continue my march down the almost deserted high street, the cold November wind whipping through my hair. I shiver, not just from the chill in the air, but from the memories of Will. There was a time when my life was simple, when the future stretched out before me like an endless road, full of promise, opportunity, and happiness.

Before Will.

I look back on the last three years and all I see is a twisted mess of lies and betrayal, a path that has led me here, to the ruin that is now my life. Why complicate it further by obsessing over a dead man whom I can do nothing about?

I keep up the pace, glancing around me to see a couple holding hands, strolling along on the opposite side of this pedestrianised street, a woman in front of the large brightly lit window of Marks & Spencer studying her phone. Nothing out of the ordinary. Nothing to see here.

Let it go, Abi, let it go.

Yet still the feeling of being watched persists, growing stronger with every step.

I could stop walking everywhere, or at least stop doing it in the dark. I'll get my driving licence back in a couple of months so I can buy a car, get back to normal, whatever that is. Get a new job, restart my career. Until then I can use a taxi or a bus because it's not as if I go anywhere very much other than work.

Give in to the fear, in other words. And the police are not going to help me because someone doesn't want Dominic Newton found. Forget it, move on with my life. Realistically, this is my only option, yet it doesn't sit right.

I've let too many things go.

Because I'm a coward.

I never used to be a coward. Before Will. I would stand my ground. I had principles.

I turn the corner and there it is; the red brick and blue painted exterior of The Rifleman's Arms. No more dwelling, I decide, at least not tonight. I stride towards the doors, past two men huddled over cigarettes, plumes of smoke billowing from their mouths into the cold night air. The warmth hits me as I step inside and pull the door closed behind me. Despite being early evening, the low murmur of voices and the clink of glasses greet me. It's familiar, like an old friend. This is normal life. There's no one watching me or following me. I'm in a town centre pub, and I'm safe. The people in here are shopworkers, or from one of the numerous office blocks nearby. People work late and come here straight afterwards. Didn't I used to do that? When I had a life? I did; after-work drinks were the normal thing to do, a reward after a taxing day, a stress-inducing meeting, or a new business opportunity. Or just because we could. Because we wanted to. A quick glass of wine before heading home for the evening, or a precursor to a meal out somewhere.

But that was before Will.

I scan around the bar but see no sign of John and when I check my watch, I see why; it's 6.35 and I'm not meeting him until seven. I'm early.

There are several spare tables at the far end of the bar, and I decide to get myself a drink and sit at one of them to wait for him. I might seem too keen arriving early but there's nothing I can do about it now. The other option is to hang around outside in the cold and I'm not going to do that. I wait at the bar and after a few minutes the barman appears and I order myself a glass of wine, slip off my coat and drape it over a bar stool. My skinny jeans and oversized jumper in pale blue cashmere are casual and I know I look good; my hair is thick and naturally wavy and luckily the walk here hasn't affected it. I've made an effort; I've even put make-up on although I stopped short of buying anything new to wear. It seemed a waste because I have jeans and jumpers galore.

When my wine arrives, I tap my card, pick up the glass and take several gulps. As the warmth hits my stomach, it feels good. I could stay here, then when John arrives, it'll look as if I've just got here myself. There seems something very sad about sitting at a table alone. I perch on one of the bar stools and scroll through my phone, sipping my wine as I do so; it can't hurt because it's not whisky, is it?

Sensing a presence behind me I turn slowly, my heart racing, to see John standing there. He smiles, and then frowns.

'Sorry, did I startle you?'

'No, no, I'm fine,' I force a smile. 'I didn't hear you.'

He smells of fresh air and, as he slips off his jacket and places it over mine, I catch a hint of aftershave. He turns and smiles at me as he settles himself onto the stool and my stomach flips, surprising me. He's attractive. Very. In jeans and a thick fisherman's jumper, the casual look suits him and I'm glad I didn't wear a dress.

'Another?' He glances at my wine glass and I'm surprised to see that it's nearly empty.

'Please.' I smile. I should order a soft drink, but the thought is unappealing.

He catches the barman's eye and orders me a glass of wine and himself a beer. I'm pleased; I don't want to be the only one drinking alcohol.

'You look nice,' he says, studying me. 'Blue really suits you.'

My face grows hot; pathetically, I'm blushing. It's been a long time since a man paid me a compliment.

'So, have you had a good day? Done anything exciting?' he asks, and I stare at him for a moment in confusion. 'You said you're on annual leave this week?' he adds.

'Oh, yes.' I laugh. 'Nothing exciting. I went for a run, did a few jobs around the house.'

How deadly dull my life sounds. I've forgotten the art of small talk and how to make myself sound interesting.

'You run?' He smiles. 'Is that a regular thing?'

'Three times a week usually, give or take.'

'Wow. You put me to shame. I can just about drag myself to the gym. What's your distance?'

'Around five miles. Nothing too taxing.' Truth be told I don't have a set distance, mostly I just run until I've had enough, even if I estimate my regular morning route is about five miles. I also lied: I run nearly every day if I can, so why didn't I say that?

Because it sounds obsessive, that's why.

'I should take up running, save the money I spend on a gym membership that I don't use enough.'

'You look pretty fit to me.' The words are out of my mouth before I think about it and I'm immediately embarrassed.

'Ditto.' He grins and I find myself grinning back.

'So how was *your* day?' I ask.

'Deadly dull. Work. Same old. Blackmores isn't exactly exciting.'

'No Spanish trips in the offing, then?'

'Not sure. Annoyingly, they always seem to pop up without much notice.'

'Whereabouts in Spain is that?'

The barman appears with our drinks and John pays for them before answering.

'Madrid. Although I'm pretty sure I won't be wowing them with my Spanish.'

'Well, at least you'll know a few words.'

'Hmm. I wouldn't count on it. How about we find a table? I don't know about you, but these stools are agonising.' He stands up, grabs both of our coats and his drink, and I follow him. He picks a table nearest the fake fire that looks surprisingly real and pulls out a chair for me. A gentleman. I sit down while he busies himself putting our coats on a spare seat. He sits down on the chair next to me and I sense his closeness.

'So.' He turns to me with a smile. 'I suppose we should deal with the elephants in the room.'

'Elephants?'

'Yep.' He bites his lip. 'The "I'm single now but I have history" elephants.'

I nod, unsure of what to say.

'Okay,' he says. 'Me first. I was married, but I'm now divorced.

Old story: Jane and I met at uni and stayed together. We were happy and there was no drama, really. I just woke up one day and realised that we were more like friends than husband and wife.'

'I'm sorry.'

He shrugs. 'I won't lie. It was sad. Mostly because I hurt Jane. She wanted a family, everything. All those years together and then it's all over. We could have stayed together, but marriage shouldn't just be about friendship, should it? So I'm free and single, though not so young.' He grins.

'Not old, either.'

'Thirty-eight, which apparently is the new twenty-five. Jane's moved on and met someone else, and I'm the one who's alone now, but I'm glad it's worked out for her.'

I'm pleased that he hasn't slagged her off; I went on plenty of dates, pre-Will, where the guy spent the evening moaning about how badly their ex had treated them. There's a lull in the conversation and I know it's my turn to tell him my history.

'No drama here either,' I lie. 'I lived with my partner for three years and then we just grew apart, I suppose. The spark was no longer there, so we decided to go our separate ways.'

He picks up his glass and holds it in front of me. 'Here's to the future.'

We chink glasses. I'll definitely drink to that. 'So how long ago was your divorce?'

'Two years. How about you? When did you split up?'

'Nearly a year ago.'

'So you're ready to move on?' His piercing blue eyes search my face.

'Yes,' I say, truthfully. 'I am.'

My words hang in the air and the moment is full of promise, full of hope, and I wonder how I can feel so close to a man whom I've only just met.

I feel like I know him; like I've known him for a long time.

The evening passes quickly and we chat so easily, but if I had to pinpoint exactly what we've talked about, I couldn't. Nothing and everything. We had another drink – Coke for John as it turns out he's driving, and another wine for me, even though I thought I shouldn't. But I had to remind myself to drink it because I didn't need liquid courage, as I thought I might. When the barman calls 'Time', somehow our chairs are close together, our knees and arms touching.

I like it.

'He wants us to leave,' John whispers, looking over my shoulder. I turn to see that we're the only people left here and the barman is leaning over, staring at us.

'Oh God, I didn't realise.' I laugh. 'We're stopping him from closing. We should go.'

'Let me drive you home,' John offers as he passes me my coat.

I'd been planning on walking, or getting a taxi, but without hesitation, I accept.

'Thank you, if you're sure you don't mind.'

'My pleasure.'

We head outside and it seems the most natural thing to link my arm through John's as we walk down the high street to the multi-storey car park. It's only as we go through the entrance to the car park that I begin to have doubts. The place is deserted, not a soul around. Am I being foolish, getting into a car with a man I barely know? I've told no one where I am tonight or that I'm with John. I haven't even told Mel that I'm on a date with him. What if he's like Will? I could get into his car and never be seen again, and no one would have a clue what had happened to me.

I glance up at him as we walk towards the car. He clicks his key to open the door and smiles, the edges of his eyes crinkling, his smile warm.

I smile back. Not every man is like Will. He's the exception, not the rule. I climb into the car and strap myself in. I need to start living again; stop imagining that every man in the world is another Will. I need to trust my instincts in the way I used to before I met him. I'm perfectly capable of using my own judgement about whether something is a good idea or not, because I managed perfectly fine before Will came along and nearly ruined my life. It's time to stop hiding away and start living again.

'All okay there?' John asks as he starts the engine and manoeuvres out of the car park.

'All good. Just admiring your car,' I reply, running my fingers over the leather upholstery.

'I'm such a cliché.' He laughs as we zoom through the darkened streets. 'The minute my divorce was finalised, I bought myself the flash car that I'd always wanted but seemed too self-indulgent to have when I was married.'

'And why not?' I say. 'Because it's gorgeous.' It is, too. I should treat myself to something nice, not a car, not yet, but a holiday, even if it's just a spa break. I've forgotten how to enjoy myself, forgotten that I *should* enjoy myself. I'm young, I have a lot of living to do.

When we pull up outside my house, he kills the engine and turns to me.

'Thank you for a lovely evening.'

'Thank *you*.'

He stares at me for a moment and leans closer. I assume he's aiming for my cheek, a chaste kiss that won't overstep the mark, but somehow his mouth finds mine and his arms are around me, drawing me close. I don't resist and relish the moment. I feel safe, safer than I've felt for a very long time. When we come up for air, it seems too soon for the evening to be over, and I'm so tempted to invite him in for coffee but I don't; I can't trust myself. There's a strong connection between us and I don't want to rush things or do something that I'll regret in the cold light of day.

'I should go,' I say.

'Yes.' He draws away from me and I push down disappointment that he agreed so easily.

'See you tomorrow?' He smiles.

'Tomorrow?'

'Spanish night?'

'Of course, I'd forgotten which day it is. One of the perils of having time off work.'

I open the car door and the closeness of a few minutes ago seems to have vanished, and I wonder if I imagined it. I clamber out of the car and lean in to say goodnight.

'Abi?'

'Yes?'

'What about Saturday? Would you like to go out for dinner?'

His expression is unsure and I suddenly realise that he's as new to all this as I am.

'I'd love to.'

He grins and I find myself grinning back like an idiot.

'I'll watch you go in,' he says. 'Make sure you get in okay.'

I walk up the path to the front door, the grin still on my face.

I might just have met the perfect man.

17

As I pull on my leggings, I think back to last night. Did I imagine the connection between me and John? No, I'm sure I didn't. There's definitely something there. I wasn't looking to get involved with anyone yet, but when is the right time? There is no set time, because you can't plan for feelings, or fate, or have any idea who might walk into your life.

Listen to me; fate, feelings, chance. I sound like a character from a soppy romantic novel. I smile to myself as I pull a T-shirt over my head. One date and I'm behaving as if I've met the love of my life. But I once thought Will was the love of my life and look how that ended. I push the thought away; I'm not going to allow the past to ruin my future. I slip my feet into my trainers, tie the laces, and pull my tracksuit top on. As I slip my phone into my pocket, it chirrups and I glance at it to see it's a message from John.

JOHN

Morning, hope I haven't woken you. Thank you for last night. I really enjoyed it. I've booked a table at Fabio's for Saturday at 8, is that okay? You do like Italian, don't you?

I stare at the screen. Will I appear too eager if I reply straight away? Should I leave it a while and play it cool? I decide I don't care. I can't be bothered to play games.

> ABI
>
> Sounds perfect! I love Italian.

JOHN

Great! What plans do you have for today? Anything exciting?

> ABI
>
> Out for a run and then Spanish tonight. I know how to live!

He responds with a smiley face and a thumbs up. I'm going to treat myself to something new to wear for Saturday, push the boat out, as Dad would say. I haven't bought any new clothes, apart from running gear, in a very long time. My phone chirrups again and I should leave it but I can't, curiosity gets the better of me.

JOHN

Should we keep it to ourselves at Spanish that we've been out together?

The image of Jax and Caro's grins and constant innuendo pop into my head. If they get the slightest idea that John and I have been on a date, there'll be no stopping them. What if the dates fizzle out and it all comes to nothing? I quickly type a reply, telling John that yes, we should keep it to ourselves, press the send arrow, and put my phone back into my pocket.

Time to run off some energy before it starts raining. I jog down the stairs, unlock the front door, and let myself out. It's cold. More than cold, but at least it's dry. I jog gently on the spot as I close and lock the door, keeping my gentle pace up all the way down the street to the end. Instead of turning to the right and crossing the road, which is my usual route to the industrial estate, I turn left.

I slowly build up my speed, aware of the cold. I'm reluctant to pull a muscle. My usual routine is to warm up outside with some stretches, but the toing and froing with the messages to John has distracted me. It'll be strange seeing him tonight and pretending we've not been out together. Luckily, I don't sit near him so it shouldn't be a problem.

I power along the edge of the estate, cross the road into the older part of town and past the Civic Offices. The houses here were mostly built in the thirties and forties, with some of the smaller terraced ones dating back to the turn of the century. I keep up a steady pace and in no time at all, I'm at the end of Mum and Dad's street. I don't go down it but carry on past. I'm not visiting them today. I run along the next four blocks until I reach Lakeside Road, a wide street of 1930s semi-detached, bay-fronted houses with large front gardens and driveways. Despite the name, there's no lake anywhere near here, but perhaps there was in the distant past. I turn into the road and slowly jog down it. There's no one around and at the end of the street, there's a narrow walkway that leads through into a large field. It's common ground, popular with dog walkers and runners, like me, who jog around the path that encircles it. I remember the visiting fair which always used to set up here, and the excitement I felt going to that as a teenager with my friends. I head towards the walkway and jog slowly down the path until I reach the field. I came here a lot when I was a child. The streets around my parents' house were our playground and I know them like the back of my hand, although I've not been here for a long, long time.

I slow to a walk and aim for the wooden bench that's in front of the path. I arrive just as an elderly man with an ancient dog settles himself at one end of it. He glances up at me as I sit down and I say good morning to him. He doesn't answer, regarding me with suspicion before inching slightly away towards the opposite end.

I never normally stop when I'm running, but today, I need to think.

Dominic Newton lives on Lakeside Road. Number 16. At least he did until he was murdered. That's the beauty of social media; if you want to find out anything, check your socials. His address isn't actually stated, but there are enough clues to piece it together if you've lived in this town all your life, as I have. There are also several blurry pictures of his house, which I've studied so often that they're imprinted on my brain. As I ran down the street taking a good look at the houses, I noticed that Number 16's block-paved driveway and black front door with distinctive handles match the photos exactly. I even found out his wife's name – Holly – and that he has two children: Leo, aged seven, and Grace, five.

Dominic Newton's disappearance is a hot topic on social media and it seems that everyone in the world has a theory about where he is. They range from running away with another man, or woman, to being abducted by aliens. It's not lost on me that amongst the numerous bizarre and outlandish theories, no one has hit on the truth of him being deliberately mown down by a car.

I sit back against the bench and close my eyes. The slats on the bench move slightly as the elderly man stands up. I open my eyes to see he's staring right at me. I smile at him and after a moment, he smiles back.

'Lovely day,' I say. 'Cold, though.'

''Tis,' he agrees, as he walks slowly past me, his ancient terrier reluctantly following him. 'Don't you overdo it with all that running. Too much exercise isn't good for you.' I smile and watch him as he flaps his hand in a clumsy wave and trudges off. How easily we make assumptions about people. What I took for suspicion was probably concern and loneliness. He might not have heard me when I said good morning; he could be deaf.

The police made assumptions about me based on a fake statement. Now, they won't believe a word I say because I'm marked as a drunk, a liar, a woman with mental health issues.

I'm not completely sure why I came here today. What was the

point, because what, exactly, can I do? Before I got here, I had some vague notion of talking to Dominic Newton's wife, of seeing if she had her own theory about what's happened to him.

Sheer madness.

It's doubtful she would open the door to me, let alone talk to me. Why would she? I'm a complete stranger to her. She'd think I was mad, just as the police do.

Even Mel and Owen, my oldest friends, think I've imagined it.

I stand up and stretch. Time to go home. I jog on the spot and head across the field towards the far side. It'll bring me out onto the main road. There's absolutely no need to go back down Lakeside Road, because I am absolutely not going to knock on Number 16's door.

I should go into town this afternoon to buy that new outfit for Saturday night. Or practise my Spanish. Clean my house. A million and one things that don't include speaking to Holly Newton.

But even as I run, although the idea of speaking to Holly Newton is mad, it won't go away. It's begun to take root in my head, and like a seed that's been planted, it's starting to grow.

* * *

I make myself busy when I get home, vacuuming and dusting, changing the sheets on the bed. All of the housework that was left unattended all week is now done. When I can't find anything else that needs doing, I sit down, go online and order new clothes from Next. I buy far more than I intended, and I probably won't even keep it all, but I'm picking it up from the shop tomorrow. It would have made more sense to go into the shop and try it all on but I couldn't find the motivation.

I shower, wash and blow-dry my hair even though, strictly speaking, it doesn't need it. Usually for Thursday night Spanish, I scoop it up into a ponytail, but this evening I don't, because I want it to look nice. For John. I pull on jeans and a jumper and glance at the clock to see that, despite being busy all day, it's still only five o'clock. Spanish doesn't start until seven. I should eat. All I've had is a bowl of soup at lunchtime so I should cook myself something before I go out.

Except that I have no appetite.

And the ridiculous thought that I have enough time to go and see Holly Newton before I go to Spanish won't go away.

It's a stupid idea, but it won't budge. And let's face it; the thought has been there all day. The non-stop activity has been an attempt to keep myself from acting on it.

But it hasn't worked because I'm going.

She'll answer the door, tell me to go away, and that'll be it; I'll have tried and can do no more.

End of.

I go out into the hallway, pull on my boots and big coat, grab my bag and leave the house.

I must be walking extra fast without realising it because all too quickly, I'm walking down Lakeside Road. It's dark, and I'm thankful for that, because I'm not so conspicuous. The street is quiet and most of the houses have their curtains drawn and some are in total darkness, the owners not yet home from work. Number 16's lounge light is showing through the closed curtains and there's a Ford Fiesta parked in front of the garage. I stop on the pavement in front of the house, trying to imagine what I can say that would make Holly Newton talk to me. I don't want to alarm her, or frighten her, but I need to talk to her.

What will I achieve by talking to her and what am I even going to say? I've no idea. The police will have questioned her endlessly, so why would I be able to find something out if they can't? I don't know; but something tells me I have to do this and then I've done all I can.

Holly Newton should know what I saw, despite what the police think of me.

Taking a deep breath, I walk up the driveway, past the Fiesta and up to the front door. I put my finger on the bell and press it twice.

Silence.

I press the button again, keeping my finger on it for longer this time. The lounge curtains move slightly and after a few minutes, there's the sound of the door being unlocked. Holly's face appears through the gap as she pulls it open just enough to peer out at me. She stares at me with a questioning look and although I've seen her and Dominic's wedding picture on social media, the woman in front of me bears little resemblance to the fresh-faced girl of ten years ago. The bouncy red curls are stretched back into a severe ponytail and her huge brown eyes are etched with fine lines and dark shadows. She looks exhausted and at her wits' end. Worry will do that to a person.

'Hello Holly, my name is Abi Redmond. We've never met but I need to speak to you about your husband.'

She frowns, takes a step backwards. I sense that the door is about to be firmly closed in my face.

'Please,' I say, moving closer. 'It's really important. I just need a few minutes of your time to explain.'

'I'm not interested,' she states flatly. 'I've already told your newspaper that I've got nothing to say, so go away and leave me alone.'

She pushes the door to close it, but I quickly thrust my foot into the gap between it and the doorframe to stop her.

'How dare you!' She looks shocked. 'Go away before I call the police!'

'Please, all I need is five minutes and then I'll go. I'm not from a newspaper. I'm just a member of the public, but I have information about your husband. I want to help. Please. I've already been to the police but they're not interested. That's why I've come to you, because they won't listen.'

She stares at me for a moment, a range of emotions flitting across her face. I wait, and then she opens the door to let me inside.

18

THEN

'I'm not dead,' he said quietly. And then he laughed, actually laughed.

I desperately wanted to hang up, pretend he really was dead, and I was safe.

But I couldn't.

'I'm not coming back,' I managed to say when I found my voice. 'Not ever. No matter what you do or say.'

'I'll decide if and when you come back, not you.' His voice was cold and fear gripped my insides.

'If you come near me, I'll kill you,' I stuttered.

He laughed again, but I detected an uncertainty in his laughter, a hesitancy. I had the strangest feeling that something indefinable had shifted in our relationship and that the balance of power had swung ever so slightly my way. Maybe there was a tiny part of him that was afraid of me now; he'd had no idea what I was capable of and now he did. He could still kill me or try to force me to do as he wished by threatening my parents, but despite that, in that moment, I knew I would never, ever, go back to him.

I would rather die than be with him.

'I've got evidence of everything you did to me,' I went on. 'It's all documented. The date of every attack, photographs of my injuries, the threats you made to me, all of it. Each time you raped me when I repeatedly told you no. And it's all in a safe place, so there's no way you can get to it. Even if you kill me before I can report you to the police, Will, you won't get away with it because I've instructed a solicitor to send all the evidence to them if anything happens to me. You're going to be arrested and charged. You're going to prison and I'll never have to see your fucking face again.'

I was breathing heavily by the time I'd finished speaking and I waited for the shouting, the insults, the threats.

But I was met with silence. I waited, sure that at any moment the promises of how he would make me pay would come. The graphic description of the violence he'd inflict on me, on my parents. He always used to do this; it was his precursor to an attack. He'd instil such fear in me, and enjoyed watching me become more terrified by the minute.

When the silence had stretched to breaking-point, he finally replied, his words and calmness taking me by surprise. 'So you've got evidence? Big deal. I have evidence, too. You tried to kill me, Abi,' he said, evenly. 'You stabbed me. You planned it. You hid the knife and had it ready, so it was premeditated. And the hospital has it all on record. They questioned me after they'd stitched me up and repaired the damage you did. I lied and told them I stabbed myself accidentally and of course they didn't believe me because it was patently obvious that I hadn't, but what could they do? I stuck to my story, but it's all logged. It's attempted murder and if I report you, there's no way you're going to get away with it.'

'I don't believe you. You're alive, you survived. It was just a flesh wound.'

'No, it wasn't. I was lucky I didn't die. You left me for dead and for that, I'll never forgive you. If my phone hadn't been in my pocket, I wouldn't be here now. I managed to call Doug and even though I lost consciousness before I could tell him what had happened, he came round and found me. He saved my life. He's a witness, too. But for him, I'd have bled out on that floor, just like you wanted me to, you murderous bitch. You walked away, turned your back on me and ran.'

I laughed then. It was partly hysteria, but also Will's indignance that I'd dared to attack him after all of his violence towards me, when he'd constantly told me he could kill me whenever he wanted to. He was offended that I'd tried to kill him.

'It's not funny.' I recognised the dangerous tone in Will's voice; I'd heard it many times before and it always preceded violence. Memories of his fists, his words, his hatefulness, flashed through my mind.

'I hate you,' I spat at him in a sudden burst of anger. 'And I wanted you dead. My only regret is that I didn't drive that knife into you hard enough and you survived. I walked away because I thought you were bleeding to death and if I'd known there was any chance of you living, I'd have come back and finished you off. I've spent the last two years praying for you to die, you vicious, disgusting bastard.'

He laughed then, and even before he spoke, I realised that he'd tricked me and, like a fool, I'd walked right into his trap.

'You stupid cow. I'm recording you, Abi, and you've just confessed to attempted murder.'

I had; and when I thought back over our conversation, Will hadn't admitted to anything at all. Not a thing. But I still had the evidence of what he'd done to me. All of his attacks on me were documented and that had to count for something, didn't it?

'So what is it you want?' I asked. 'You can't make me come back.'

'Do you think I want you back, you mad bitch? After what you've done? You stay away from me and I'll stay away from you. That's it. That's all. No police, no charges.'

He had no idea how relieved I felt when he said that he didn't want me back. I still wonder, now, what would have happened if I hadn't had all the evidence, if he'd have forced me to go back to him.

'So, that's it?' I asked. 'You leave me alone and I leave you alone? Seems too easy. How can I trust you?'

'Because that way, we can get on with our lives and never see each other again. That's the deal. But I'm warning you, if you try to make trouble for me, if you spread any rumours or I hear one single word of you badmouthing me to anyone, I'll come for you. You need to know that. You can't tell anyone what happened. No one else can know about this, except for us. As far as the rest of the world knows, we broke up because we grew apart.'

I'll come for you. Did he mean he'd kill me or go to the police? I didn't know. I didn't ask.

'Okay,' I said.

'You're sure? Because there's no going back on this.'

'I'm sure,' I said.

And that was the last time I spoke to him.

19

'Come through to the kitchen,' Holly says as she closes the front door and walks into the lounge. I follow behind her. A young boy and a girl are seated on the sofa watching a cartoon on the huge television on the opposite wall. They stare up at me as I go in, the little girl's eyes round with interest.

'Mummy's just got to talk to the lady for a moment,' Holly says to them. 'It's work, so nothing to worry about. You can watch the rest of the cartoon and then it's bath time, okay? I'll just be in the kitchen, so I'll hear if you start fighting.'

The children stare at me for a moment and then the little girl puts her thumb in her mouth and turns her attention back to the TV screen. The boy stares at me and his eyes follow me as we go into the kitchen. Once inside, Holly pushes the door until it's nearly closed and walks over to the sink and turns to face me.

'Okay. You've got five minutes.' She folds her arms and waits.

She doesn't offer me a seat at the large dining table filling the space in front of sliding doors that lead onto the back garden and I stand awkwardly, wondering where to start. The kitchen is warm and cluttered; children's paintings are taped along one wall and a jumble of school bags clutter one end of the table next to a discarded school jumper. The logo on it is for the same primary school I attended when I was a child. This is a home, just like millions of others across the country, except that Holly's husband, Leo and Grace's father, isn't here.

And he's never coming back.

I take a deep breath and begin to speak, my voice shaky. 'I was a witness to an accident and your husband was involved.' She looks stricken and I realise what I've just said, but what other way is there to say it?

'What sort of accident?'

'A hit and run. I saw someone run over. I'm certain that it was your husband.'

'When was this?' Her voice is sharp, but her face has paled.

'The second of November. It was in the early hours of the morning. Still dark. I run when it's dark. I was running up Tydeman Road where it goes past Hyton industrial estate when I saw a man come tearing out of a side street. A few seconds later, a car came out of the same street and ran him over. When the car stopped and two men got out, I thought they were going to help him, but they didn't. They looked at him and then got back in the car and drove off.'

'And what did you do?'

'I ran to him to see if I could help. He was lying in the middle of the road. It was only later, when I saw your husband's picture on the news, that I realised it was him.'

Any minute now, she's going to throw me out.

'I ran to a phone box to call an ambulance because I didn't have my mobile on me. It took me about thirty or so minutes and by the time I got back, your husband was gone. It was as if the accident had never happened.'

'You can leave now.' She walks past me to the kitchen door.

'Please.' I step closer to her. 'I'm not lying. It was him, it was. I recognised him.'

'You're lying. If what you're saying was true, the police would be investigating and they haven't told me about any of this. You say you called an ambulance, which means the police would have been notified, so why haven't they done something about this so-called hit and run? They wouldn't just ignore it, would they?'

'It's complicated. There was a policeman there when I got back and I told him everything that I'd seen. He convinced me that your husband couldn't have been injured and had got up and walked away. I believed him.'

'Look, I don't know what your game is, but you need to leave. If you're telling the truth, why aren't the police investigating it?'

'I'm not lying.' I shake my head. 'I'm not.' But I can't tell her about the fake statement because that'll really convince her I'm a liar. I should never have come. I've wasted my time. I've upset her and for what? It's not as if I've achieved anything.

'I'm sorry.' I turn towards the door. 'I'll go.'

'Wait.' She's confused, and who can blame her? 'This man you saw run over, why are you so convinced it's my husband? If he walked away, where is he now? You're not making any sense. Shall I call the police and you can explain yourself to them?' She walks over to the countertop and picks up her phone.

'No, please don't do that. I'll leave.'

She ignores me and unlocks her phone. I should run, now, but she'll give them a description and when she tells them what I've said, they'll know it was me.

'I think they're in on it, the police,' I gabble, in an attempt to stop her from calling them.

'What?' Her face is a picture of disbelief.

'Your husband was wearing a suit and a tie, a striped one. He looked as if he'd just left work, but it was five o'clock in the morning. It was him, I'm sure of it. I'm not lying. I knelt down next to him and stared right into his eyes. I put my tracksuit jacket over him to try to keep him warm until the ambulance arrived. I gave the police a statement and told them all this, but they altered it.'

'Altered it? Why on earth would they do that?'

'I wish I knew.'

'Was he conscious? Did he say anything?'

I can't meet her eyes. How I wish now that I hadn't come. I've made it worse for her.

'Well?' she demands.

'I thought he was dead,' I blurt. 'He was just staring up at me, not blinking.'

The words hang in the air and after a moment, tears roll silently down her face.

'You're lying. You're some sort of bloody fantasist and God only knows what sort of sick thrill you've got out of coming here. But I think you're right about one thing: he's dead,' she says, quietly. 'Because he wouldn't leave us. He wouldn't. He loves me and the kids more than anything, and I don't care what everyone is saying and splashing all over social media. Dominic would never leave like that. He wouldn't do this to us.'

'I'm so sorry.' I move closer to her, unsure of what to say. 'But I am telling the truth.'

'I don't know why I'm telling you this, but the police aren't interested. They've tried to tell me he's run off with another woman. They say it happens all the time, and that the wife is always the last to know. But I know my husband and he's not capable of that. We were happy. Okay, he'd changed lately, but that doesn't mean he had someone else, does it? Stupidly, I told the police something was troubling him, though I wish I hadn't. Everything was fine until he started that fucking job at Wildings...'

A yell from the lounge interrupts us. 'Mummy! The cartoon's finished. Can we have another one on?'

'How had he changed?' I ask.

'Mummy!' Leo pushes open the kitchen door and stares up at his mother.

'I'm coming darling, the lady's leaving now.' She swipes the tears from her face with her hands and flashes me a warning look. I follow her into the lounge. She picks up the remote control, points it at the TV and another cartoon begins to play.

'Last one,' she says, as Leo jumps back onto the sofa next to his sister. I follow Holly into the hallway and she pulls the lounge door closed behind us.

'Holly, I...'

'Go,' she hisses quietly. 'And don't *ever* come back, because if you do, I'm calling the police.'

* * *

As I power along the streets, my mind is in turmoil.

I want to cry. Holly's husband is dead and she and their children might never find out what happened to him.

Why won't the police do something? Dominic Newton has been murdered and whoever killed him is getting away with it.

My conscience keeps telling me I should do something more, but what? There is no one I can go to for help. I have no choice but to let it go. But I don't want to; it's important, it matters. It's a man's life we're talking about, so how can I just pretend that it never happened?

Because I have to.

I shouldn't have gone to see Holly because all I've done is cause upset. I've achieved nothing. I haven't helped her; in fact, I've made it worse. What a stupid, pointless thing I've done. What gives me the right to crash into her life like that and tell her that her husband was mown down by a car? Did I think I was going to solve the mystery of what happened to Dominic Newton?

Yes. On some level, I did.

Aside from it being an utterly selfish thing to do, I'm fortunate that she didn't call the police and get me arrested. The police are not going to give me any more chances.

I march along on autopilot, having no idea of the time and it's only as I enter the classroom that I realise I'm the last to arrive. Everyone turns their head towards me as I say my *holas* and take my seat. John catches my eye and I find myself transfixed and have trouble tearing my gaze away from him. God, he's so gorgeous. Let all the other stuff go, my brain tells me, and enjoy what might be the beginning of something good. I pretend to be busy getting my folder and Spanish dictionary out of my bag so that I can avoid making eye contact with him.

'Not like you to be late.' Jax leans closer and I turn to see her staring straight at me with a questioning look on her face.

'Been busy. Time just got away from me.'

She sits back and purses her lips.

'You seem different,' she says, her head on one side. 'It's your hair. I never realised it was so wavy and thick. You can't see how lovely it is when it's all scraped up into a ponytail.'

'Thanks,' I say with a laugh. 'I think.'

'Yeah, you look very different tonight. Whose benefit is that for?'

'*Buenas noches, amigos,*' Josie announces loudly, preventing me from answering.

I turn my face to the front, but I can sense Jax's eyes on me. Good God, what is she, a witch? How could she possibly know? Am I that obvious? Making an effort with my hair when I don't usually bother, and I put make-up on, too. I might as well have hung a big sign around my neck and be done with it. My phone bleeps loudly from my bag and everyone's eyes swivel towards me.

'*Lo siento,*' I apologise, pulling my phone out and flipping it to silent, glancing at the screen as I do so.

> JOHN
>
> Do you want a lift home after the class?

I slide my phone back into my bag and glance over at John, giving the slightest nod of my head. He raises his eyebrows slightly. I lower my bag to the floor and fix my gaze on Josie as she starts the lesson.

Concentrate, Abi, and forget about Dominic Newton.

It's not your problem and you've done all you can.

20

Marks & Spencer's cafe is busy. Mel has bagged us a table whilst I queue for our lunch. As I wait in the slow-moving line, I question why we came here instead of somewhere else. Although it's a Saturday lunchtime, so everywhere will be heaving.

Suddenly, an overpowering sensation of being watched comes over me and I turn and scan the room, convinced that Mel must be trying to catch my attention.

She's not.

I scan around the cafe, studying the people. No one is staring at me, no one is watching me, but how would I know if they were?

I wouldn't.

The person behind me coughs and I jump. The cough is a hint because the woman in front of me has moved and there's a massive gap. I move forward, select my baguette and Mel's carrot cake, a pot of tea, milk and cups, and put them on a tray.

I'm being paranoid, which isn't surprising after everything that's happened. When Mel and I were wandering around the underwear department, I had the distinct feeling that someone was following me. Nobody was, of course, because every time I looked around, all I could see were normal people going about their business. Nevertheless, even though I keep telling myself that I'm being ridiculous, the feeling won't go away.

'Thirteen pounds seventy-five, please.'

I tap my card, pick up the tray and carry it carefully over to the table.

Get a grip, Abi, and stop being so bloody dramatic.

Drama llama, Will's voice says.

'Oh my God, that cake looks amazing.' Mel pulls the plates off the tray while I offload the teapot and cups before sitting down opposite her. 'So, has he told you where he's taking you tonight?' she asks, digging her fork into the cake.

'Fabio's,' I say through a mouthful of bacon baguette.

'Ooh, very romantic. Don't eat too much garlic then.' She giggles.

'How can I *not* eat garlic in an Italian restaurant, hmm? Anyway, as long as he has it too, it won't be a problem.'

'And what are you wearing?'

'Well, I've treated myself to a nice little dress. Long sleeves, scoop neck, not too low but just a hint of cleavage, and it sits on the knee to show off my legs.'

Mel puts down her fork and gazes into the distance. 'God, I've forgotten what it's like to get dressed up and go out somewhere nice for dinner. It's not quite the same when you're the size of a small family car.'

'A bit of an exaggeration,' I laugh. 'And I can't remember the last time I got dressed up either, so it's going to be a bit weird.'

Mel puts her hand on my arm. 'I'm just so glad that you've met someone nice after the way Will treated you.'

'Me too.'

'Anyway, talking about things you've not done for a long time... Have you and John done the deed yet?'

'Mel! Of course not. I've only been out with him once.'

'Yeah, but you see him at Spanish as well, don't you, so that counts? And I can tell you really like him. And from what you've told me, he's super-hot. And it's the 2020s, not 1920s. It's not necessary to get married before having sex.'

She's not wrong about me liking him. When I'm with him, I can't take my eyes off him. When he dropped me home after Spanish, we sat in his car chatting for ages, all thoughts of my trip to Holly's house earlier, forgotten. Okay, not forgotten, but I managed to put them to the back of my mind. The chatting soon turned into passionate kissing and I was sorely tempted to invite him in, but managed to stop myself. I don't want to rush things. I don't want to mess it up, although I sensed that John wanted to continue the evening just as much as I did. Or perhaps that was wishful thinking.

'So, what have you done with your time off, apart from seeing your hot new man?'

'Nothing, really. A lot of running. Cleaning and sorting out. I cleared my wardrobe out and took a load of old stuff to the clothing bank. Visiting Mum and Dad. I suppose it's a bit of a waste of annual leave, but I had to take it because I'm not allowed to carry it over to next year.' If I'm even there next year. I'm back at work on Monday night but I don't mind, actually, because having too much time on my own sends my brain into overdrive; makes me imagine that I can solve crimes that the police say don't exist.

Makes me believe people are following me.

'Not running in the dark, I hope.' Mel looks stern.

'Of course not,' I lie. Although I do take my phone with me now, so I suppose that's a step forward. If anyone attacks me, I can ask them to hang on a minute while I call the police. 'And what about you? How much longer are you going to carry on working for? Are you going to be one of those mums who work right up to the last minute and gives birth the day after they finish work?'

'No chance. Originally, I wanted to keep working until as close to the birth as possible so I could take the maximum maternity leave afterwards, but I'm having second thoughts now.'

'Why? Is there something wrong?'

'No.' Mel laughs. 'I'm absolutely fine.' She leans across the table and lowers her voice. 'I haven't told anyone else, but Owen keeps saying "Why not finish now?". Enjoy a bit of time to myself before the baby arrives, a last bit of freedom. I've not told work yet, but I'm probably not going back after the baby's born. By the time I've paid for a nursery place, it'll hardly be worth it, because it'll eat up a huge chunk of my salary and that's even with Mum childminding a couple of days a week, too. And Owen says what's the point in having a baby if I can't enjoy being a mum? Now he's got his new job, we're not reliant on my salary so I don't *have* to go to work. And actually, I don't like my job that much, anyway.'

'You're going to be a stay-at-home mum?'

'Yeah, I am. Is that bad? Am I letting the side down? Should I be going back to keep my foot on the career ladder, not lose all the years that I've built up?' She bites her lip.

'No, definitely not. What could be more important than bringing up a child? You can get back on the ladder in years to come – if you want to. Work isn't the be-all and end-all. If you'd asked me the same question a year ago, I'd have thought differently, but I've had a massive life change since then. I'm working somewhere I'd never have considered working before and it's put things into perspective. Essentially, we all go to work for the same reason – money – but we tend to forget that, because we're so caught up in having a career. Work shouldn't be the most important thing in our lives.'

'No, it shouldn't. Mum doesn't understand why I'm agonising over it and says to just do it. She says why bother working if I don't need to? It was different for her, though. Most women stayed at home when they had babies unless they had fantastic, highly paid jobs to go back to.'

'You should do what makes you happy. And there's nothing to stop you restarting your career later on.'

'That's what I thought. I mean, you've had a career break, of sorts.'

'True,' I agree. 'Although Celia keeps messaging me to remind me to put in for that job she told me about. I'm still thinking about it.'

'Well, once you get your licence back, you can apply for any job you want.'

'Yes.' I take a bite of my baguette. 'Although it doesn't mean I'll get it.'

'Do you reckon your sister-in-law will go back to work?'

'She's not mentioned it and before she got pregnant, I'd have said she definitely would, but now I'm not so sure. It's not that they've actually said it, but I get the impression they've waited a long time for this baby, so who knows?'

'Well, it's the same for me and another reason for not going back. The IVF took over our lives and what was it all for if I hand my baby over to a stranger every morning?'

'You're right. You should enjoy it and luckily, you've got the choice. And there's no need to tell work what you've decided yet. Wait until after you've had the baby.'

'I won't change my mind, but no, I won't tell them yet. I'll just start my maternity leave sooner rather than later. They don't need to know any more than that. And I *am* lucky, because most people don't get to have a choice. Although Owen has to work stupid hours, so he's not going to be at home as much as I'd like, but you can't have it all. I mean, honestly, here we are, Saturday afternoon and he's at work. How mad is that? It's not as if he works in a shop, is it?'

'Well, they're not paying him all that money for nothing, are they?'

'No, they're not, and it's my duty to keep spending it, so let's finish our lunch and head up to that new baby shop that's just opened.'

'Sounds like a good idea. We can see if there's something I can buy you that you haven't already got.' I pop the last of my baguette into my mouth.

Mel laughs, and I'm relieved that there's been no mention of her suspicions that Owen's having an affair. Hopefully she's getting some perspective on it at last.

Like me; I'm getting perspective, because I can't do anything about the accident I saw. I'm letting it go. No, I've *let* it go.

It's done. I'm not even going to think about it any more. Every time it pops into my head, I'm pushing it firmly away.

And no one is following me, either.

* * *

I slip my feet into my black heels, stand up and practise walking across the bedroom. It's been a while since I've worn heels; mostly I'm in trainers or boots. After a couple of wobbly passes up and down the room, my walk becomes steadier as I become more confident that I'm not going to trip over my feet. I walk slowly to the full-length mirror next to the wardrobe and appraise my appearance.

Not bad, though I say so myself. Pretty good, actually.

The dress just skims my knees and there's a slight swing to the skirt which shows off my legs, which I'm rather proud of because the running has made them toned and shapely. I swing around and look over my shoulder and smile at myself. I can't help it. My hair looks lush and full and my face is glowing.

Tonight is going to be a good night.

My phone bleeps with a message from John to tell me that he's just pulled up outside the house. Picking up my handbag and fake fur coat, I head down the stairs. Quickly turning out the lounge lights, I slip my coat on and open the front door, letting in the freezing air. Pulling it closed behind me, I shiver with the cold. My quilted puffa coat would have been a better idea but it's not exactly glamourous.

John has the car door open for me, and I slide into the passenger seat as elegantly as possible.

'Wow, you look stunning,' he says quietly as I pull the door closed.

I turn to him and smile.

'You do too.' He does. The blue of his shirt and dark jacket show off his good looks to perfection.

'All strapped in?' he asks, slipping the car into gear.

'Yep, all done.' We accelerate down the street and turn smoothly onto the main road into town.

'Done anything exciting today?'

I tell him about my shopping spree with Mel, and how we bought several bags of baby clothes and assorted bits and pieces from the new baby shop. I got them a sleep nest to go in the pram, which apparently guarantees they sleep well from birth. I tell John this.

'How does that work?' John asks.

'No idea,' I laugh. 'Because I know nothing about babies.'

'Me neither.'

After we've parked up and we begin our walk to Fabio's, which is just a couple of streets away, I slip my arm through John's and he immediately drops his arm. Embarrassed, I'm about to tuck my hand into my coat pocket when I feel the warmth of his fingers wrapping themselves around mine and I can't help grinning to myself. We hurry along through the cold streets and when we arrive at Fabio's, we make ourselves comfortable at the cosy table in the corner of the restaurant that John's specifically booked.

It seems as if John and I have known each other for much longer than a couple of weeks because we're so comfortable in each other's company. We slip into easy conversation and when the waiter appears to take our order, he has to cough several times to get our attention.

'Didn't even realise he was there,' John says, as the waiter walks off.

'Nor me. He seemed a bit sniffy.'

'He did, didn't he? Maybe we should have gone to a Spanish restaurant. We could have practised what we've learned, which in my case would have amounted to asking for a beer.'

I laugh. 'I'm not much further ahead than you and without my notes, I'm pretty rubbish.'

'Not so; I've heard you in class, remember?'

I laugh. 'Now you're making me sound like a swot.'

'I'm so glad I signed up for the course.' John reaches across the table and takes my hand. 'Because if I hadn't, I wouldn't have met you.'

He holds my gaze and for the first time in a long, long time, I'm truly happy.

* * *

I snuggle down underneath the duvet. John has asked me over to his place on Friday so he can cook me dinner. He was mysterious about what he was going to make, only telling me that it was his signature dish.

I'm not sure why I didn't invite him in tonight. It's still in my head that I shouldn't rush into things, but there's no set schedule to do things by, is there?

But what if he's like Will?

He's not; I'm sure of it. What are the chances of meeting two men who are sadistic abusers? Very small, the logical part of me says. And I've agreed to go to his house on Friday and I wouldn't have done that if I didn't trust him.

I *do* trust him; I'm safe with him.

I remember Mel's remark about *doing the deed* and I smile to myself. Who knows what Friday night might bring? There was a lot of passionate kissing again at the end of the night and it took all of my willpower not to invite him in. He's awaken feelings in me that have been dormant for a very long time. Will killed any sexual feelings that I had stone dead with his abuse, although I had to pretend I still wanted him.

I push the thought away, determined not to let him in, I close my eyes, picturing John's face instead of Will's. As I'm drifting off to sleep, I suddenly open my eyes and stare into the darkness, remembering something else that Mel said to me this afternoon.

She said that Owen's always at work, even on a Saturday. But it's not that. It's where Owen works.

He works at Wildings.

Holly Newton mentioned Wildings.

Everything was fine until he started the job at Wildings.

Dominic Newton worked at the same company as Owen.

21

Incredibly, it's Thursday morning already and my working week is now finished until Sunday evening. This week has flown by, the routine of working and running eating up the hours, and I prefer it that way. When I was on leave, I felt adrift without my regular schedule.

Keep busy, that's the best thing, and then there's less time for my mind to go off on a tangent and for me to take stupid, ill-advised actions.

I pick up a bag of salad and drop it into my basket. Although I've finished my shift, I'm in the supermarket shopping. Sally and I treated ourselves to a slap-up English breakfast from the little cafe next door. It was nice to have a good gossip together without looking over our shoulders every five minutes to check if Kelly was creeping up on us. Once I've picked up my few bits of shopping, I'll be heading home for a nice long sleep.

This store opens at seven and now, at just twenty past, the early-bird shoppers are here. Most are people on their way to – or, like me, from – work, but there are a few young mums with babies, too, who come early to miss the crowds. It seems strange to be in the store with customers when I'm so used to it being just staff. I meander around the aisles, picking up a few items. I'm going to John's for dinner tomorrow night, so I don't need to buy any food, but I should definitely get a nice bottle of wine to take with me. I wander around to the alcohol section, debating whether to buy red or white. John hasn't divulged what he's cooking, only that it's his signature dish. He's been working away in Spain this week and isn't back until late tonight, so he won't be at Spanish class. We've messaged each other every day. Many times a day. I've missed him. Apparently absence really does make the heart grow fonder.

White; definitely white, I decide.

As I scan the shelf, the hairs on the back of my neck prickle. I slowly turn my head from side to side; there's a woman studying the wine shelf further down the aisle and a lone man putting six bottles of red into his trolley. Neither of them are even looking in my direction.

Get a grip, Abi. It's all in your imagination. Again.

I grab a bottle of Sauvignon Blanc and then turn and walk briskly to the nearest till. I unload it onto the belt and resist the urge to check behind me to see if anyone is watching me. Of course they're not; it's all in my mind.

But try as I might, I can't shake it off.

I think I'm being watched.

* * *

When I wake up that afternoon, I don't bother showering, but get straight into my running gear and leave the house. The wind cuts through me as I pull the front door closed, and it takes all of my willpower not to go straight back inside and forget all about going for a run. I jog down the street, heading towards the industrial estate. It's already starting to get dark and the sky is low with clouds, but I power on and increase my speed.

As if I can outrun my thoughts.

Ever since I realised that Owen works at the same company as Dominic Newton had been working at just before he died, I've been trying to figure out why Owen has never mentioned this fact. We've had conversations about Dominic Newton, despite Owen not believing he was the man I saw run over.

So why did Owen never say that he'd worked with him?

Though it *is* a big company. Why should Owen have any knowledge of Dominic Newton working there? It's not as if he has to personally know every single employee of the company, is it?

Only I think he must have.

Because I couldn't stop myself; I read the news reports online and Dominic Newton worked for a firm of auditors. When he disappeared, he was working as an external auditor in the finance department at Wildings.

Owen is the head of Finance.

This thought has been whirling around in my head all week, and I've driven myself mad about it. Mel rang for a chat on Tuesday and all the time she was talking, I was trying to find a way to ask her if Owen knew Dominic Newton.

Madness.

Luckily, I managed to stop myself because how would it look if I'd dropped that into the conversation?

As if I were accusing Owen of something, that's how it would look.

And what, exactly, would I be accusing him of? I've known Owen for years and common sense tells me that there will be a perfectly reasonable explanation as to why he never mentioned Dominic Newton working at Wildings, so do I really want to ruin our friendship by asking him why he didn't?

No, I do not.

I have no intention of doing so, but I also never intended going to see Holly Newton and look how that turned out. As I keep reminding myself, I'm lucky that she never called the police. They already have me down for a madwoman; one call from her and I'd be done for.

No. I'm not asking Owen anything, or Mel. I've made a promise to myself and I'm going to keep it.

They're my best friends and no way am I jeopardising that by asking stupid, pointless questions about something I can do nothing about.

* * *

I stop my eyes from looking in the direction of John's empty seat when I arrive in the classroom. I call out '*Hola*', slip my coat off and sit down next to Jax, who's deep in conversation with Caro.

'Isn't John coming tonight?' Jax asks loudly.

It takes me a minute to realise that she's asking *me*, with an expectant expression on her face.

'I don't know.' I shrug, feigning surprise.

She grins and stares at me. Honestly, how can she know? John and I haven't told anyone that we're seeing each other and we deliberately ignore each other in class.

I busy myself arranging my notepad and pens on the desk, but I can sense her studying me.

'What?' I eventually ask when she makes no secret of the fact that she's looking at me.

'Are you sure you don't know where John is?' she asks.

'Why should I?'

'So you're not seeing each other?' She grins.

'Whatever gives you that idea?'

'Oh, well, it could be the way you avoided looking at each other the whole time last week in class.'

Thankfully, I'm prevented from having to reply because at that moment Josie calls for everyone's attention. I concentrate on her and try to ignore the fact that Jax is now whispering to Caro, who is glancing at me with interest.

The evening crawls by and for most of it, I can sense Jax studying me from the corner of my eye. She's desperate to get my attention, and it's wearing. She doesn't miss a thing, and John and I are obviously deluding ourselves that we can keep our relationship private.

Relationship... Is it? Yes, I think it is. There's no set time to get to know someone. Will and I hadn't been seeing each other for very long when we moved in together and although that was a disastrous relationship, it doesn't mean that this one is.

John is not Will.

Ten more minutes and the class will be over.

'Abi,' Jax hisses.

I ignore her.

'Abi.' She accompanies it with a nudge this time and I reluctantly turn to her and raise my eyebrows. 'Caro's asking if you want a lift home.'

It's only so they can trap me in the car and interrogate me about John.

'No, I'm fine, but thanks for the offer.'

'It's going to chuck it down. You'll get soaked.' Jax stares at me with a challenging look on her face. I smile and as Josie finishes the lesson, I pull my coat on, grab my bag, and hurry out of the classroom. I don't bother waiting for the lift, but race down the stairs two at a time. As I burst out of the double doors into the car park, it's already spitting with rain. Crossing the car park as quickly as possible, I march through the pedestrianised town centre. I don't want there to be any possibility of Caro pulling up alongside and badgering me to get in.

The small droplets of rain soon turn into a downpour and as I trudge home, I wonder why I was so stubborn; why didn't I accept the offer of a lift and let them question me, because at least I'd be dry. By the time I turn into the end of my street, the rain is driving down, the wind is howling and I've given up trying to hold the hood of my coat over my head. My hair is sodden, my coat is clinging to my legs and my hands are so cold that my fingers are numb. Even my socks are wet. I squelch up the path to the front door, huddle underneath the canopy and fumble in my bag for my key. At last, my frozen fingers find the familiar contour and I grasp hold of it with relief. As I put it up to the lock, a noise from behind startles me and I swing around in shock. A dark clothed figure is walking up the path towards me. I move backwards and hit the front door. I can't get away.

'Who are you?' I shout.

The figure draws closer and I bunch my fingers around the key, knuckleduster style.

'Abigail?'

It's a woman. She comes to a halt in front of me and I peer through the darkness to try to make out who it is. The voice isn't familiar.

'Who are you?' I ask, my voice sounding much weaker than I intended.

'I just want to talk to you.'

'What, now? Look, I don't know who you are but you frightened the life out of me. What do you want at this time of night?'

'Just to talk to you. Please.'

I stand immobile. Her voice is soft, hesitant. She sounds frightened. But who is she? What stranger turns up at ten o'clock at night to talk? She could be an axe-murderer for all I know.

'Tell me who you are and what you want.'

'My name is Georgia. Georgia Trent.'

Is that name supposed to mean something to me? It doesn't.

'Well, Georgia Trent, why don't you come back tomorrow, in the day? Although I have no idea why you want to talk to me.'

If I pretend that I'll talk to her tomorrow, she'll leave. Although there's no way I'll be talking to her at any time.

'I can't.' Her voice is pleading. 'This is the only time I can get away. Please. Help me.'

Help? For what? Does she want money? I've heard of this sort of thing; scammers pretending they're in trouble or have had an accident.

'You need to leave,' I bark at her, 'or I'll call the police.' I turn and quickly push the key into the lock, readying myself to get inside.

'Just five minutes, that's all.'

I don't reply but open the door and slip in, pushing it closed behind me. Before I can get it fully shut, her face appears in the gap.

'Please. Just give me five minutes and I'll go.'

'GET OUT!' I scream.

'I'm Will's girlfriend!' she shouts at me, desperation in her voice. 'And I need your help.'

22

We stand in the hallway staring at each other.

I've let her in.

I shrug my coat off, lay it on the stairs and pull off my boots. They're soaked right through, as are my coat, jeans, hair and feet. I keep hold of my handbag because it has my phone inside and I may need to use it. I'm acutely aware that I've allowed a complete stranger into my home and what's more, no one but me knows that she's here.

'You should take yours off,' I say, walking into the lounge.

I stand in front of the sofa and wait while she takes off her coat and lays it carefully on the hallway floor before removing her shoes. This is how Holly Newton must have felt when I doorstepped her. She stands uncertainly in the hall before coming into the lounge. There's something about the way she stands that's vaguely familiar.

'Have you been following me?' I ask.

'Yes. I'm sorry. I've been trying to find the right moment to speak to you.'

'You were at the supermarket this morning, weren't you, in the wine aisle?'

'Yes.' She nods. 'And the other day, too, in the town centre. I wanted to talk to you then, but you were with your friend.'

When Mel and I were shopping. So I *didn't* imagine I was being watched; I actually was. Strangely, this gives me comfort; I can trust myself, I'm not paranoid.

'Why are you here? Will and I finished a long time ago.'

'It's the only time I could get away from him. I've told him I'm away at a work conference, at a presentation dinner where I can't take calls.' She shivers, her voice on the verge of breaking.

'I'll make tea,' I state. 'Sit down.'

She lowers herself onto the sofa and I go out into the kitchen, fill the kettle and switch it on, throwing teabags into mugs. When the kettle boils, I pour water into the mugs and a splash of milk, not asking her how she takes it. There's silence from the lounge and when I walk back in, I half expect her to have gone. But she's still there, hunched on the sofa, her hands clamped around her knees.

'Thank you,' she says quietly as I give her the tea.

I take several gulps and let the warmth course through me before sitting on the chair opposite her.

'So, what is it you want?'

'You were Will's girlfriend, weren't you? Before me?'

'Yes, I was, what of it?'

'He talked about you.' She places the mug on the table.

I'm surprised he told her.

'He says he threw you out because you were an alcoholic and you cheated on him. He called you a slut.' She says the words quietly, her eyes fixed on my face. 'He showed me the news article about how you crashed your car into the school.'

Anger surges through me. How typical of him to lie and make me look bad, although he could hardly tell her the truth, could he? Although he could – and should – have said nothing, because we had a deal.

But it doesn't matter. I don't care what he says about me.

'I knew he was lying,' she says. 'Because he lies all the time. And I don't think you were the first, either. There was someone else before you but he doesn't really say much about her. He did it to you, didn't he? Lock you up?'

I stay completely still.

'I don't know what you're talking about,' I say after a moment.

She looks sad but not surprised at my lie and I experience a pang of guilt; he's doing the same to her, because why else would she be here? She wants my help. But I can't give it. Will and I made a deal and even though he's reneged on that by lying about me – because I had to promise not to badmouth him, so I expected the same from him – I don't want to give him any reason to come after me.

She stands up and gives me a shaky smile.

'It's okay,' she says quietly. 'I understand. I shouldn't have come and I've no right to ask you for help because I'm a stranger to you. I'm nothing to you. You got away so why would you risk your new life to help me?' She walks out to the hallway.

She'll go in a minute and I'll never have to see her again.

I force myself to stand up and go to the doorway, watching as she slips her feet back into her shoes. She puts her hand on the door and turns to me with a wan smile.

'I won't follow you again, so you needn't worry. And I don't blame you for not wanting to help, not at all. If you could tell me how you got away from him maybe I could do the same, because I can't see any way out.'

When I don't respond, she opens the door and I want to stop her, but I'm afraid to. Why open up that nightmare again? I'm free of Will; I escaped. She's not my problem.

She steps outside. It's stopped raining at last, so there is, at least, that. She's reached the end of the path before I call out to her. 'Georgia?'

She turns, her expression invisible in the darkness.

'Come back. We can talk.'

She stands still for a moment and then walks slowly back towards me. I take a deep breath, wondering why I'm getting involved. She's nothing to me; an absolute stranger. There's no reason why I should help her. But as I let her in, it hits me that if I don't, Will is going to kill her.

And I can't live with that.

She follows me into the lounge and we resume our seats; her on the sofa, me on the chair. What if this is a trick – what if Will has sent her to find out if I'll stick to my side of our deal?

'What makes you think he locked me in the cupboard?' Did he tell her? I can't imagine he would.

'There are dents inside the door of the cupboard. I think they're from where you hammered on it to try and get out because there are more now, that I've made. And I found a clump of hair in the corner, underneath a box. I thought it was mine at first; a handful that he'd pulled out, but it was the wrong colour. That's when I knew for sure that he'd done it before. He says it's my fault, that I make him do it, that he's never done anything like it before, but he's a liar.'

'What does he do to you?'

She bites her lip at my question and I see her fighting with her emotions. 'Locks me inside the cupboard. Threatens to go away and leave me there to die. It was two days the last time. I thought I was going to go mad with thirst. He phoned my manager and told him I was ill in bed with flu and my absence wasn't questioned.'

She draws a shuddering breath and I wait.

After a moment, she begins to speak again. 'He's getting worse. But he's not stupid because he never leaves marks on me where they can be seen. Sometimes our life is normal; Will is almost normal. Except that he's not; I'm constantly waiting for him to turn. I'm living a nightmare. He's nothing like the man I met and fell in love with and I wish I'd never met him. We'd been living together for a month when it happened the first time.' She stops and puts her head in her hands.

So much more quickly than it happened with me. He's escalating, getting worse.

'Can't you leave him?' I ask, as if she still has a choice. 'Run away? Go somewhere he'll never find you?'

'No.' She shakes her head. 'If he can't find me, he'll take revenge on my family. I have a younger sister and he delights in telling me what he'll do to her if I ever leave him.'

'He did the same to me,' I admit. 'Threatened my family, said he'd make them pay. I stayed with him for three years.'

'Oh my God, three years. How did you bear it?'

I shrug.

'He's going to kill me,' Georgia says in a rush. 'It's building, the violence. I'll never be free of him. God, how I wish I'd never met him. He seemed like the perfect man and now...' She pauses. 'I just don't see how I'm ever going to escape him. If I go to the police, he's promised me I'll never see my family again. But you managed to get away, didn't you, so there must be a way? How did you do it? Because I don't believe for one minute that he threw you out. He's lying about that because he won't want to admit you got the better of him. You managed to escape and if it worked for you, it could work for me.'

Flashbacks of the night I crashed the car bludgeon their way into my head. He will kill her if she stays, of that I'm sure. It's just a question of time.

I begin to talk, and for the first time, leaving nothing out, I confess everything that happened on that night.

* * *

'Wow, I'm impressed.' The slice of beef Wellington on my plate, nestled next to new potatoes and green beans, looks as if it's come straight out of the kitchen of a professional chef. The beef is pink in the middle and the pastry light and crisp.

'You haven't tasted it yet,' John says, but there's a confidence there; he's quite sure it's going to be as delicious as it looks.

'Only one way to find out.' I slice through the pastry, spear it onto my fork and put it into my mouth.

John watches intently as I chew and I hope I haven't got food all around my mouth.

'Well?' he asks.

'Perfect,' I say, taking a sip of wine. 'But I think you knew that.'

He laughs. 'It's the only dish I ever cook so I should be good at it by now.' He picks up his knife and fork and proceeds to tuck into his own meal.

I'm not sure what I expected from John but the perfectly laid table, along with candles and napkins, tell me that he's no stranger to cooking for others.

We continue eating and in no time at all, our plates are clean, not a scrap left on either of them.

'That,' I say, placing my knife and fork in the middle of the plate, 'was amazing. I'm already feeling inferior. My cooking is no match for yours.'

'Well, that's it, the sum total of my cooking skills. One dish only. Dessert is from Marks & Spencer and all I've done is take it out of the box.'

'Thank God for that, otherwise you'd be too perfect.'

There's silence and I feel embarrassed at my own words. 'So,' I say, filling the gap, 'is it nice to be home again? Apart from the rotten weather?'

'It is.'

'Did you try your Spanish out whilst you were there?'

'A little. I felt really self-conscious doing it, but they were all very complimentary about it. They attempted to teach me a few more words but it was in one ear and out the other. I'm never going to be a linguist.'

'Well, your absence was noticed on Thursday night. Jax asked me where you were.'

'Did she? God, she doesn't miss a trick, that one. What did you say?'

'Told her I had no idea, although I could tell she didn't believe me.'

John picks up his wine and studies me from across the table. 'I missed you, you know. A lot.'

'Me too. I mean I missed you, not myself.'

'Really?' He looks into my eyes and I can't look away. 'You seem a bit preoccupied tonight, Abi, is there something bothering you?'

The urge to unburden myself is tempting; Holly Newton, my suspicions about Owen, Georgia Trent, the whole sorry saga of my disastrous relationship with Will.

But I can't.

'It's been a bit of a week; quite a few things going on, but it's over now.'

'Like what? You can tell me. I promise you I'm a good listener.'

'Honestly, it's fine, I won't bore you with it all. It's my own fault for interfering, I should learn to mind my own business.'

'Sounds ominous.'

'No. It's really not,' I laugh, trying to make light of things. 'I just got involved in something that I wish I hadn't, but I didn't have a choice.' I remember last night's visit from Georgia. She wants me to help her but I don't see what I can do.

'Involved in what?' John is looking at me, a serious expression on his face. Why am I bringing the evening down by even mentioning it? Would John's opinion of me change if he knew about Will? I don't want him to see me as a victim. I've been looking forward to tonight and I'm not spoiling it with stories of my violent ex.

John's eyes search my face and I force a bright smile. 'Honestly. Ignore me. I'm just a drama llama.' I laugh and wonder why I'm saying the hated phrase that Will always used about me.

'If you're sure. I'm here, if you want to talk.'

'I know, and thank you.' I pick up my wine glass and hold it up.

'We should toast your excellent cooking skills.'

'So.' John raises his glass and we chink them across the table. 'Do you want dessert now or do we need a breather?'

'Definitely a breather.' I swallow the last of my wine.

'Okay.' John refills our glasses. 'Then I suggest we retire to the lounge for a while so we can have our breather in comfort.'

I follow John down the hallway. For some reason, I imagined him living in a super modern bachelor pad, but that couldn't be further from the truth. His house is a 1930s three-storey, bay-windowed terrace just outside the town centre. It looks tall and narrow from the outside, but inside, it's huge. The kitchen, where we've eaten, is at the back of the house and is modern and spacious, but the hallway has unpainted walls, the wallpaper stripped off, revealing multicoloured plaster.

'Work in progress,' John says. 'There were about twenty layers of wallpaper to scrape off. The hallway's much wider now.' He laughs, rubbing his hand over the wall.

'Did *you* do it? Are you a do-it-yourselfer?'

'I wasn't, but the builder I employed wasn't stepping up.'

'Oh, what did he do?'

He frowns. 'Let's just say he's not coming back.'

'Sounds ominous.'

'It was.' He stares at the wall, his expression angry. I've clearly hit a nerve.

'Anyway,' he says, just as the silence is becoming uncomfortable, 'the house is getting there, albeit very slowly.'

He turns and continues down the hallway and we go into the lounge. I gaze around at the dark velvet drapes covering the front bay window which dominates one wall. A large brown velvet sofa faces a tiled, black iron fireplace with an open fire and it feels warm and cosy.

'This is lovely.'

'Thank you.' He smiles at me, his anger of only minutes ago, gone. He strides across to the fire, picks up a poker from the hearth and prods the coals, the flames shooting skywards towards the chimney. Throwing himself onto the middle of the sofa, he pats the cushion next to him and I smile and sit down. He takes my glass from me and places it on the table and I relax into his arms.

And somehow, we never get around to eating that dessert.

23

I place the last jar of honey onto the shelf, lean back and push my fingers into my back and stretch my spine. Another half hour and that's work done until Sunday evening. John's coming to mine for dinner tomorrow evening and I've yet to decide on a menu, let alone buy the ingredients. There's no way I'll be able to compete with his beef Wellington. But I could cook lasagne, I guess. I've never yet managed to mess it up.

I can't help smiling as I remember last Friday night; I ended up staying at John's that night, and the next night, too. Although we did call in at mine the next morning on the way out to lunch to pick up some clean clothes. We spent a cosy Sunday cooking a roast together and watching old movies cuddled up on the sofa. I lied to Mum and Dad to explain my absence from my usual visit to them; I told them I was in the middle of a big sort out of my house and would be over to see them during the week. They accepted my excuse easily as I knew they would; they're not ones to question or interfere and I felt a pang of guilt for deceiving them.

John and I have given up the pretence that we're not in a relationship and whilst there's been no mention of love, because it's far too soon for that, there's no doubt in my mind that I've fallen head over heels for him. We've not seen each other since Sunday and I've missed him, despite messaging each other constantly. I can't wait to see him again.

I just hope he feels the same way.

He's picking me up tonight for Spanish, so we'll be arriving together. Jax will be delighted and whilst I find her nosiness annoying, there's no avoiding it and actually, why does our seeing each other have to be a big secret? Neither of us has anything to hide.

My phone vibrates in my overall pocket and after a quick glance around to check that my manager isn't hiding somewhere, ready to pounce, I pull my phone out to check it. When I see who the message is from, my heart sinks.

Georgia.

GEORGIA

> He's going away skiing for a whole week before Christmas. This is my chance. I'm making a plan.

I slip my phone back into my pocket without replying. What do I say to her? I told her I'd help but in all honesty, what can I do? I'm suddenly afraid; I've promised help and now I'm going to have to go through with it and I don't want to.

I told Georgia how I'd attempted to kill Will and left him for dead. She was horrified and said she could never do anything like that. She gave me the impression that by telling her what I'd done, I was suggesting she do the same, but I wasn't.

Although if she were to kill him, it would solve a lot of problems, wouldn't it? But despite Will deserving it, I shouldn't wish him dead, because my conscience tells me that karma will get me if I go down that route.

I confessed what I'd done to Georgia because I wanted her to see how desperate I was to escape, how bad it had got and that she wasn't alone. But that wasn't the only reason; it was such a massive relief to actually speak the words out loud for the very first time and to get them out of my head.

I told her to do what I did; start documenting the abuse with photographs, times and dates, the specifics of everything he'd done to her. Then she could take her evidence to the police.

She said she couldn't do that because he'd go after her family and exact his revenge by doing all the vile things that he'd promised. Police investigations take time. He wouldn't be kept in custody so would be free to do whatever he liked. These are the very same reasons that I didn't go to the police, and I knew she was right; they'd release Will, and she'd be at his mercy.

So I promised I'd go to the police with her.

Because they'll have to take notice of two of us, won't they? Two women saying the same thing with a lot of evidence to back it all up. They wouldn't be able to ignore us; they'd be forced to arrest him and hold him in custody. They could even track down the girlfriend before us, because he surely did it to her, too.

It sounded so feasible when I said it to her, but now, in the cold light of day, is it? The police can't hold him forever, can they? And as soon as he was freed, he'd come after us.

He'd come after me. Because he'd blame me.

Although he'd have to be stupid to do that, because if anything happened to Georgia or me, the police would know it was Will. So would he actually come for me, even knowing he'd go to prison? I think he would; because despite Will appearing like a normal human being, I'm quite sure he's mad. Psychotic.

But even if he kept away, and the police believed us, selfishly, I wish I'd stayed out of it all and told Georgia that I couldn't help her. I could have not let her in the house, ignored her, because Will was no longer my problem – I'd escaped. Yet again, my stupid, do-gooding-can't-keep-my-nose-out-of-stuff attitude is going to bring everything crashing down around me, just when my life is starting to come good again.

'Penny for them?' Sally appears from the next aisle, a big grin on her face. 'Dreaming about your hot new man?'

I summon up a fake smile. 'Maybe.'

'God, you're so lucky. There's nothing like those first few months of overwhelming passion. Make the most of it, because once you start washing his underpants and socks, the romance will be well and truly dead.'

I laugh.

'It's early days.'

'That's the best time. I can tell when someone's smitten and you most definitely are.' She puts her head to one side and studies me. 'Seriously, though, I'm pleased for you. You look good on it and he sounds like one of the good guys.'

'Yeah, he is,' I say.

It's just the rest of my life that's an absolute disaster.

* * *

I move the bag over to my left hand and wiggle the fingers of my right hand to try to get the blood flowing through them again. I wish I'd split my shopping between two bags, so it was easier to carry.

That's what happens when you do the groceries when your mind is clearly elsewhere.

I've promised myself that once I get home, I'm not dwelling on Georgia's situation for a minute longer. It's all been going around in my head but the minute I step through that front door, I'm putting it out of my mind. No more. Because it's not as if I've achieved anything. I've replied to Georgia, to tell her I'm here for her, but I haven't made any suggestions about what she can do.

That's for her to decide.

I'll help her, but she has to make the decision as to how she's going to leave Will. I can't do that for her. It's two weeks until Will goes skiing, so nothing is going to happen until then.

Two weeks for me to tell John about my past. Because it's all going to come out, and I want to prepare John for that. I didn't want him to know about Will and what happened with him; I want him to see me as *me*, not a victim, but it looks like I don't have any choice but to tell him.

It would be much easier if Georgia had never contacted me, but my conscience won't let me turn my back on her. How much easier my life would be if I didn't have a conscience.

I reach the house and fumble in my pocket. I find the key and push it towards the lock, but instead of it going in, the door swings inwards.

The door is open.

I freeze, and slowly lower the bag of shopping to the ground. How can the door possibly be open? Last night when I left, I came out of the house, pulled it shut, locked it, and walked to work.

I'm sure I did.

I've been burgled.

I take a deep breath and fully open the door. I step inside, but I don't close it behind me before going into the lounge. If there's still someone here, I need a way to escape quickly. I prepare myself for the sight of the room having been ransacked. Visions of spray-painted walls and overturned furniture force their way into my thoughts.

It's a few moments before I realise that everything appears normal. My laptop is still on the coffee table where I left it, the television is on the wall where it should be, nothing has been disturbed. If a burglar had been in here, surely the laptop and TV would have been the first things taken.

I look around the room again, more slowly this time, but can see nothing out of place.

Did I leave the door open? Did I not close it properly?

I have been preoccupied; when not worrying myself sick about the Georgia situation, I've been mooning over John like a lovesick teenager. Daydreaming. I could have forgotten to lock the front door, it's an old wooden one and when it rains, the wood swells and it requires a bit of force to secure it. It's entirely possible I didn't shut it right because it happened once before, not long after I moved in, when I went out for an early-hours run. I came back to exactly the same thing.

I walk through into the kitchen. Everything looks normal; my plate from last night's dinner is still in the sink, the knife and fork next to it. Exactly as I left it. I walk to the back door and try the handle; it's locked, as it should be. I rarely go out into the back garden. It's winter, it's cold, and there's no reason to, except when I drag the dustbin out to the front for collection and get it back in the next day, and that's about it. I haven't been out in the garden for several days. I peer through the glass in the door; the garden looks just as it always does. Annoyed at my own stupidity, I go back into the lounge, through into the hallway and pick up the shopping that I've left outside, close the front door and lock it. I take the shopping through to the kitchen, unpack it and put it all away. I usually put the TV on and eat breakfast before going to bed, but I'm not hungry at all, despite not having eaten since break time last night. I decide not to bother. I'll cook myself something before I go to Spanish tonight.

I'm furious with myself for being such an idiot. How fortunate that a random opportunist didn't come in and help themselves to anything they could find lying around. Or trash the place.

Imagine explaining that to Mel's dad.

Checking that the back door is still locked – as if it could have unlocked itself somehow! – I repeat the process on the front door before trudging upstairs. Checking the spare bedrooms on the way to my room to find that they look like they always do; unused, dusty, slightly sad and neglected. I go through to my bedroom, pull the curtains closed and set my alarm for 3.30. The curtains are thick and block out most of the light. Not fully black-out, but good enough. I strip off my clothes, toss them into the laundry basket and pull on my pyjamas. I'll shower and wash my hair when I get up. For now, I'm getting straight into bed because I'm absolutely exhausted. I've worn myself out with too much thinking and now I've started doing stupid things without even realising.

From now on, I'm concentrating on the here and now. I need to stop wasting time dwelling on what ifs.

Pay attention, Abi.

I pull back the duvet, plump the pillows, then head to the bathroom to brush my teeth. As I press down the handle to open the door, it registers at the back of my brain that the door is closed.

I never close it.

One step inside the bathroom and I come to an abrupt halt; the hand basin is right in front of me, an age-spotted mirror fixed to the wall above it.

All the air has been sucked out of the room and I can't breathe. When I at last manage to draw in a shuddering breath, the letters written on the mirror in red lipstick sear themselves into my brain.

KEEP YOUR MOUTH SHUT.

24

I stare in horror at the mirror, my legs feeling as if they're going to crumble beneath me. Turning, I close the bathroom door, ramming the bolt across with trembling fingers. I stumble to the bath and lower myself onto the side of it.

KEEP YOUR MOUTH SHUT.

I see then that the lipstick used to write the message is lying in the basin, the once smooth tip jagged and broken. It's one of mine; taken from the basket on the windowsill where I keep what little make-up I use. The thought of someone delving through my belongings makes my stomach lurch. I jump up and just manage to reach the toilet before I throw up violently. Holding my hair back from my face, I vomit until there's nothing left in me.

What else have they been looking through and touching?

My first instinct is to run, to escape from this house and get as far away as possible.

But I need to think.

I stand up and flush the toilet, lower the seat, and sit down on it.

Think, Abi, think.

Someone is trying to frighten me.

They've succeeded.

But who? Who wants to send me such a message that they'd go to the lengths of breaking into my house? They're telling me that they can get to me any time they like, that I'm not safe in my own home. But who is it?

Will.

It must be him, because who else could it be? I recall the message from Georgia earlier. Was it really from her, or has Will got her phone? Is he trying to trick me? I remember how he used to take such pleasure from terrifying me; the more frightened I became, the more aroused and violent he became.

He could have found out that Georgia came to see me and made her tell him where I live. Or has he always known? Will would have made it his business to find out where I am, because that knowledge would make him feel he still has some sort of control over me. He could easily have taken Georgia's phone and be pretending to be her. She could be locked in the cupboard.

What if she's dead?

I close my eyes as if that will help. I'll never escape him; he'll always be there, watching and waiting for me to slip up. The nightmare of living with Will resurfaces and a doubt begins to niggle: is this really Will's style?

No; the Will I knew wouldn't be able to contain his fury at me. If he'd been in here, the furniture would be smashed into pieces, every item of my clothing ripped to shreds. Then he'd have lain in wait for me to come home so he could take his rage out on me.

So if it's not Will, who? Whoever did this didn't need to break in, they had a key or they picked the lock. Could it be something to do with Dominic Newton? I'm no threat to whoever ran that man down, but do the people who did it know that? Have they somehow found out that I visited Holly Newton?

The thoughts whirl around in my head and I give up on the

possibility of getting any sleep. I stand up, take a deep breath, and stare at the bathroom door. If whoever has left the message wanted to harm me, they could easily have already done so. Would have done so. No, this is a warning that they can get to me whenever they want.

I turn and open the bathroom cabinet and take out a packet of wet wipes. Pulling out several, I bunch them in my hand and rub the mirror, smearing the lipstick across the glass. I throw them into the bin, pull out more and clean it again. When I'm done and there's no trace of lipstick left on the mirror, I pick up the broken lipstick from the basin and toss it into the bin.

Should I have taken a photograph of the message, given it to the police, reported that I'd had a break-in?

Maybe. But I went to them for help once before, and look how that ended.

I come out of the bathroom and walk down the landing towards my bedroom, resisting the urge to recheck the spare bedrooms to make sure there is no one in them. I can't allow myself to do that because once I start, I'll be checking everything constantly, forever. Once in the bedroom, I strip off my pyjamas, pull on my running gear and scoop my hair up into a ponytail.

Tucking my phone into my pocket, I head downstairs. Again, I fight the urge to go out to the kitchen and check.

There's no point.

I push my feet into my trainers, take my key from the hook, open the front door and step outside. It's cold but dry. I jog gently down the path and along the street before heading towards the industrial estate. The roads are getting busier, I run around people on the path who are on their way to work, but I keep up a steady pace as I run my usual route. Falling into the familiar routine of breathing and pacing myself, I begin to feel slightly better.

But I don't want to go home. Not yet.

I'm tired and I haven't slept since yesterday but instead of going home, I carry on running. I go past the turning for my street and head to the outskirts of town, pounding along unfamiliar streets, running farther than I've ever run before. When I eventually begin to flag, I turn back the way I came and continue running but more slowly; my energy is waning and fatigue is setting in. Eventually I find myself at the end of Mum and Dad's street. My stomach growls and a glance at my watch confirms that, incredibly, it's one o'clock in the afternoon. I've been running for hours. A visit won't seem unusual because I often pop in unannounced. I head down the street, relieved when I see their car parked in the driveway. That means they're at home. I fix a pleasant expression on my face and jog up to the front door.

'What a lovely surprise!' Mum looks delighted as she lets me in.

'I was out for a run so thought I'd drop by as it's such a nice day.'

'It is. Cold though.' She steps aside to let me in. 'Your dad's just doing some lunch if you want some.'

The smell of bacon wafts from the kitchen.

'Yes please, I'm starving.'

Dad's standing in front of the stove, frying pan on the hob.

'Brown sauce?' he asks, looking up.

'Please.' I settle myself at the kitchen table while Mum busies herself, pouring me a cup of tea.

'I thought you'd be sleeping. Didn't you work last night?'

'I did, but they're digging the street up and it was too noisy to sleep, so I thought I'd come out for a run.' Mum doesn't question me and I'm surprised at my capacity to lie so easily and quickly.

'Who's digging it up?' Dad asks with a frown.

'Not sure.' I shrug my shoulders. 'A broadband company, from the signs. No one I've heard of.'

And there it is again, the easy lying.

Mum puts a mug of tea in front of me, and I take a good few gulps. Running is thirsty work. Dad places a bacon sandwich on the table, brown sauce oozing between the slices of crusty bread.

'Hey, I can wait, Dad. Eat yours first.'

'No, you have it.' He drops more rashers into the pan. 'You'll have worked up an appetite running all the way over here.'

I tuck in, relaxing in the warmth of the kitchen, the familiarity of home, the easiness of it.

The safeness of it.

* * *

I pace the lounge and look out of the window for what seems like the hundredth time. John should be arriving at any minute because he's messaged to say he's on his way. I have my coat and shoes on ready, as they have been for the last half an hour. I'm ready to go the minute he arrives.

After lunch at Mum and Dad's, we settled in the lounge, and without meaning to, I fell asleep. Over two hours later, I woke, and for a moment, had no idea where I was. Yet I did feel better for it, even though I'm tired now. At least I've had some sleep. After yet another round of tea – my parents can drink tea for England – Mum proudly showed me what she's been knitting for Adam and Eve's baby. The little jacket and hat were beyond cute and I felt so pleased for them at their barely concealed excitement about soon having a grandchild. She's also crocheted a lovely blanket for Mel's baby and Dad found a bag with long handles to put it in so I could loop it across my back when I ran home. He offered to drive me back and, tempted though I was, I had to say no because Dad would have known then that I'd been lying about the street being dug up. I didn't relish the thought of returning to the house but the run home gave me time to think of a plan.

Mum asked what I'd been up to, and I told her about Spanish and seeing Mel and all the other trivia, but I never mentioned John. There's a superstitious part of me that thinks if I mention him, I'll jinx it. Because he doesn't know about Will yet, and that could change everything.

By the time I left, it was already beginning to get dark and as I ran through the streets, I thought how wonderful it would be if I could outrun parts of my life. When I arrived home, I quickly showered – avoiding looking at the mirror the whole time – and got dressed, then packed a bag with several days' worth of clothes. When I got downstairs, I went straight into the kitchen and turned off the heating and sat down. After an hour, the house has rapidly cooled down and all the radiators are now stone cold. Which isn't surprising because it's zero degrees outside. Another couple of hours and this house will be absolutely freezing. I check the window again and this time when I pull the curtain aside, John is parked out in the street. A man is leaning down into the open window of the car and talking to him. I lean closer to the glass and am trying to make out who the man is when he straightens up. I think it's my neighbour who lives next door but one. I've spoken to him briefly a couple of times and from what I remember, he lives with his wife and a couple of young boys. There's a sudden roar of the engine and John's car surges forward at the same time as my neighbour leaps backwards. I peer through the darkness to see my neighbour shouting something at John and waving his fist before turning and going into his house. What was that all about? I go into the hallway, pick up my bag and go out to the car.

'Can I put this in your boot?' I ask, opening the passenger door.

'Yeah, sure. I'll unlock it.' John looks up at me, his face unsmiling. After a moment he flips a lever and I hear the boot release. I go to the back of the car, throw the bag in and pull the lid down.

'Why was he shouting at you?' I ask, as I clamber into the seat and plug in my seat belt.

'What?'

'My neighbour, I saw him waving his fist at you and shouting.'

'Fucking moron,' he says, his expression grim. 'He's fortunate I didn't get out of the car and punch his face in.' He says the words quietly and evenly with barely contained rage. I'm stunned; this is a side of John that I haven't seen before, a side I would never have imagined.

'Oh,' is all I can manage to say.

John is silent and the tension in the air is almost palpable. I wish now I'd not mentioned it. My neighbour has clearly overstepped the mark.

'Oh, God...' He suddenly turns to me. 'Whatever must you think of me? I'm so sorry, I must sound like some sort of thug, but I won't tolerate people threatening me. It doesn't sit well, especially when I'm trapped in a car and they're invading my personal space.'

'He threatened you?'

'He did. Said if I didn't move my car away from his driveway this second he'd take a hammer to it and me as well. Said if I dared to do it again there would be no warning.'

'No!' I gasp in shock.

'Yep. A complete nutjob. Didn't you see the hammer he was waving around?'

'No, I couldn't see a lot, what with it being dark. I can't believe it, he seems such a nice, normal guy.'

'Believe it.' John shrugs. 'Because sadly, psychos tend not to go round wearing a label.'

'God, that's awful. I'll make sure to keep out of his way in the future.'

'I would, because he's clearly sick in the head. I'm just sorry you had to witness it.' He puts the car into gear and we drive down the street, then pull onto the main road.

'So, what's in the bag you put in the boot?' he asks as we pull up to the traffic lights.

'Oh, that? Clothes. Toiletries. The usual.'

'Are you going somewhere?'

'Well,' I sigh, sounding annoyed, 'typically, as we're having the coldest winter for years, my heating has decided to break down. I've contacted my landlord who is my best mate's dad and a really nice guy, but unfortunately, demand for plumbers is high at this time of year and the earliest he can get one to me is the middle of next week.'

'That's not good.'

'No, it's not. He offered me some portable heaters, but I can't imagine they'll be much good, especially because I'm used to central heating. So I'm going to stay with my parents until it's fixed. I was kind of hoping you'd give me a lift there after Spanish.'

'Yeah, of course I will. No problem.'

'Great. Thanks. I mean, I haven't actually asked them yet, but I'm sure it won't be a problem. Mum has the spare room set up as a sewing room but I'm almost sure they have a put-you-up bed up in the attic they can get out.'

The car slows and I see we've arrived at the college already. I usually walk, which makes it seem like a long way away, but the journey takes only minutes by car.

I unplug my seatbelt in readiness to get out, but John hasn't moved. 'Something wrong?' I ask, as he sits looking at me.

'No, nothing wrong.' He smiles. 'Seems a shame to put your parents to all that trouble when you could come and stay with me.'

I look at him as if I'm surprised, as if it's not exactly what I was hoping for.

'Stay with you...' I pretend to give it some thought, 'that would be great. If you're sure you don't mind, because you know I work weird shifts and I wouldn't want to disrupt you too much.'

'No problem,' he says with a grin, unclipping his seat belt and leaning across to kiss me on the lips. 'I like you and your weird shifts. Stay as long as you like.'

25

I've been at John's house for over a week.

He likes having me here, and that's not just my wishful thinking, because he's repeatedly said that I can stay as long as I like. He hasn't asked once about the heating and when I lied and said the plumber was waiting for a vital component to come into stock before he could fix it, John said why worry when I can stay with him. In fact, he continued, I should stay, because this way we were being green and saving the planet by heating only one house. My concern that my shifts might be a problem was unfounded because he's at work during the day, so I've slept undisturbed until three o'clock, just as I normally do.

I like coming home in the morning and John is still here. The first day, I crept around downstairs in an effort not to disturb him, but he came down, bleary-eyed with sleep, clearly having just that minute got up. I was surprised he was awake, and he confessed that he was usually up by now but had stayed in bed, keeping it warm for me. The next morning when I came home, I went straight upstairs and got into bed with him. I'll miss that special time with him when I go home.

If I go home.

Our relationship is much too new to be saying stuff like that out loud, so for now, I'm keeping my thoughts to myself. But I am hoping. The sensible part of my brain is shouting that it's too soon; less than a year ago I was still with Will. But the other part is saying that you can't put a timer on how you feel; you can't plan fate.

John is already making plans for this weekend, assuming that I'll be here, and I'm going along with that. He's organised dinner out at a nice restaurant tomorrow night – which is why I'm on my way to my house now to pick up some more clothes – and a Sunday roast with all the trimmings that we'll cook together after we've taken a brisk walk around the common, weather permitting.

I am aware that I can't hide here forever. Even if our relationship becomes permanent, there are things I need to do before I can properly move on in my life. One of them is to find out who broke into my house and wrote the message on my mirror; I need to find out who's trying to scare me.

Keep your mouth shut.

I am scared. Not when I'm with John, not at all, but when I'm alone. Walking to and from work, I'm constantly looking over my shoulder to see if I'm being followed.

Soon, I'll have to tell John about Will, because I can't keep putting it off, no matter how much I might want to. The abuse, the drink driving, the whole sorry saga. And about Dominic Newton, too, because I won't keep anything from him, not if we're going to be a proper couple. But I do have a fear that it'll spoil what we've got. We're so happy and at ease with each other and all of that stuff will just throw a big, ugly curveball into our budding relationship.

What if John decides that my life is too messed up for him to be involved in? I don't think he's that shallow; in fact, I'm sure he's not, but there is a tiny niggle in my head because we're so happy together that I'm just waiting for something to spoil it.

So I will tell him.

But not yet.

My phone pings with a message. It's from Georgia.

GEORGIA

> Not long now. I'll ring you soon, when it's safe to
> talk. I think I know what I'm going to do.

Is it really from Georgia or is it Will pretending to be her? The message is ambiguous. It could mean anything, and it's exactly what Will would write if it were him. I wish now that I'd asked Georgia where she works because I could have rung her there without Will being aware. I've searched for Georgia Trent on social media, but the profiles I found definitely weren't hers. I type 'okay' with a thumbs up emoji and press the send button. All of my replies to her have been like this. If it is Georgia, the reply will look cold and uninterested, but I can't put anything else in, in case it's Will who's messaging. If the message really is from her, I'll know soon enough when she rings me.

I've arrived.

I turn into my street and head towards my house, scanning the surrounding area as I draw closer. The street is quiet, as it usually is, and there's no one around. What, exactly, am I expecting to see? I honestly have no idea. I walk up to the front door, quickly open it and step inside, closing it behind me before fear gets the better of me.

Nothing feels different; nothing *is* different.

The house is freezing. My breath forms white clouds when I breathe out as I climb the stairs and go along the landing to my bedroom. Pulling down a holdall from the top of the wardrobe, I open it, grab two dresses and chuck them in, followed by fresh underwear and two jumpers. The blanket that Mum knitted for Mel's baby goes on the top. It's super soft and cuddly and I imagine Mel's baby snuggled inside it. I zip the bag up and lift it off the bed. Not too heavy. I'm going to Mel's for lunch after I've finished here so will give her the blanket then. The closed bathroom door taunts me as I go past, and I try to remember if I shut it the last time I was here.

Obviously I must have, because it's closed now.

But I normally leave it open.

The worm of doubt starts to grow. In one swift movement, I step forward, grasp the handle and turn it roughly, shoving the door open as I do so. The mirror stares back at me and the only thing on it is the reflection of my face. No lipstick, no scrawled threatening message.

Nothing to see here.

Annoyed that I've let myself get so rattled, I head down the stairs. In a few days, if Georgia rings me, it means Will isn't out to get me and that he hasn't been in my house.

Great.

Though... if it wasn't him, who was it?

* * *

'So you've moved in with him already?' Mel's eyes are wide with surprise. We were chatting, and I mentioned how nice it is to have John waiting for me when I get home from work, completely forgetting that she doesn't know. That's the trouble with lies. They trip you up.

'No, of course not.' I laugh, but Mel's not fooled. She stares at me steadily, raising an eyebrow. 'It just sort of happened.'

'How's that?'

'Well, we go to Spanish class together and it was easier to stay over at his place, and I'm still there.' It sounds lame, but I can't tell Mel the same lie that I told John. Mel's dad owns the house I rent and he'd never leave me without the heating working.

'Yes, I can see how impossible it must have been for him to pick you up from your house and take you.' We both laugh and I sense a 'but' coming. 'You're sure about him, are you? I mean, you haven't known each other very long.'

'Says the girl who jumped into bed with Owen the night she met him.' The words are cutting but I say them in what I hope is a light-hearted way.

'Ouch.' Mel pulls a face. 'You're absolutely right. I did, but I didn't move in with him after a few weeks. I'm just concerned for my best friend, that's all.'

'Honestly, you don't need to worry. Apart from being absolutely gorgeous, John is kind and considerate and we think the same about so many things. I actually think I've found the perfect man.'

'Sounds like you might have. When do we get to meet him?'

'Soon,' I promise. 'Very soon. I haven't introduced him to anyone yet, not even Mum and Dad.'

'Well, that's because you're all loved up and haven't got room for anyone else. That'll wear off.'

I laugh; she's sort of right because I haven't met any of John's family or friends either. It's completely normal to want to spend every minute together in the first throes of a relationship when you can't get enough of each other. Other people aren't even on the radar at the moment.

'So he's not like Will? He was never interested in socialising with me and Owen, was he?' Mel says. 'I always got the impression he couldn't be bothered with us.'

He couldn't. We all went out for dinner a couple of times, but those occasions soon tailed off. I made excuses by telling Mel that he wasn't a very sociable person. Defended him.

'He could only be bothered when it was his friends,' I say. 'He was a completely selfish prick. God knows why I couldn't see it at the time.'

Mel looks shocked and I realise it's the first time I've deviated from the *we fell out of love* story. 'I've never heard you slag him off before.'

I shrug. 'I didn't want to get into it all because it brings me down. But what I will say is that John is nothing like him and you'll be meeting him very soon because he's heard all about you.'

We're interrupted by the sound of the front door opening. Seconds later, Owen walks into the lounge.

'So, this is what you do all day?' He grins at Mel and kisses her. 'Sit around gossiping?' He leans over and gives me a peck on the cheek. 'How are you doing, Abs?' Owen asks.

'Oh, not so bad. How about you?'

'Busy.'

'He's checking up on me,' Mel says. 'He keeps popping in to make sure I'm okay.' She rolls her eyes, but she can't hide that she likes that Owen is concerned about her.

'I'd be here a lot more if it weren't for work. It's manic right now.'

He looks tired; no less handsome than usual, but there are dark circles underneath his eyes and the merest hint of frown lines on his forehead.

'Do you want a coffee? Something to eat?' Mel asks.

'I didn't come home for you to wait on me. Besides, I have to get back. It's only a flying visit.' He checks his watch.

'You've got time for a quick sandwich, though? I was going to do us some, anyway.'

He hesitates for a moment and then smiles.

'Yeah, why not? But let me make it. You stay there.'

'Absolutely not.' Mel pulls herself off the sofa, holding her bump. 'It's time I moved. I've been sitting in one position for far too long. Sit down and chat with Abi and get her to tell you about her new man, John. I'll bring it all in on a tray and we'll have a coffee table picnic.'

Owen shrugs his suit jacket off and throws himself onto the sofa.

'So, who's this John? Got yourself a new bloke?' he asks with a grin.

'I have. It's early days, though.' I cross my fingers and hold them up. 'I don't want to jinx it, but let's just say I've got high hopes.'

'That's great, I'm pleased for you. Bring him around here so I can give him the once-over. Make sure he's up to standard and me and Mel approve.'

I laugh. 'I will.'

His phone bleeps from his hand, he glances at it and frowns.

'Work hassle?'

'Yeah. I expect Mel's told you how full-on it is. Absolutely mental. We've got some new investors and they're extremely high maintenance.' He rubs his hand over his face and I see how tired he looks. Obviously, he doesn't get paid lots of money for nothing. He seems a different person to the carefree Owen I've known for years.

'Cheese and pickle or ham?' Mel appears in the doorway, knife in hand.

'Ham,' we both chorus.

'You don't know what you're missing,' Mel says as she walks off. 'I'm obsessed with cheese and pickle.'

'You don't regret the big promotion, then?' I ask.

'How could I when it's bought all of this?' His smile doesn't reach his eyes and I wonder if he misses the days of their two-bed terrace and the local pub.

'It's finance you head up, isn't it?'

'Yeah. Financial Control.'

'So you would have known Dominic Newton?'

'Who?' He looks down at his phone but he isn't quick enough; I caught it, the slightest flicker in his eyes.

'Dominic Newton. The missing man I told you about. The one I saw run over when I was out running.'

'I'm not with you.' He gives me a puzzled look. 'Why would I know him?'

'Because he worked at your company.'

'Abs.' He sighs. 'No offence, but Wildings is a massive company. I don't personally know every single person who works there.'

'But you'd know everyone who works for you in your department, yeah? Because you are the boss.'

'Yeah, course,' he says, looking at his phone again. 'Although it's a pretty big department.'

'Dominic Newton worked in your department. He was an auditor.'

'I've got to go. Director's apparently just turned up at the office.' Owen jumps up from the sofa, putting his jacket on.

'So you definitely didn't know Dominic Newton?'

'No, Mel, I didn't,' he snaps. 'The man never worked in my department and I never met him, okay? Didn't the police warn you about all this nonsense? If I were you, I'd take their advice and let it drop. Because you got away with wasting police time before, but they might not be so forgiving if you start doing it again.'

I stare after him in disbelief as he strides into the kitchen. How dare he speak to me as if I'm some sort of hysterical time-waster who constantly pesters the police? I hear him saying goodbye to Mel and seconds later, he walks back into the room.

'Right, I'll be off. Nice to see you, take care,' he says breezily, holding a foil-wrapped sandwich up in the air – as if he hasn't just accused me of making things up.

'I'm not imagining things, Owen,' I stand up and say, as he passes by to go out into the hallway.

'Of course you're not.' He stops and turns around to face me. 'But maybe you're a bit confused. Or overtired, because you've been under a lot of strain, what with breaking up with Will and the driving conviction and losing your job. Whatever it is, I'm concerned about you. I don't want you getting into trouble again.' He smiles, but doesn't make eye contact and it suddenly hits me.

He's lying.

'I spoke to her.'

'What?'

'Dominic Newton's wife, Holly. She told me he worked at Wildings. As an auditor in the finance department. *Your* finance department.'

He doesn't answer.

'She said everything was fine until he started working there. I don't believe you've never met him, Owen. I think you're lying.' I'm shocked at my own words. I hadn't planned on saying any of that, but now I'm glad that it's out in the open. Owen can admit he knew him and tell me what the hell he's playing at.

Eyes glittering with anger, Owen steps towards me and roughly grabs hold of my arm. I try to shake him loose, but he tightens his grip, his fingers biting into the flesh. 'Keep out of it,' he says quietly, glancing over at the doorway to check Mel isn't there.

'Let go of me,' I demand.

'Keep your voice down,' he hisses. 'And stop sticking your nose in where it's not wanted.'

I stare up at him in shock.

'Take my advice and keep your mouth shut.'

'Keep your mouth shut,' I repeat. 'It was you, wasn't it?'

'I don't know what you're talking about.'

He does though, I can tell by the way he won't look me in the eye.

'You've been in my house, haven't you?'

He stares at me for a moment and then pulls me roughly out into the hallway, pulling the lounge door closed behind him.

'Just leave it, Abs, for your own sake.'

'So you admit it? You broke into my house and frightened the fucking life out of me!' I hiss at him.

'Yeah, I did.' He moves closer. 'And I didn't break in, I borrowed Mel's key. I was trying to do you a favour because you don't know what you've got yourself involved in. I was trying to stop you from getting hurt. You have to leave it alone, Abs. You have to. Forget Dominic Newton, forget what you saw, pretend it never happened.'

'Or what?' I demand. 'What are you going to do to me if I don't?'

He sighs. 'I'm not going to do anything. I'm your friend and I'm trying my best to protect you but if you don't leave it, you're on your own. I won't be able to save you. These are bad people, Abs, very bad. So please, just let it go.'

26

'Too big?' John stands back, hands on hips, and we gaze up at the huge Christmas tree he's just manhandled into the corner of the room next to the fireplace. The very top of the tree brushes the ceiling and the heady smell of pine needles mixed with wood smoke fills the room.

'No,' I say. 'It's perfect. A small tree wouldn't look right in a room this size.'

'Hmm, yeah, you're right.' He grins. 'It's a bit of a beast, though, isn't it? The top is skimming the ceiling. Going to have to bend it over to get the star on.'

'I hope you've got plenty of decorations to go on it,' I tease.

'Yep. Loads of them. Somewhere. Anyway, we deserve a glass of wine to reward ourselves for all our hard work.' He flops onto the sofa, pulling me down with him. I briefly melt into his arms before pulling away, forcing myself to say the words I've been avoiding for weeks.

'So. My heating's working now. All fixed.'

'Oh.' He seems surprised.

'It's actually been fixed for over a week,' I lie.

'I see. So what you're saying is, you're going home?'

Disappointment crushes me. I was hoping he'd ask me to stay. More than hoping. Praying. I open my mouth to say 'yes, I'll pack up my things', but he beats me to it.

'Why don't you stay for Christmas?'

'Christmas?' I echo.

'Yeah, why not? You should stay because it's a waste of time going back to your place when we'll be spending Christmas together anyway, won't we? So why not just stay here? I mean,' he goes on, 'I have to go to sodding Spain again, but it's only for a few days. Four max. I'll be back in time for Christmas Eve.'

Should I play a little hard to get? No; I'm not playing stupid games. I've already lied about the heating. From now on, I'm playing it straight. Total honesty.

'Although you've probably already made arrangements.' John says, taking my silence for hesitation. 'Of course you have. I shouldn't have just assumed you'd want to stay for Christmas, although if you did, I'd be more than happy for your parents to join us if you'd planned on spending the day with them. I'm going to meet them sometime, right?'

'I haven't made any arrangements,' I say, gazing up at him and thinking how perfect he is. He wants to meet my parents, which must mean he's serious about me. My heart lifts as I realise that he feels the same way about me as I do about him. 'And I'd love to spend Christmas with you. My parents are celebrating the day at my brother and sister-in-law's, but we can schedule in another date with them.'

I was invited to Adam's as well, way back in the summer, but I declined. I told him I'd already accepted an invitation for Christmas dinner with my old boss Celia and her partner. It wasn't a complete lie. Celia did invite me, but I turned her down, too; I had been intending to spend Christmas Day alone because I didn't feel like celebrating.

But that was a long time ago; things are very different now.

'Brilliant.' His face lights up. 'This Christmas is going to be so good.'

'It is,' I agree.

'I suppose I should go and find the tree decorations so we can make that beast look festive.'

'You should. And you'd better have a truckload of them, because all those branches are going to take some covering.'

'I've got plenty. My parents offloaded all their old ones onto me when they downsized. I didn't have the heart to tell them I didn't want them, because they behaved as if they were endowing me with the family jewels.'

'That's so sweet.'

'Not as sweet as you.' He kisses me and then pulls away and grimaces. 'That was so cheesy, but I mean it.' We lock eyes and right at this moment, I couldn't be happier.

'Should we make a start on that tree?' I ask, breaking the spell.

'We could,' John whispers. 'Or we could celebrate the fact that you're staying?'

'We could.'

And perhaps I'll be staying for more than Christmas, because right now, I never want to leave.

* * *

I click my phone screen closed.

Georgia.

She just rang me and she's absolutely fine. Growing increasingly worried as the days went by without hearing from her, I became convinced that Will had found out about her contacting me. The date she'd said Will was going skiing had long passed, and I feared the worst.

But I had no idea what to do about it.

What could I do?

And now everything is okay and there was no need to worry at all. With only five days until Christmas Day, Will has already been away for several days and Georgia is staying with her family. She did sound a bit odd though and I couldn't quite put my finger on her mood. Excited, almost, and hyper; gabbling away, stumbling over her words in her hurry to tell me how she's taking control of her life and is so optimistic for her future. But she ignored my question when I asked if she'd told her parents about Will, so I assume she hasn't. Perhaps it's the relief of Will actually going away and her knowing she's safe for the first time in ages, even if it is temporary. I don't know. I forced myself to ask her about us going to the police together and she told me breezily that I wasn't to worry because it was 'all in hand' and that she 'had a plan', whatever that means.

I accepted that, because what else can I do?

Also, it was easier.

I can't lie; I'm massively relieved. Do I really need to tell John about Will now? What would I actually achieve by telling him? Nothing, that I can see. It's a part of my life that's over and done with; some things are best forgotten.

Besides, I have other things to worry about.

Owen.

It was a week ago, but his words are still raw and fresh in my memory.

He's in on it.

Does Owen know who murdered Dominic Newton? Was he involved in his murder? The idea is ridiculous, unthinkable; sweet, loveable Owen who would do anything for anyone.

Except that it's not ridiculous, because he's warned me to keep out of it and told me that the people involved are very bad.

He's admitted that he wrote on the mirror, that he was trying to stop me from asking any more awkward questions, stop me going to the police.

He says he was trying to protect me and rightly or wrongly, I believe him.

So now I know there's something going on at Wildings, the question is, what am I going to do about it?

Nothing. Because there is nothing I *can* do. I've thought about it for a week and come to the conclusion that I can't do a thing. The police don't believe a word I say, and if I report Owen, what do I tell them? It's my word against his because there were no witnesses to our conversation. He lied to me about knowing Dominic Newton but that's hardly compelling evidence of wrongdoing, is it? The police are hardly going to launch an investigation on that and maybe he didn't lie about Dominic Newton to them. Maybe he only lied to me.

And whoever is behind this has already killed one man. What's stopping them from killing me if they think I'm stirring up trouble?

Nothing.

Even if there were something I could do, would I? No, because Mel is my best friend and I won't do anything to cause her any kind of distress. Thinking about Mel was the only way I got through the rest of that afternoon. When she came back from the kitchen, I somehow managed to pretend that nothing was wrong; as if Owen was still the same man he's always been and not someone who's involved in something terrible. It makes sense now, the massive change in their circumstances. The plentiful supply of money hasn't come from a huge promotion but from somewhere much darker. Mel would be heartbroken if she knew the truth about it and I'm not going to be the one to tell her.

So that's it, I have to forget it all. Memories fade.

If I'll let them.

I feel bad for Dominic Newton, particularly for his wife and two children, but my hands are tied. Putting myself in danger won't bring him back.

I'll occupy my mind with other things and eventually, it'll be a distant memory, like it never happened. I wish John were here with me now because when I'm with him, nothing else seems important, but he's gone away to Spain for work again, and I'm on my own for the next few days.

I might as well make myself useful.

The tree is still bare, so I'm going to hunt down the box of decorations and make it look pretty. Luckily, I've finished work until after Christmas. I booked annual leave months ago; so long ago that I'd forgotten all about it until Kelly reminded me. She spoke to me about it because she wanted me to change it to another time because, of course, they're short-staffed as everyone wants time off at Christmas. I took great pleasure in reminding her that I couldn't do that as we're not allowed to carry leave over into the next year. The expression on her face was priceless, but she couldn't argue. I didn't tell her that if she hadn't reminded me, I'd have gone into work as usual because I didn't remember I'd booked it.

So I have two or three days to fill with activity before John comes home.

Home. That's how I think of this house now, with John.

John said that the tree decorations are in one of the spare bedrooms, so all I need to do is find them. I go upstairs and open the first door off the landing to find a large room with tins of paint, a stepladder, and assorted decorating paraphernalia dumped in the middle of the floor. There's nothing else so the decorations clearly aren't in here. I move on to the next bedroom. Much smaller than the first one, it's filled with huge, square cardboard boxes dumped haphazardly around, with just enough room to walk between them. Some of the boxes are closed, gaffer tapes sealing them shut, others are open with stuff spilling out of the tops. I ignore the closed ones and go to the nearest open box and poke around. Books and magazines litter the top; I pick up an issue to see it's dated from three years previously. I unload the volumes to find they're hiding a jumble of battered trainers and shoes beneath. I root around before moving onto the next box; a toaster with the plug cut off, DVDs and yet more magazines that are years old. I don't delve too deep because I'm hoping the Christmas decorations will be easy to spot. John said there were lots of them so I'm hopeful they're in a box of their own. The next few boxes contain kitchen utensils, storage baskets with clothes stuffed inside, and yet more ancient magazines. I'm shocked; John's house is neat and tidy, but clearly, he's a secret hoarder of useless junk that belongs in the dustbin.

The next box I sort through contains an old-fashioned flowery dinner service, each item carefully wrapped in yellowing newspaper. Is this from John's parents? More hopeful now, I'm disappointed when the next box is yet more assorted junk; glasses, threadbare towels and discarded clothing. I stand back and survey the room, seeing if I'm missing the obvious.

And I am.

The very first taped-up box that I ignored and walked past has 'Xmas Decs' written in thick black pen on each side.

I rip off the tape and open it up and sure enough, inside are cartons of baubles, bags of tinsel and tangled strings of lights. I take some of them out, ferry them downstairs into the lounge and then head back upstairs for more.

This will keep me busy.

* * *

I take one last look at the picture of the Christmas tree I sent to John and put my phone on the bedside table to charge. The tree looks amazing, although it took forever to get all the decorations downstairs, let alone arrange them on the tree. It's a riot of colour and it won't win any awards for design or colour coordination, but its twinkling multicoloured lights and old-fashioned baubles look perfect in this room. It was so worth doing and I'm immensely proud of it; the room feels cosy and Christmassy and I can't wait for John to see it for real. When I'd finished hanging the decorations, the carpet was so covered with pine needles and shreds of tinsel that I had to vacuum the entire room.

John messaged back immediately to say that I'd done a tremendous job of decorating the tree and that he was missing me. We couldn't speak to each other because he's attending the staff Christmas function at a posh hotel. It's a formal meal with speakers afterwards so I totally get why we can't speak whilst all that's going on. He's been super busy since he arrived and aside from all the work he has to do, he's expected to fully participate in their social events, too. Apparently, Spanish Christmas celebrations start much earlier than ours and they take them very seriously. He's going to ring tomorrow, though, when he gets an opportunity. It's easier for him to ring me rather than me ringing him and going to voicemail.

I turn out the lamp, snuggle down underneath the duvet, and close my eyes. A few more days and John will be home and our Christmas can begin. We're going shopping together for the food but I haven't yet bought John's present; I want to get him something special but am still thinking about what it's going to be. I have a few ideas and maybe tomorrow I'll go into town and buy it. This Christmas is going to be so very different from last year's; I was on tenterhooks the whole time in case Will flipped, and him being at home instead of work all over Christmas made it even worse than usual. He'd insisted on just the two of us having Christmas together and made no secret of the fact that he found my parents old and irritating. It seems incredible that my life can have changed so much.

This year is going to be wonderful.

I begin to drift off to sleep, but there's something niggling at the edge of my consciousness that just won't let go.

There's something important, my brain insists on telling me, that I've forgotten.

I open my eyes and run through things it could be. Did I turn off the TV, the lights, the cooker? Did I lock the doors? I mentally retrace my steps; yes, I'm sure it's all done.

So what is it?

I think back over the day and try to remember because I won't be able to sleep until I do. I go through everything I've done; the phone call with Georgia, my resolution to let things go, Owen. Will.

Nothing.

Finding the decorations, dressing the tree, cleaning up, vacuuming, dinner. No, there's nothing important about any of that.

And then I remember that there is.

I lie completely still for a moment before throwing back the duvet and clambering out of bed. I pad out of the room onto the landing in bare feet, not bothering to turn the light on. It's nonsense; a stupid thought that means nothing.

Go back to bed, forget it. Go to sleep.

Except I can't. I need to satisfy myself that my overactive imagination is playing tricks on me. I'll go and look, confirm that I'm being ridiculous and then I'll be able to sleep.

I walk along to the spare room, go inside and flick on the light. It's cold and I shiver. The heating has gone off. I scan around the room until I see what it is that's been aggravating me like an unscratched itch. An open box in the corner has odd shoes and old clothes spilling out of the top of it. I move closer and study the clothing. A blue nylon sleeve with a black cuff is hanging over the edge of the box. I tug it and pull it out. It's a tracksuit jacket, a popular brand. There must be thousands of them around, probably hundreds of thousands. They're common, and unisex, and I used to have one just like it. The last time I saw it was when I laid it over Dominic Newton's chest to try to keep him warm while I ran to the telephone box.

It's John's and there's no reason at all why he shouldn't have one exactly the same as mine. Except that it's way too small for it to be his; he's six foot three and there's no way this would fit him. I check the label inside to confirm that my eyes aren't fooling me; it's the same size as the one I used to have.

Put it back in the box, Abi, forget it. Why are you always trying to spoil things, my brain asks? *Just leave it. Put it down and walk away.*

I want to, I really do, but I can't. I've seen it now and I have to be sure. Running my fingers along the length of the zip, I find the end. My jacket's zip had a loop of blue cord on the metal tag to pull it closed when I bought it, but the cord broke when I was out running and I lost it. I remember being really annoyed about that and I was tempted to return it to the shop for a refund, but laziness won. I replaced the cord myself with a piece of black ribbon that I'd kept from a fancy gift I'd been given. I threaded the ribbon through the hole, tied it in two neat knots and snipped off the ends to make it look better.

I force myself to look at the end of the zipper. There's no cord on it but black ribbon, tied in two knots, the ends uniform, as if they've been cut. I don't want it to be true, but there's no doubt in my mind.

It's my jacket.

27

I stare at the jacket, trying to make sense of it.

I'm suddenly freezing and I begin to shiver, so much so that my teeth chatter.

It's not that cold, it's shock.

I force myself to move and quickly stuff the jacket back into the box, pushing the other clothes on top before switching off the light and leaving the room. I close the door and stare at it.

Why did I go in there?

Why did I have to find it? Why couldn't I just leave it alone? Why did I have to notice it?

I hurry along to the bedroom and climb back into bed, pulling the duvet up to my neck and closing my eyes. As the warmth of the bed engulfs me, the shaking gradually subsides and my teeth stop chattering. My jaw aches.

My heart aches.

Stop, I tell myself, *stop catastrophising. There must be a million perfectly innocent explanations for my tracksuit jacket being in John's spare room.*

So why can't I think of a single one?

Maybe it's not mine, maybe someone else had a jacket just like it and replaced the cord. I expect the cords fall off them all the time. It'll be a design fault. That jacket could belong to John's ex-wife.

See? There's a perfectly logical explanation for it.

But seriously, what's the probability of it being his wife's? A million to one? Ten million to one? I desperately want to believe there's an innocent explanation for it, because if that jacket *is* mine, it can only mean one thing.

John is involved in Dominic Newton's disappearance. His murder.

I refuse to believe it. It's preposterous. What are the chances of me meeting John and him being involved in it? John *and* Owen?

It's insane.

John doesn't even know I witnessed the accident, because I've never told him; he knows nothing about it.

Unless he knew before I met him.

I feel sick. What if John got to know me deliberately because I witnessed what happened to Dominic Newton? What if he doesn't care about me at all but is just pretending, to make sure I don't stir up trouble? What if meeting John wasn't a coincidence at all?

No. I don't believe it. John cares about me. He does.

But he joined the Spanish class after everyone else. Was that to target me? I was all too willing when he showed an interest in me.

There's a simple solution to this; I'll ask him, just come right out and ask him. We're close, we've been living together for three weeks, sharing a bed, sharing our lives. I'll be able to tell if he's lying.

I'd know.

I pick up my phone to ring him. I can ask him, right now; get this all sorted out with one telephone call and then I can go back to sleep even though it'll be embarrassing to ask him because he'll know I'm doubting him. I open the screen and see that it's 12.30. It'll be 1.30 in the morning in Spain; he's most likely asleep and has his phone on silent so it'll go to voicemail. I can hardly leave a message about it, can I?

I place the phone back on the bedside table. This isn't a conversation for over the phone, I need to see him, speak to him properly, look at him.

My head hurts from running it all through my mind. I lay down and think about tomorrow; do I try and ring John, although he's warned me that it's easier if he rings me, as he's in and out of meetings? Can I bear to wait for him to call me? Backwards and forwards, around and around my thoughts go like a mental washing machine. And somehow, incredibly, I fall asleep.

* * *

I'm showered, dressed, and downstairs by eight o'clock.

I make myself a coffee but can't even think about eating anything. What am I going to do if he calls me? Should I wait until he gets back to speak to him? Can I wait?

Common sense tells me I should wait. I drink my coffee and go upstairs and into the spare bedroom and pull the tracksuit jacket out of the box and study it. I take it over to the window and hold it in the light. It's definitely mine and I have to face the fact that John could be lying to me. I don't want it to be true but I need to know for sure. I go into our bedroom, pull open the top drawer of the chest of drawers and take out my laptop. I carry it downstairs and set it on the coffee table, open it up and log on.

I search on the internet for Blackmore Services where John works. I open up their website and study it. They offer 'practical solutions for all businesses for safety, compliance and business support'.

Whatever that means.

For the first time I realise that I don't know very much about John. He's told me he's a project manager, but what does he actually *do*? He's mentioned getting the Spain office 'up and running' but exactly what part he plays in that, I don't know. He's similarly vague about his ex-wife and family. But I've never thought anything of it because I've been deliberately vague about Will. He's mentioned friends but I've never met any of them. But he hasn't met any of mine either, so if that makes him suspicious, then I am, too.

If Blackmore Services has done work for Wildings, then maybe John could have met Owen. If John's involved, does he know Owen? When I've talked about Mel and Owen, I don't recall John seeming uncomfortable or trying to change the subject.

But I wasn't looking, was I?

I scroll through the website, it's slick and professional. I click on the 'Offices' tab to see that they have premises here, in London and in Newcastle.

No mention of Spain.

I go back to the search engine and type in Blackmore Services Spain. Lots of results come up, but none match. The office there could be under a different name; it could be a subsidiary. I change my search and try all possible combinations to find an office in Spain.

I find nothing.

I go back to Blackmore's website, pick up my phone, punch in the telephone number from the screen and hit the call button. After several rings, a voice replies.

'Blackmore Services. How may I help?'

'Oh, hello. I wondered if you could tell me, does your company have an office in Spain?'

'No, we don't,' she replies after a moment. 'Can I ask who's calling?'

'No office in Madrid?' I hear a muffled conversation and then she replies. 'No, Blackmore is British-based only.'

I'm about to end the call but change my mind. 'Could you put me through to John Fletcher, please?'

'John Fletcher?'

'Yes. I've lost his direct number. He's a project manager.'

'Putting you through. Who shall I say is calling?'

'Jane,' I say. 'Jane Smith.'

I wait for her to tell me there's no one of that name working there, but she doesn't; there's a click and then I hear the line ringing. After several rings, it's picked up.

'Projects.' The voice is impatient, the accent, Scottish. He sounds in a hurry.

'Oh, hello, can I speak to John Fletcher please?'

There's a muted conversation as whoever is on the end of the line puts his hand over the receiver while he talks with a colleague. 'Sorry.' He's back on the line. 'Who's calling?'

'Jane Smith.'

'Hello Jane, how can I help?'

'I'd like to speak to John Fletcher please, the project manager.'

'Speaking.'

But it's not; it's not the John Fletcher I know.

With shaking hands, I end the call.

I stare numbly into space. Once again, I've fallen for the wrong man. John's lied to me from the minute we met. Every single word has been a lie.

John.

Is his name a lie, too? He doesn't work at Blackmore. So where is he is now?

My brain feels as if it's spinning around and the beginnings of a headache are burrowing their way in. I want to scream and sob but lean back, close my eyes and try to think logically. Hysterics won't help me now; I need to think calmly.

Part of me still doesn't want to believe that John isn't the man I thought he was. When we're together he's so gentle and kind, so caring. I feel so close to him, so safe with him. Can anyone be that good an actor and fake that? Is there a rational explanation for my jacket, for him not being the John Fletcher who works at Blackmore? I can't think of one but it's possible.

Anything is possible.

Think, Abi, THINK.

I care about him and I don't want us to be over but what else can I do? A warning voice in my head reminds me that I was like this with Will. I refused to believe what he was capable of, preferring to believe that the first time he abused me was a blip and not the real Will at all. But what if I've got it all wrong and there is an explanation for all this, as mad as it sounds to even think that? The one thing I do know is that I can't make the same mistake as I made with Will, I can't.

How can I possibly know the complete truth about John? And as I think that, it comes to me, there is a way to find out.

Owen.

28

The run back to my own house barely registers in my brain. I pound along the pavements, my body on autopilot, my head full of thoughts of John. One minute I'm persuading myself that he's innocent, the next, that he's guilty. By the time I let myself in the front door and close it behind me I feel as if I'm going mad, that my brain has turned into a never-ending loop of the same thoughts. The house is freezing. It's almost as cold as it is outside and yet I've run all of that way with no notice of the chilling wind, without even noticing that my fingers are red and itching from the icy temperature.

I go into the lounge, sit down on the sofa and wait. It's strange to be back here again, to think that when I left here to stay with John, I trusted him completely and had no doubts at all.

It seems like a lifetime ago.

There's a quiet tap at the front door and I jump up and go out into the hallway. I unlock the door and before I can open it fully, Owen pushes his way inside and closes it behind him.

'Why have you got me here, Abs? What's with the threatening messages?' He's angry, his face flushed as he hisses the words at me.

'I had to make sure you'd come,' I say.

'Well, you achieved that. What do you want?' He glares at me. 'What the fuck is going on that you threaten to lie to Mel that I'm involved in Dominic Newton's death if I don't come here right away?'

'So you weren't involved in his death?'

'Of course not. What do you think I am? Is that why you got me here? So you could question me? You're treading on dangerous ground, can't you see that? Have you got a fucking death wish?'

'No, of course not.' I stare at him in shock. 'I've let it go. It's not that, it's something else.'

'What?' he demands. 'Just get on with it.'

'It's about John.'

'What?' He looks puzzled. 'Your new bloke?'

'Yes.'

'Fuck's sake, Abs.' He laughs harshly. 'I've got a meeting I have to be at in about ten minutes and you drag me over here to talk about your new boyfriend?'

'I think he might be involved with what happened to Dominic Newton.'

He sighs and shakes his head.

'Aren't you getting a bit obsessed with it all? Trust me, someone you met at an evening class is not involved in anything.'

'I think he might be. I've found out he's not who he says he is, and he doesn't work where he told me.'

Owen stares at me.

'His name is John Fletcher.'

'And? I don't know a John Fletcher.'

I feel a tiny sprig of hope; perhaps I have got it all wrong. Maybe there is a perfectly good explanation for what I've found out.

'I'm going now, if that was all you got me here for?' Owen goes back out into the hallway and I follow behind him.

'Wait, please, just wait for a minute.' I pull my phone out of my pocket and flick through the photographs. 'Just look at his photo.' What if Owen knows him by a different name?

I have to be sure.

I scroll through to the photograph I took of John after we'd chosen the Christmas tree at the farm shop. He's standing in front of the tree, his arms spread wide, a huge grin on his face.

'This is John,' I say, holding my phone up in front of his face.

Owen stares at the picture and he doesn't even need to speak because the answer is written on his face, his horrified expression telling me that he knows John.

'You know him?'

'Yes.' He swallows. 'But not as John Fletcher.'

'Who is he and what's he got to do with it all, Owen?'

He turns, reaches for the handle on the front door. 'His name's James Ford. He's involved, and that's all you need to know. Don't confront him with what you've found out and please, don't tell him you've talked to me about any of it because if you do, I'm a dead man.'

'You're frightening me, Owen.'

'You should be afraid.' He turns and he looks beaten, his voice a whisper. 'Lie to him, make something up to get away from him. Run, Abs, as far away from him as possible but whatever you do, don't tell him what you know.'

* * *

How John must be laughing at me, what an absolute fool I've been.

John. That's not even his name.

On the night of the accident, I saw two men getting out of the car. Was John one of those men? I think he was either in the car that ran the man over, or he came back for the body and that's why he has my jacket.

Anger suddenly engulfs me and I want to smash something, let my rage out. My pathetic life that I thought was getting back on track is now even worse than before, I may as well be back inside that cupboard, because I'm helpless, powerless.

Alone in the dark.

I can't go to the police because they don't believe me and because of that, Dominic's family will never find out what's happened to him.

John has got away with murder.

Unable to keep still, I go back into the lounge and begin to pace the room to release my pent-up anger. There must be something I can do. There must be. It's not right. John, Owen, PC Cameron Malone, they shouldn't be allowed to get away with it. Someone must be held accountable. When the ringtone shrills on my phone which I'm still clutching in my hand, I stop in my tracks, my heart pounding. Taking a deep breath, I hold it up and look at the screen.

It's John.

The temptation to answer it and scream at him that I know what he's been doing is almost overwhelming; tell him that I'm not a fool, that I hate him.

I throw the phone onto the sofa where it bounces and lands, then ball my hands up into fists, my fingernails cutting into the palms of my hands. I need to think before I speak to him. I'm so angry that I'm afraid I'll confront him and tell him what I've found out, and that would be the worst possible thing I could do.

The ringing stops and I let out my breath, uncurl my fingers. Seconds later, it starts to ring again. I force myself to walk past the sofa and go out into the hallway and close the door. I stand and listen to it ring, it seems like forever but eventually it stops and doesn't ring again. And then I hear the familiar tone of a message coming through.

He'll wonder why I didn't answer. I'll have to make an excuse, say I was showering or something. I don't want to make him suspicious because once he knows what I've found, there'll be no going back and my life will be in danger. I thought he cared about me but I see now that he wanted to get closer to me to find out what I knew, stop me from making any trouble.

And I fell for it like a lovesick fool.

How quickly life can change, feelings can change. Yesterday, before I found the jacket, I thought John was the man I was going to spend the rest of my life with. Despite everything that happened with Will, I let John into my life because I wasn't going to allow Will to ruin my future with anyone else.

I thought I was falling in love with John.

But now I hate him.

How can my feelings for John have changed so quickly? Because I see him for what he is. He tricked his way into my life; charmed me, flattered me, became everything that I was looking for.

He took me for a stupid, gullible fool and he's no better than Will.

I have to get out of John's house, be gone by the time he comes back.

Run.

I can't stay with him; the thought of being with him, seeing him, makes me physically sick. I stare at the stairs, desperately trying to think of some way that I could make the police believe what I've found out about him. I could go to a different police station, speak to another detective. Somehow, convince them to start an investigation. But I come back to the same facts; my statement. I'm on record as a liar, a fantasist, a drunk. And Owen won't back me up; he has too much to lose and he's afraid, too.

I have no evidence. My tracksuit jacket isn't evidence.

And then it hits me; John thinks I'm stupid, too. He made no attempt to hide my jacket; he could have destroyed it, to be certain there was no possibility of me finding it, but he didn't bother.

He's so sure of himself.

Which shows he's careless. So there *could* be evidence, something that would make the police look at him in a new light; look at *me* in a new light. I have to search for something, anything, that will incriminate him. With no idea what I'm even looking for, I know that I still have to try, because I have nothing to lose.

Which means I have to go back.

I go into the lounge, pick up my phone from the sofa and tuck it into my pocket. I leave the house, lock the front door and jog down the path to the gate. Once I reach the end of the street I break into a run, my legs pumping up and down as I head back to John's house. I speed along, eating up the miles and with each step, I feel more optimistic; I will find something, I *will*.

By the time I reach John's house my lungs feel raw from breathing the freezing air. Twice, I've slipped on the icy pavements that haven't thawed all day, just managing to stop myself from falling. I open the front door and step inside, and the warmth engulfs me. My mouth is parched and I go out to the kitchen and draw myself a glass of water from the tap, gulp it down greedily and immediately refill the glass and drink that, too. I pull my feet out of my trainers and wiggle my toes, feel the tingling as the circulation returns to my fingers.

My stomach growls noisily and I realise I should probably eat something, but the thought of food is unappealing. Besides, I don't have time; I have things to do.

Evidence to find.

It's time to take this house apart.

29

I've found nothing, but quite honestly, what did I expect? A signed confession? I started searching immediately when I arrived back yesterday, taking only a brief break at eight o'clock to eat something because I was feeling light-headed and nauseous. Aside from that, I didn't stop and finally fell into bed at 11.30. Sheer exhaustion made me sleep without waking until six o'clock this morning and once showered and dressed, I resumed my search, going back over places that I'd already looked.

Nothing.

I flop onto the sofa, lean my head back, and close my eyes. What the hell am I going to do? I should eat something; I forced a slice of toast down this morning, but it's now past two o'clock. Food might help me feel better but I can't be bothered. Zero appetite.

There's nothing to find here. I should leave. Soon. I won't be here when John gets back in a couple of days.

Unless he comes back early, because he could be anywhere, couldn't he? Spain was yet another lie. I eventually replied to his message yesterday, pretending that I'd missed his call because I'd been in the shower. I kept it brief because I couldn't bring myself to tell him that I missed him or couldn't wait for him to get home. He'll notice my coldness and I want him to. He needs to believe I'm having second thoughts about our relationship; that being alone has given me time to reflect and for doubts to surface. I'll tell the lie that it's all moved too fast for me and I need time to think. When we talk, which we must, we'll do it by phone because I never want to see him again. I'll use Will as a reason but not the truth, of course. I'll lie that it's too soon for me after ending one relationship to start another, that I'm afraid of having a rebound relationship when I've barely got over the previous one.

In other words, I'll use the old *it's not you, it's me* excuse and pretend that I've gone because I'm not sure about us, not because I've discovered the truth about him.

The big question is, will he believe me?

I hope that he does, because it's all I've got.

But I'm not going to tell him yet. That can wait until I'm safely out of here.

I jump up, unable to settle. I'll go and pack my bags and then call a taxi because I can't walk home carrying all my clothes. I should get on with it because there's an amber weather warning for snow and the worst thing that could happen right now would be getting snowed in here. I go upstairs, passing the bedroom full of boxes. I went through every one of those boxes, again, even the sealed ones, carefully resealing them all afterwards.

Nothing.

Not that I have any clue what I'm even looking for.

Aside from the boxes, the remainder of the house was easy to search because there was nothing much to look through. I found no bills or letters stuffed into drawers, no insurance documents, none of the usual detritus of paperwork that grows and accumulates with each passing year. Nothing, not one single thing. No photographs, either. Even though most of my finances are paperless, I still have letters and old stuff that I've hung onto, but I found nothing like that here. And John's divorced, so there should be paperwork for that somewhere too, solicitors' letters, finance stuff. I found nothing. Which is suspicious; although the ex-wife is most probably a lie, too.

I continue on to the bedroom, pull out my holdall from the wardrobe and throw it onto the bed. I head across the landing to the bathroom and collect up my toiletries and toothbrush, taking it out of the stand next to John's. I take a last glance around the bathroom, checking that I haven't forgotten anything. I unscrewed the bath panel this morning to check if anything was hidden behind it. There wasn't, and it took me ages to get it back on. I crouch down and check that it's secure and that I've left no clue that I've been searching this house.

I throw the toiletries into my bag, pull clothes out of the wardrobe and pile them on top. I checked the pockets of John's suit jackets and took everything out of his drawers to check nothing was hidden underneath.

A bang makes me jump and my heart races but it's only the loft hatch on the landing. The wind is getting up and because this is an old house, nothing fits properly. It's done the same thing several times already today, but such is the state of my nerves that I still jump each time. I cram a pair of trousers and my laptop into the holdall, and pull the zip closed with difficulty. There is no more space, so the rest of my clothes will have to go into carrier bags. Not very elegant, but I have no choice. I head downstairs to the kitchen and find a bundle of them underneath the sink. I take two out and take them back upstairs with me. I'm crossing the landing when the loft hatch rattles again. Predictably, I jump, again.

Opening up the bags, I roll up more clothes and am stuffing them inside when a thought strikes me.

The loft.

I never searched the loft.

I walk out to the landing and stare up at the hatch. The ceiling is high, so I'd need a ladder to get up there. There's one in a spare bedroom with the decorating stuff but is it worth the effort? What are the odds of anything being hidden up there?

Not high; because aside from all the useless junk in the boxes, I found no trace of John in this house. But it's the one place I haven't searched so I should look to satisfy myself.

I go into the spare room, drag the stepladder onto the landing and open it out underneath the hatch. The steps are rickety, but seem solid enough when I put my weight on the first one to test it. I climb up and when I get to the second rung from the top, I push upward on the hatch with my fingers. It moves slightly so I climb higher, but once on the top rung, there's nothing to hold on to. I look down to see the chasm of the stairs below me. A fall from here could easily break my neck.

I raise my arm towards the hatch and the ladder wobbles. My stomach lurches as I grab the loft surround with one hand, and put my other hand on the ceiling. Maybe this wasn't such a great idea. Committed now though, I push the hatch to one side, grab hold of the other side of the surround and haul my upper body inside the loft.

It's dark. I wait for my eyes to adjust, slowly lower my hand to my jeans pocket and pull out my phone, carefully bringing it up in front of my face. I press the torch on and grip the phone tightly, aware that right now would be the worst possible time to drop it.

I direct the beam around the loft.

It's completely empty.

Thick, spongy insulation is wedged between the joists, but aside from that, there's nothing; no boxes, no old junk. I click off the torch and carefully tuck it back into my pocket. Time to get down from here without breaking my neck and finish my packing. I put my hands on each side of the hole, and try to forget about the long drop down the stairs below.

Clutching onto the sides of the hatch, I tell myself it'll be fine, providing I take it slowly. Gripping tightly, I promise myself that on the count of three, I'll move.

And that's when I touch something wedged in the gap between the inside of the hatch and the first joist.

Not wood or insulation, because the top of whatever it is is smooth, soft. Pulling myself upwards, I carefully push my hand underneath the insulation around the hatch and pull out a black object. It looks like a man's washbag and has a zip along the top; it feels heavy in my hand. I force it down the front of my jumper so my hands are free and lower myself back down and drag the cover across the hole, letting it drop into place. It just misses my fingers. It could be nothing, I warn myself, don't get too excited.

So if it's nothing, why hide a man's washbag in the loft?

As soon as I'm off the stepladder, I hurry along to the bedroom, sit down on the bed and turn the bag over in my hands and study it. Whatever is inside bulges outwards, but it's not tightly packed because there's space around the edges. I carefully tug the zip open and shake the contents out onto the bed.

A handgun, a USB stick, three British passports and some sort of black casing. I pick up the casing and see that it has bullets clipped inside it.

I open one of the passports. It's in the name of John Fisher. The picture is of John, though he told me his name is Fletcher. The second passport is for John Fiennes, the third James Ford. Owen knows him by the name of James Ford. Each has the same photograph. Are any of them real or are they all fake? They all look real. He must have another passport with him; that's if he's even in Spain.

I close them and stare at the gun, touching the handle with the tip of my finger. I don't pick it up. I'm afraid to, what if it goes off? I know nothing about guns, my knowledge is limited to movies and TV programmes. The fact that John has a gun is terrifying, not least because there are several empty spaces in the clip of bullets, which must mean the bullets have been used.

I pick up the USB stick. Most people use the cloud for storage now but what if you don't want to leave a trail of evidence waiting to be found? Don't want to take the chance of someone hacking your account? A USB stick is perfect; no one else has access to it unless they have the stick itself. I look at it for a moment and then drag the holdall towards me, unzip it, take out my laptop and open it up.

There's only one way to find out what's on it.

Once my home screen appears, I push the USB stick into the port and navigate to it. There's only one file on it. I click to open it, hoping that it's not password-protected.

It's not.

A spreadsheet opens in front of me, the first tab labelled simply 'Bank'. I open it to see a column of initials, with a company name in the column next to them and next to that, a column of figures that look like bank account numbers and sort codes. Are the initials people? I think they are. I scroll down the page, unable to believe the volume of people that must be involved in this. The next tab is labelled 'A'; I click on it to see columns and columns of figures that make no sense to me; the next tab, labelled 'B', is the same.

I pull the USB stick out of the port with trembling fingers as the scale of what I've uncovered sinks in.

I have to get this to the police because surely this is evidence, and they can't ignore it, or me, now. At the very least, the gun and fake passports will make them question John because they show that he's a dangerous man. Once they start looking into him, surely they'll find out what he's been doing.

I'm elated that I've found something that the police can't ignore, no matter what they think of me. But I'm also scared; what if this evidence disappears just like Dominic Newton's body did? My statement was faked, and I was made to look a liar. What's stopping the same thing happening again?

I need a witness; someone whom I can trust totally, who will stand by me, no matter what.

And there is only one person: my brother, Adam.

I'll call him. Because, for all our differences, I know he will never let me down.

But not yet, because I'm not staying in this house a minute longer, I have to get out of here. I'll ring him on my way to the police station.

I put the passports back inside the bag, followed by the USB stick. I'm loathe to touch the gun, but force myself. I pick it up by the handle and push it inside, next to the passports, and zip the bag shut. I close my laptop, stuff it back into the holdall and put it inside the wardrobe. The carrier bags are sitting on the floor with my clothes in them and I grab them and stuff them next to the holdall, squashing them in with my foot so I can get the door shut. Suddenly gripped by an overpowering feeling of panic and urgency, I'm desperate to get as far away from here as quickly as possible. I stand up straight, draw a deep breath into my lungs, and slowly exhale. I feel light-headed and spaced out and I remind myself that there's absolutely no need to panic. Nothing has changed. John has no idea what I've found.

Calm down.

Inhale, exhale. I repeat the process several times until my breathing has slowed and the dizziness has gone.

Taking John's bag with me, I go downstairs and once in the hallway, I put on my quilted puffa coat. I try to push the bag inside one of the large zip-up pockets, but it won't fit, it's too big. I open it and remove the gun. Now it fits into my pocket. I slip the gun into the other pocket, zipping it closed. I pull on my boots and pick up my key. I'll ring Adam when I'm halfway there. He works in town so can be at the police station within minutes. I could ring him now and he'd come and pick me up, but I can't wait for him.

I have to get out of here.

I'm ready with my hand on the front door handle when I hear the unmistakable sound of a car pulling up outside. No, I tell myself, it won't be John, he's not due back yet; it'll be one of the neighbours. I'm panicking, that's all. Hurrying into the lounge, I peer through the slats of the blind, look out over the street and recoil in horror.

It's John.

He's outside in his car and at any minute he's going to walk through the front door. But he's not making any move to get out of the car yet; he's looking down at something. Probably his phone. I turn and race through the lounge and out into the kitchen. There's a gate at the bottom of the garden that leads to a back alley. If I'm quick, I can get out before he comes in.

Thankfully, the key is in the back door. With shaking hands that refuse to work properly, I unlock it, slipping outside at the very moment I hear the front door opening. I pull the door closed behind me as quietly as possible and run down the path to the back gate, praying that John doesn't come into the kitchen and see me through the window. As I open the gate into the alleyway, I glance back at the house, but I can't see if John is watching or not. Venetian blinds cover the window and it's impossible to tell. I close the gate, relieved that I'm now out of sight of the house. The gate is six feet high and made of wooden slats, as is the fence, so there's no way he can see me.

I run to the end of the alley and slow down to start the walk into town. There are other people around, witnesses, if John comes after me. I'm safe.

John doesn't know that I've found out about him, I remind myself; he has no reason to come after me. Once I'm a safe distance from the house, I'll ring Adam. It'll all take some explaining, as he has no idea that I've been seeing John, let alone living with him. Staying with him, that's how I'll phrase it. Visiting.

Even now, I care about my brother's opinion of me.

I stride along and when I reach the outskirts of the town centre where the tall Victorian houses give way to flat-fronted terraces opening straight onto the pavements, I take my phone out and go into the nearest bus shelter. Luckily, there's no one waiting for a bus because I don't want anyone to hear what I'm going to say. My phone rings before I can scroll to Adam's number, and I nearly drop it in shock.

It's John.

I should answer it; lie, tell him I'm visiting my parents. Pretend everything is normal. I regret, now, my brief message to him yesterday.

Did I make him suspicious?

No. I'm overreacting. I press the button to accept the call.

'Hi, how's Spain?' I ask in as cheerful a manner as I can manage, keeping up the pretence that he's still there.

'I'm back.'

'Oh, really? What a shame I'm not home,' I gabble. 'I'm at my parents'. You should have let me know you were coming home early. I'd have stayed in.'

There's silence, and then a heavy sigh. 'Stop with the lying.'

'What?'

'I saw you. Running down the garden. It didn't take long to find out why, so I know you have it. I know you're not with your parents.' I hold my breath, wondering if I should hang up now. 'Anyway, enough chit-chat. Where is it?' His voice is loud, aggressive, demanding. I'm shocked at the way he's speaking to me, despite everything I've found out about him. 'What have you done with my bag?'

'What bag?'

'Don't fuck me around, Abi.' I hover my finger over the button to end the call. 'I let you off the visit to Newton's wife because she has you down for a nutjob, but you've gone too far now. Tell me where my bag is.' His voice is cold, nothing like the John I thought I knew.

How can he know I went to see Holly Newton? Has he been following me?

'You're too late, John,' I say. 'I gave it to the police.'

'No, you didn't. You're not that quick. You're on your way there now, aren't you?'

'No,' I gasp. 'They already have it. I took it there.'

'You can run, Abi, but you can't hide.' He laughs and ends the call. He's coming after me. I tear out of the bus shelter and onto the pavement, looking wildly around me in panic. I need to ring Adam. Now. I scroll through my phone until I find his number.

'Lampton and Co.' The voice is Judith's. She's worked as Adam's secretary for as long as I can remember.

'Can you put me through to Adam, please?'

'I'm afraid he's in a meeting. Can I take a message?'

'It's me, Abi, his sister. It's an emergency. A family emergency.'

She doesn't reply and the next thing I hear is a click and Adam's voice.

'Abi?' There's fear in his voice, terror that something awful has happened.

'I haven't got time to explain, but I need your help. I'm in trouble, Adam, big, big trouble. Meet me at the police station. I'm on my way there now. Please. Just meet me there.'

He starts to speak, to ask me what's going on, but I end the call and push the phone back into my pocket. It immediately begins to ring, but I ignore it; there's no time to answer it now.

I take a deep breath and start to run.

30

Going through the town centre will take longer than running along the road that leads directly to the police station, but it'll be safer; the stores will be busy with Christmas shoppers and I can mingle, lose myself in the crowds. It'll be nearly impossible for John to find me. Out here by the road he has the advantage, because he has a car and I'm on foot.

I increase my speed although I'm already running; pushing myself with every ounce of energy that I have. John could drive by at any moment, and if he does, I'm done for.

I power on, resisting the urge to keep checking the road to see if he's there. Concentrating on the path in front of me, I keep going. Past the bus station, along towards the underpass that comes out into the precinct. When I reach the underpass, I want to punch the air with joy.

I slow down to a walk. There are so many people that it's impossible to run around them and even if I could, a woman running would stand out. I need to blend in. Once I'm out of the town centre, it's only a short run on an open road to the police station. Even if John does manage to find me, now I've come this far, I'm confident I can get to the police station before he can stop me. He's in a car, and faster, but I'll have the advantage because the roads will be busy there and he'll be fighting his way through traffic.

I've crossed the precinct and am heading for the high street when I spot him. He's standing in the walkway, his height making him stand out from the crowd. I stop in my tracks, trying to decide what to do. His head is down and I guess he's studying his phone. He hasn't seen me yet. How the hell did he know I'd come this way?

Not that it matters. I force myself to move, because staying still will make me stand out. I head towards a shop doorway, keeping my eyes on him. I can do it, I can get past him because he has no idea where I am and in a couple of minutes, I'll be around the corner and safely out of his sight. It's just rotten bad luck that he's so close to me. As I think this, he suddenly looks up, turning his head, his eyes searching the crowd.

And then he spots me, and with a grin, begins to walk towards me.

Run, Abi, run.

I swivel and go back around the corner into the precinct, retracing my steps. Not running, but walking fast, weaving between the streams of people. Safety in numbers.

I can lose him. I can. There's no need to panic.

Once around the corner, I pull my hood over my head to change my appearance. I skirt around the edge of the precinct and along the front of Birkins department store. Saturday mornings spent here as a teenager, giggling and laughing as we tried on hats and wigs, first haircuts at the in-store hairdresser's, coffees in the cafe... The memories charge through my brain as I enter the warmth of the store.

Is my life flashing before me?

I head for the escalator, weaving my way in and out of the throng of shoppers. I climb onto the first step and then up the next two to stand next to a man. He turns his head and looks at me in surprise.

I've broken etiquette, sharing his step. I want it to look as if I'm with him; John will be looking for me on my own, not with someone else, and he'll only see the back of my hood. He'll have trouble finding me now; too many people, too many places for me to hide. I turn slightly to check behind me and see him standing in front of the revolving doors at the entrance.

Staring right at me.

How can that be possible?

He holds his phone up in the air with a grin and begins to head towards the escalator and it suddenly hits me.

He's been tracking me.

Of course he has; how else would he have known that I went to Dominic Newton's house?

I fumble in my pocket for my phone and with trembling fingers, I turn it off.

I can do this. I can escape. I can outrun him.

It's not over yet.

* * *

I'm going to die.

The thought runs through my head on a loop, expunging every other conscious thought from my brain.

Escape. There must be a way.

There isn't.

I'm so cold. The biting wind whips my hair around my face, covering my eyes, my mouth. I pull it away and feel wetness on my skin.

It's snowing.

Perhaps it'll be a white Christmas.

I wrap my arms tightly around my body, fumbling to pull my jacket sleeves over my fingers. I'm standing in the furthest corner of the rooftop, as far away as possible from the squat brick building that sits in the middle of this open roof. Small and square, it houses the opening of the stairwell. Double doors that open out onto the roof are opposite me and at any moment, he's going to step through them. I fleetingly considered hiding in between the huge heating pipes snaked around one side of the rooftop – they rise out of the floor and run parallel to the roofline – but decided not to. Besides being too easy to trip over, my feet would still be visible.

He knows I'm here, so it's pointless to hide. He's chased me through every floor of this department store and soon, he'll burst through those doors, intent on ending my life. I was so confident I could outrun him as I raced up the escalators, so sure I'd find an emergency exit and make my escape from the store. There must be a fire escape, I reasoned, stairs that I could use to get back down to the ground floor. I spotted the door marked 'Staff' tucked away in the corner as I'd raced through the china department; dodging around shoppers who'd tutted and glared at me with annoyed glances as I'd passed them. I shouldn't have been able to get into the stairwell because it had a keypad on the door, but someone had wedged it open with a cardboard box, so I took my opportunity and ran through, pushing the box out of the way and pulling the door closed behind me. How clever I thought I was; he couldn't follow me now. I was convinced I'd lost him.

Only I hadn't.

He's strong, much stronger than me. Seconds after I'd closed the door, I heard him on the other side as he battered against it. I knew it was only a matter of minutes before he'd get to me and in my panic to get away, I ran up the stairs instead of down. Realising my mistake, I turned to go back, but it was too late. With a crash, he was through the door and on my heels. So I ran. Up and up.

And now I'm trapped.

I look around again, praying that in my panic I've missed another doorway that offers an escape from this roof. There isn't one, of course, because no one comes up here except for the maintenance men, and why would they have another exit?

I don't want to look down over the edge, but the brightly coloured lights from the shopping centre far below draw my eyes to them like a magnet. They stretch high across the square, twinkling prettily in the darkness, and the faint sound of Christmas carols carries on the wind. Or maybe I'm imagining it; my brain playing tricks on me. From here the shoppers look like swarms of ants scurrying around. The last-minute panic-buying has begun in earnest.

A Christmas I'll never get to see.

I'm sad about that, but much more than that, so very afraid.

Will it hurt, the moment that I hit the ground below? Will death be instantaneous, or will I feel every agonising second of it? As I plummet towards my death, will each millisecond seem like forever?

I'm not brave; I never have been.

I don't want to die but it's inevitable, so *make it painless*, I pray to a god I don't believe in, *make it quick*.

Is this building ten storeys high or eight? I'm not sure, there are four shopping floors and I've spent a large part of my life shopping in them. This store has been here for as long as I can remember, a constant in this ever-changing retail environment. What are all the other floors for? Offices, stockrooms? I've always assumed so and I still don't know because all I've seen of them is the scruffy, cold stairwell.

Not that it matters, eight floors or ten; it's high enough to ensure my death. I hope. Lying half-dead with appalling injuries would be worse than dying. What if I land on one of the shoppers below? Will I kill them, too? As if it's not bad enough that I have to die, will I murder an innocent person in the process?

A noise breaks through the howling of the wind and I tear my eyes from the scene below to stare at the door. Is he here already?

I've pushed a wooden mop through the handles of the doors that lead onto this roof. It was sitting in a bucket nearby as I burst out of the doors, running for my life. I felt a glimmer of hope when I saw it; a lifeline was being thrown to me. Was this an omen that at last, luck was on my side? With a hoot of hysteria, I grabbed hold of it, sending the bucket spinning around like a top. Although I knew the mop would only stall and not stop him, I thought it would be enough.

That would give me the vital minutes I needed to get away.

Except that there is no escape, nowhere else to run, no other way out. The only way off this rooftop is back through the door I came out of, or over the low wall that runs around the edge.

The quick way.

A bang echoes around the rooftop, and I watch as the doors bow inwards, shaking the mop.

He's here.

Maybe someone will hear him and come and help me, but I instantly banish the thought and hope that no one does. They'll die too, he'll make sure of that. No witnesses. No comebacks. The doors swell outwards again, and there is loud thudding as he batters against them. There's a splintering sound and it won't be long now before the mop handle snaps. He's strong; a thin wooden pole won't hold him for long. I open my mouth wide and draw in a deep breath and scream as loud as I can, but the sound is snatched away by the wind. No one is going to hear me up here, no one can help me and if anyone tries, I've just signed their death warrant.

But it feels good to scream, so I do it again and as I do so, I wish I could go back in time; return to that day, change what I did. Relive that moment again and make it different; make this not happen, make it all go away. Because life is about choices; there is always a choice.

I made the wrong one.

In just one second, I ruined my life.

There's a loud bang and the doors fly open and he's there. He comes towards me and I whimper with fear; this is it, the end. He stops several feet away from me, puts his hand out towards me and smiles.

'Hey, don't look so frightened, I'm not going to hurt you.'

I'm shocked; wrong-footed. This isn't what I was expecting.

'I don't believe you,' I gasp. 'If you're not going to hurt me, why have you chased me up here?'

He laughs softly.

'I wasn't chasing you, I just wanted to talk to you. You're being a bit dramatic, Abi. You ran away and all I wanted to do was explain everything.'

'Explain?' I shout, suddenly angry. 'Okay, I'm listening. Tell me why you have fake passports and a gun. Tell me why I found my jacket in your house – the jacket that I last saw when I put it over a dying man to keep him warm. Tell me, John, because I'm all ears to hear exactly what will explain all of that away.'

He sighs, and gazes up at the sky, at the snowflakes flurrying around, and then looks at me.

'Honestly, he wasn't meant to die; it was an accident. We were just trying to make him understand why he couldn't go to the police. He ran off and then it all went horribly wrong. We're not violent; that's not the way we do business. If he'd just taken the money like everyone else, it could all have been avoided. And I wasn't aiming for him in the car but, you know, these things happen.' He shrugs.

'So you were driving the car?'

'Yeah. And then when we realised he was dead, we couldn't just leave him lying there in the road but we couldn't fit him in the boot, so we had to go and get a bigger car. And then I saw your jacket and I had to take it in case any of my DNA was on it. I should have got rid of it and that was careless of me. My bad. But like I said, it was an accident and it would have been fine if you hadn't had the bad luck to see it.'

'Fine?' I demand. 'You killed a man and if no one knew, it would have been fine? Not fine for his wife and children though, is it?'

He shakes his head.

'That was unfortunate but like I said, we don't resort to violence unless we have to.'

'I thought you said it was an accident?'

'It was. Look, we've been doing this a long time and until you came along and started poking around, we were good. People keep quiet if you pay them enough so it's a win-win for everyone and no one needs to get hurt. Owen can vouch for that; he has a lifestyle he could never dream of affording on his salary. He didn't need much persuading once he saw the benefits. All Dominic Newton had to do was turn a blind eye and we'd have rewarded him for it. But like you, he wouldn't let it go.'

'And what about Cameron Malone, the policeman? Did you pay him to make me look like a liar?'

'No. He was another one with rigid morals. We wanted his help because you were a loose end that we could do without, but he wouldn't play ball. All he had to do was make you look unreliable. So we had to resort to threats, which never sits well with me.' He shakes his head sadly and for a moment, I'm almost fooled.

'Everything you've ever said to me was a lie, wasn't it?' I ask. 'You set out to keep me close so you could watch me, make sure I wasn't getting near the truth.'

'No,' he moves closer, eyes wide. 'No. I've never lied to you about my feelings for you. Never. Yeah, at first I wanted to check on what you were doing but that soon changed. I've fallen in love with you, Abi, and I'm not lying about that. You're overreacting, making too much out of all this. Let's forget about it and put it behind us, go back to how we were. None of this is important, it's not about *us*.'

He sounds so sincere, so believable. So reasonable. But then he always did.

Just like Will.

'I don't believe you love me. You're a liar. You're lying to me now.'

He studies me for a moment and sighs.

'Why are you being so difficult?'

'Difficult?' I laugh. 'You think telling me you love me are the magic words that will make all of it disappear? I'm not a fool and I'm not weak, not any more. You're a liar and a murderer and I see you, John. *I see you.*'

His expression changes and despite the dim light, I see his eyes glittering with anger. The eyes I once thought so warm and attractive are now ice-cold and menacing. We stand silently and I tense my body, waiting for him to make his move.

'Okay. Have it your way. I'm done trying to be nice. Give it to me, Abi.' He moves closer to me. 'And I'll let you go.'

For a second, I have no idea what he's talking about and then I remember; of course, his bag. He holds out his hand and I realise he needs to get it from me before he pushes me off the roof. He won't be able to get to it once I'm lying dead in the precinct with hundreds of witnesses around. How will he explain the fake passports and gun that will lead the police straight to his door once the bag is discovered on me? He's never going to let me go.

'Okay,' I say. 'You can have it.'

He watches as I unzip my pocket and pull out the bag. I hold it out towards him.

'I'd like to let you go, Abi,' he says as he takes it from me. 'Because I really like you, I do. I wasn't lying about that because there's real chemistry between us and you can't fake that. And I'm honestly sad about that, but I can't trust you now.' He unzips the bag, pushes his fingers inside and roots around. 'Where's the gun?'

'Here,' I say, pointing it at him.

He looks up at me.

'Give it to me.' He moves closer. 'We both know you're not going to use it. You don't have it in you to pull the trigger.'

'Stop. Don't come any closer.'

He laughs, reminding me of Will. 'It's not even loaded.'

But he's lying, again, because if it weren't loaded, he'd just take it from me.

I move backwards and feel the wall cut into my calves. This is it, the end of the line, there's nowhere else to run.

'Stop there!' I shout, as he steps towards me. 'Just stop.'

He's still grinning as I squeeze the trigger.

31

TWO MONTHS LATER

I settle down on the seat, preparing myself for a long wait. There are several other people who were here before me. I'm sitting in the same seat that I sat in all those months ago when I came here to tell Sergeant Timpson that the man I saw being run over was Dominic Newton.

A lot has happened since then.

I've been staying with Mum and Dad since I shot John. I couldn't go back to my house, even after everything had settled down. Not with the way things were with Mel, what with my house belonging to her dad and everything. All too awkward.

Mel won't speak to me.

I get it, I do, because she needs someone to blame for her life being ruined and it was never going to be Owen. Even so, it stings a bit, because I never mentioned his name to the police, not once, even though I knew he was involved. I did my best to keep him out of it but as soon they started investigating in earnest, there was nowhere for him to hide. Owen's in prison on remand. The charges are money laundering and financial irregularities, with a question mark hanging over whether he had any involvement in Dominic's death. Owen's defence is that he was coerced into doing what John told him because of the threat to his wife and child-to-be, but the fact that he profited massively from it isn't helping his case. He may get off with a lighter sentence, but their house will be sold nevertheless. Proceeds of crime.

I have my doubts about Owen's innocence; I remember how disgruntled he was with his salary, how he was always complaining that he was underpaid and how 'those at the top' kept everything to themselves. So I don't know, but he did try to warn me off in his own warped way, and I think he genuinely had no idea that I was living with John. But whatever happens to Owen, he's not going to be around to see the birth of his daughter, who is due any day now, as the trial won't start for another year, such are the complexities of it all. I want to be there for Mel, be the friend she needs, but I'm staying away for now and letting her process it all. I hope that in time we can be friends again and get back what we had.

John, whose name isn't John Fletcher or any of the names on the passports I found, is also in custody. His real name is Robert Sanderson and he was one the 'mid-level' men, as the police call them. They have a second man in custody, but so far, no one at the very top has been arrested as not surprisingly, neither John nor the other man are willing to talk. The company Owen worked for – Wildings – was being used to launder money but it was much bigger than just Wildings. From what the police have divulged to me, there are ongoing investigations into several other local businesses, as well as many others throughout the country. The investigation has mushroomed to countrywide and the scale of the money laundering is ever growing. I'm guessing that John was at these other businesses around the country when he lied that he was working in Spain.

John spent quite a few weeks in hospital after I shot him. He had to have extensive surgery on his hand but despite the surgeon's best efforts, he's been told he'll never regain full use of it.

A gun will do that at point-blank range.

He didn't believe I would shoot him; he was so sure that I

wouldn't pull that trigger. I told the police it was self-defence and they seemed satisfied with that, although if his hand hadn't taken the full brunt of the bullet, he'd most likely be dead. John, or rather Robert, hasn't said otherwise, hasn't tried to say that it wasn't self-defence and I'm trying not to see that as a kindness from him. He's a cold-blooded murderer, who would have pushed me off that roof without a moment's regret. After that day, when the madness had died down, I was angry with myself for the way John completely fooled me; for not seeing him for what he was. I see now that I *wanted* him to be perfect and I ignored anything that didn't match that ideal. John is a very good actor but there were signs, if I'd just chosen to notice them. The day he picked me up from the house and my neighbour threatened him; I think now, looking back, that John was the one who did the threatening, that *he* was the 'nutjob' and not my neighbour. There were other occasions, too, but I dismissed them, not wanting anything to spoil my perfect new man.

But I've learned from this, I hope, and in the end, I found the courage to do the right thing and stand up to him.

I console myself with that.

There are many others involved in the money laundering and a lot of arrests have been made, and more are expected. Apparently, investigations such as these are always long and protracted. From what the police have told me, Dominic Newton was just massively unlucky and happened to be in the wrong place at the wrong time. He was never meant to be working at Owen's firm, but was the last-minute replacement for an auditor who'd been hospitalised due to a burst appendix – a man also in the pay of the criminals, who would have overlooked the money laundering that Dominic discovered. But for that case of appendicitis, Dominic Newton would be alive today and Owen and Mel would still be my friends.

Police Sergeant Cameron Malone was swiftly arrested, once the police had interviewed me. He's claiming he was forced into falsifying my statement. I told the police what John said to me on the rooftop about Cameron, that they'd threatened him, so I hope that will help him because he didn't seem like a bad guy. He was, like me, in the wrong place at the wrong time.

When I called Adam from the rooftop of Birkins, I was screaming so much that he couldn't make sense of what I was saying and thought I was the one who'd been shot. John was rolling around on the floor clutching what was left of his hand, but I was still terrified that he was going to kill me. I was incoherent with fear and never took my eyes off him for one second while I waited for Adam and the police to arrive. I held the gun in my hand, pointed at him, ready to shoot him again.

By the time the police showed up – which was within ten minutes, I was later told, although it seemed like hours – John was lying motionless. But still, I watched, fearful he was trying to trick me. The police had to prise my fingers from the handle of the gun to get it off me whilst I sat immobile and numb to everything.

Adam wanted me to go to hospital and get checked over but I refused; it was shock and horror at what had happened, and there was no tablet that was going to fix that. He told me I didn't have to talk to the police immediately, he could speak to them and delay it until the next day. I told him, no, I just wanted it done with, although of course it wasn't done with because there were many more interviews after that first one. When the interview began it was so different from my previous visit; I didn't feel like a criminal and I had Adam beside me, which meant that I wasn't afraid. I wondered then why I didn't tell Adam about it all before, take him with me when I went there the first time? If I had done that, things might have been very different, they might have listened to me because once in full lawyerly mode, Adam was magnificent.

But you cannot change the past, only the future.

I'll have to give evidence in court, but that's a long way off as they're still preparing the case. And I don't fear it because I'm stronger than I ever believed I was.

Much stronger.

The weeks afterwards passed in a blur. I slept a lot, huddled underneath my duvet in my parents' spare room to recuperate, recover. I never went back to Spanish classes. They were tainted, spoiled. I couldn't face it.

And now I'm moving on with my life, even though there's still the trial to contend with. I get my driving licence back next month and I have an interview for a job as a regional manager, thanks to Celia's recommendation. 'A proper job', as Adam says. I don't take umbrage now when he says things like that. He's not trying to put me down when he says it, I see that now, it's just his way.

I'm beginning to feel normal again, to gain perspective.

To forgive myself.

Because I blamed myself, at first. I should have left it alone, that nagging voice told me; kept out of it, forgotten what I'd seen, kept my mouth shut, stopped poking my nose into other people's business.

Like I did with Will; pretend it had never happened. Bury it. Deep.

But I slowly began to realise that none of it was my fault, the same way that none of it was Dominic Newton's fault. I was in the wrong place at the wrong time.

I was right to not let it go.

And when I realised that, I knew that I shouldn't have let Will get away with what he'd done to me, because if we don't stand up for what's right, they've won.

Will won.

He'll carry on abusing women and he won't ever stop unless someone stops *him*. Georgia went back to him. I never helped her. She never asked me again and I was too caught up in my own woes to care.

I conveniently put her out of my mind because it was easier.

And then one day I woke up and knew what I had to do. I

messaged Georgia and she responded, eventually, telling me she was fine. I didn't believe her because I knew she was pretending, just like I used to.

Lying for him because she could see no way out.

I messaged her again, told her I'd help her; told her what I planned to do, telling her I would do it with or without her.

'Abigail Redmond?'

There's a man calling my name, standing in the open doorway that leads to the interview rooms. I can't remember his name but I've seen him here before, when I've been here with Adam.

'Okay?' I ask, turning to the woman next to me.

'Yes.' She swallows and I see that she's so very afraid. But she's also determined, like me, to do the right thing. I take hold of her hand and we stand up together and walk towards the waiting officer. When we reach him, he looks at us both with a quizzical expression.

'Which one of you is Abigail Redmond?'

'I am,' I say. 'This is Georgia Trent. She's making a complaint, too. Is that okay?'

He nods. 'Yes. Come with me.'

He turns and we follow him. I look at Georgia and she gives a hesitant smile as we enter the room.

We're doing the right thing; we're stopping him.

After today, Will won't be able to force anyone into that cupboard ever again.

No more women will be alone in the dark.

ACKNOWLEDGEMENTS

Thank you again to the wonderful team at Boldwood for all of their help and support in producing this book. Special thanks to my editor, Isobel Akenhead, for her encouragement and her ideas for writing myself out of a corner! Thank you to Peter, my husband, for his unending support and enthusiasm and, last but not least, thank you to my readers for reading my books.

ABOUT THE AUTHOR

Joanne Ryan lives in the rural county of Wiltshire, South England. She enjoys writing psychological thrillers which explore the dark secrets of seemingly ordinary people. Joanna also writes dark comedy and 'Chick lit' under the pseudonym, Marina Johnson.

Sign up to Joanne Ryan's mailing list for news, competitions and update on future books.

Follow Joanne on social media:

facebook.com/JoanneRyanAuthor

instagram.com/authorjoanneryan

bookbub.com/authors/joanne-ryan

ALSO BY JOANNE RYAN

Keep Your Friends Close

Don't Let Her In

Alone in the Dark

THE

Murder

LIST

**THE MURDER LIST IS A NEWSLETTER
DEDICATED TO SPINE-CHILLING FICTION
AND GRIPPING PAGE-TURNERS!**

**SIGN UP TO MAKE SURE YOU'RE ON OUR
HIT LIST FOR EXCLUSIVE DEALS, AUTHOR
CONTENT, AND COMPETITIONS.**

SIGN UP TO OUR NEWSLETTER

BIT.LY/THEMURDERLISTNEWS

Boldwood

Boldwood Books is an award-winning fiction publishing company seeking out the best stories from around the world.

Find out more at www.boldwoodbooks.com

Join our reader community for brilliant books, competitions and offers!

Follow us
@BoldwoodBooks
@TheBoldBookClub

Sign up to our weekly
deals newsletter

https://bit.ly/BoldwoodBNewsletter

Printed in Great Britain
by Amazon

47520247R00149